Mali Waugh has a Bachelor of Arts degree from Monash University and a Juris Doctor from the University of Melbourne. She has previously worked in a library, a chocolate shop and as a lawyer. This is her first novel.

JUDGEMENT DAY

MALI WAUGH

MACMILLAN
Pan Macmillan Australia

Pan Macmillan acknowledges the Traditional Custodians of country throughout Australia and their connections to lands, waters and communities. We pay our respect to Elders past and present and extend that respect to all Aboriginal and Torres Strait Islander peoples today. We honour more than sixty thousand years of storytelling, art and culture.

First published 2023 in Macmillan by Pan Macmillan Australia Pty Ltd
1 Market Street, Sydney, New South Wales, Australia, 2000

A catalogue record for this
book is available from the
National Library of Australia

NATIONAL
LIBRARY
OF AUSTRALIA

Typeset in 12.5/18 pt Garamond Premier Pro by Post Pre-press Group, Brisbane

Printed by IVE

MIX
Paper from
responsible sources
FSC® C018183

The paper in this book is FSC® certified.
FSC® promotes environmentally responsible,
socially beneficial and economically viable
management of the world's forests.

For my family

'Abandon hope all ye who enter here.' Dante Alighieri*

*Written about Hell but could just as easily have
been referring to the Family Law Courts

PROLOGUE

When Kaye Bailey woke on the morning of her death there were no omens on display, no clues from which her imminent murder might be deduced. There was no crow perched on the window ledge, no bells tolling ominously from St Patrick's Cathedral whose steeple pierced the view from her window. It was a perfectly ordinary April day – grey-skyed, warm but with a brisk autumnal breeze; the type of day that matched the mood of a city that had belatedly shaken off the lethargy of summer and finally returned to the work of living.

18 April 2018.

It was the eighth sitting week of the year for the judges of the Federal Circuit Court and Kaye's seventh year on the bench. She hoped too that it might be her first as chief judge. 'That tremendous prick' (as she referred to His Honour Saul Meyers privately) was turning seventy in a week and therefore retiring. Kaye knew that she was in with a strong chance to replace him. Her time at the court had revealed to her the inefficiencies in the family law system, the failures in culture and planning that had led to the court being a victim of its own success. 'If you give me a chance I can fix this.' That had been her pitch to the appointment panel, and she felt they had been receptive to it.

Kaye had always been a consummate planner. She had meticulously charted her graduation from university, the two years at a boutique law firm then three at Legal Aid before taking the Bar Reader's course and joining the Victorian Bar. How then had she not planned for an early death? If she had only known, she might have chosen a different outfit, reapplied her make-up in the afternoon, tidied her desk and telephoned her daughter to say goodbye. It was the smallest blessing that she was able, in those final hours, to sign off on the judgement that had been stalking her like a shadow since December 2017.

Sharma & Nettle – or *Mad & Madder* as her associates jokingly referred to what would be her last judgement – was the sequel to so many of the world's great love stories. He, a forty-one-year-old cosmetic surgeon, and she, a thirty-two-year-old online content creator, had the youthful looks of Romeo and Juliet, the tempestuousness of Catherine and Heathcliff, and the difference in material situation of Elizabeth Bennet and Mr Darcy. They were also both arseholes.

Kaye had started the day early, waking with unresolved exhaustion to a perfectly still flat. It was not quite light, but that pale in-between time when the world seemed alive with possibilities. At this hour she might still have been a girl waiting for her mother's clock radio to spur the day into action, or a young mother gazing at three-year-old Ama, spread-eagled between herself and Bruce in their old house in Northcote.

She thought of Ama as she dressed, and felt the melancholy pride she always did when she thought about her daughter. Ama had only left for the UK a few weeks ago but already Kaye missed her dearly. She missed her presence in the flat, the noises she made washing dishes and talking to the cat, missed her falling asleep with the television on, the smell of her shampoo, the mess of textbooks and phone chargers and half-empty lip glosses lying around.

Kaye left the house at six-thirty, having packed a change of outfit and her make-up bag for Saul's retirement party that evening. The walk from East Melbourne to the legal precinct was a little over twenty minutes and she arrived with the sun, both of them edging their way into the quiet of the city. In a laneway off Little Bourke Street a youngish man was furiously billboarding an advertisement for an anti-fascism rally to be held at the State Library that Sunday. It showed Donald Trump's face on Hitler's body. She took a photograph and sent it to Michael O'Neil, her companion (she was too old for a boyfriend). *Shall we go and invite The Boys?*

The Boys was how she and Michael referred to the club of older male barristers and judges they spent so much time around. These men were a particular breed – conservatives who hated Trump not on the basis of policy, but because of his vulgarity. It wasn't his cruelty that was repulsive, it was his use of words like 'pussy'.

Kaye found him repulsive too, of course she did, but to her mind, a man like Trump who never hid who he was, was less threatening than those pernicious characters she encountered so regularly in her professional life. Men who were one thing to the world – unassuming doctors, lawyers, carpenters or teachers, perhaps – and monsters in the privacy of their own homes. These were the men who truly scared her.

She bought a coffee at Trapski, a hole-in-the-wall cafe on the Little Lonsdale side of the court complex. As she was waiting for the barista to steam the milk, lost in thought, a car pulled up behind her. She turned at the sound of a window lowering.

'Buy a mate a coffee?'

It was fellow judge Grant Phillips, a man Kaye had known most of her professional life. Grant had a long quick face and expressive eyes that always looked to be foreshadowing a brilliant smile. He was typically referred to as a 'character' – witty in an outrageous sort of way, bright enough that he allowed himself to be lazy.

'What are you after?'

'Get me the most expensive drink on the menu – some triple-shot, almond-milk, fluffed-up bullshit thing. When they announce you later today you'll be able to afford it.'

'It's not me,' Kaye insisted, although of course she was hoping. 'I haven't heard a thing.'

Saul Meyers' replacement had been a topic of much speculation within the walls of the court. Kaye was aware that she had been widely tipped as a frontrunner, but she was also aware that her progressive attitudes on family law (and her suspected politics) put her at odds with the current attorney-general, and of course with Saul himself.

'Liar,' Grant said with a wink. 'I'll see you up there.'

He waved as he put his window back up and turned into the underground carpark of the Commonwealth Law Courts, where only judges were permitted to park their government-issued cars.

Kaye ordered Grant a strong latte, and when both orders had been made, collected them, walked through the security door and took the judges-only lift up to her chambers on the twelfth floor. The building was silent save for the murmur of old computer monitors and photo-copiers and the humming of the automated lights overhead.

Grant's chambers were next to her own and an exact replica – an antechamber for the two assistants, referred to as associates, and an inner sanctum for the judge. Grant's associates had both recently left for the bar and were yet to be replaced. Kaye knocked lightly on his outer door and, not hearing a response, entered, intending to leave his coffee on his desk. She found him halfway through changing into his court attire.

'Sorry!'

'Not to worry.' He pulled off his shirt, displaying a lean, albeit mottled, iron-man physique as Kaye placed the cup on his desk. At sixty-five he was still in good shape. 'So you're telling me Saul hasn't had a secret meeting with you?' he said as she turned to leave.

'I swear.'

'Well, that's very interesting.' Grant cocked his head as though considering her, and she was transported back to her first meeting with him many years earlier, when she had briefed him at the last minute for a very vulnerable client. That morning he had put his head to the side in the same way and said, 'Has anyone ever told you that you look like Demi Moore's sad twin?' Kaye had worried he was about to hit on her, but she relaxed when she saw his empathy towards her client, the victim of significant family violence. 'That husband of yours is a real piece of work,' he told the client. 'I can't apologise enough on behalf of the male sex.' So had begun a long friendship.

At eight-thirty Kaye's associates, Matthew and Christianne, arrived together, talking animatedly about the season finale of a reality television program. Christianne took the files for the matters in court that morning down to Kaye's courtroom, and at ten o'clock Kaye and Matthew went down to the court on level two. Matthew knocked briskly on the door behind the judge's bench and entered. 'Silence please, all stand and remain standing; the Federal Circuit Court of Australia is now in session.'

From a professional point of view, it wasn't really the type of morning any judge would choose as their last. A tedious procedural argument from a solicitor who Kaye considered incompetent and who insisted on doing his own appearances, the listing of a trial in a property matter, the finalisation of parenting orders for an eight-year-old girl that Kaye knew were ultimately doomed to fail. When the matters concluded Kaye returned to chambers with her associates and continued to work on *Sharma & Nettle*.

'I've sent the Notice of Judgement out,' Christianne told her at four-thirty.

'Well, that means I really need to finish it,' Kaye sighed.

At six o'clock the three of them joined the various judges of the court in the conference room between the two wings of the twelfth floor. Several members of the bar were in attendance, including the functional alcoholic Greg Eaves and the belligerent Graham Norman. These were Saul's cronies – the men he went to the races with, played golf with, ate lunch with most days.

The room smelled like roasted meat. Despite the early hour, the party was in full swing. Saul's heavy cheeks were bright red and Judge Virginia Maiden, his good friend, was hanging off him, her face also coloured with drink. Saul appeared to be midway through a joke, the telling of which was eliciting uproar from those gathered around him. Virginia's eyes met Kaye's own, cold and unwelcoming. Despite her gender, Virginia was one of The Boys.

'Fucking insufferable.' Grant had materialised beside her. 'Drink?'

'Several,' Kaye said. 'Thank you, manservant.' She turned to Grant's wife Harriet, who greeted her with her usual awkwardness, something Kaye had become accustomed to over the years.

Kaye urged her associates to help themselves from the over-whelmingly carnivorous platters in the middle of the room. She noticed that Saul hadn't invited his own associates, who he referred to as 'his girls'.

At seven-thirty Virginia Maiden tapped the edge of her glass with a spoon to announce the formalities. She then held forth on the brilliance of her friend, his commitment to law and justice, and his expansion of the court's jurisdictional and physical presence.

'The only things Saul's ever been interested in expanding are his stomach, his bank account and his beach house,' Grant whispered in Kaye's ear. Virginia Maiden looked at him as though she'd overheard, eyes narrowed. It was well known that she detested Grant, who she openly referred to as a 'glib showboat'.

Saul's turn to speak was accompanied by much throat clearing and pomposity. 'My friends, colleagues, brothers and sisters,' he began, 'I want to thank you all for being here today to celebrate ... well ... me.' He chuckled, and proceeded to talk at length about his time at the courts, ending finally with, 'So thank you, my dear friends, for your support and encouragement.' He waited for applause, which came after the merest hint of delay.

'Who's replacing you then?' Grant called over the dying claps.

Saul waved his hand as though shooing the question away and accidentally smacked his own cheek. He really was quite drunk.

'Tell us, go on!' one of the barristers called.

'Yes, put us out of our misery.'

'Oh, very well,' Saul said, clearly eager to regain the gravitas lost when he'd hit himself. 'I can confirm that the next Chief Judge of the Federal Circuit Court is none other than Kaye Bailey.'

'You sly fox!' Grant exclaimed, leaning in and kissing her on the cheek. Other judges followed suit, crowding around to congratulate her and offer hugs, handshakes and kisses.

At around eight, Kaye returned to chambers where her associates were hard at work. Her heartbeat reverberated too loudly and she felt wired and anxious. *Did that really just happen?* She shook her head, took a deep breath and told herself that she would think about what had transpired later. She needed to finish the judgement first.

'Time to go,' she called out to Christianne and Matthew an hour later after each of them had proofread it again. She stayed on to do her own final read-through of the hard copy.

The facts of the matter had been confirmed in painstaking detail, and the several pages after that contained a precedent that she'd used in many previous judgements that set out the relevant legislation and case law. It was the section headed 'Findings' that had changed so much as Kaye had turned the matter over in her head again and again.

'Alright, I think you're finished,' she addressed the final page. Her associates had also prepared the orders that were to accompany the judgement. She read through them carefully, signed both documents and placed them on Christianne's desk, ready to be photocopied first thing in the morning. She then set to work on the other piece of business she hoped to complete and which, with her appointment, had a new urgency.

At eleven she thought she heard a rustling in the antechamber. From under her door she could see that the lights, which responded to movement and which had turned off over an hour ago, had flicked back on. 'Hello?' she called. When there was no response she stood up and opened her office door. The noise from the party down the hall had died down and there was no sign of anyone. Maybe the cleaner, she thought, and, leaving her door open, she returned to her desk. She wondered where Saul and Virginia and Saul's barrister cronies had gone to continue their celebrations. She imagined the men all leering at some poor university student moonlighting as a barmaid, telling themselves they were just as charming as they'd been at twenty-five.

Shortly before midnight she stood up, intending to call it a night. She walked over to her window and looked out onto Flagstaff Gardens. Clouds were hovering low over the tops of the trees. It would rain any minute.

It was then that she saw her killer's reflection.

She knew what was going to happen before either of them moved. She knew with certainty that the fight was unwinnable, but she also knew that she would fight regardless, because that was what she had always done and who she was. It was over quickly. In her final moments, Kaye Bailey was left with a succession of emotions – love for her daughter, an appreciation for the privileges she had been given, but most deeply, an aching pain at the injustice of it all.

PART ONE

PART ONE

CHAPTER 1

The deluge, abrupt and insistent, began anew as Detective Senior Sergeant Jillian Basset was getting dressed.

'It's a sign,' said Aaron, his voice muffled by the pillow protecting him from the light of the bedside lamp.

She directed the light towards her wardrobe, and when she still could not differentiate between activewear and work wear, turned the overhead light on.

Her husband's body contracted into the foetal position like a slater whose belly had been poked. Jillian was dimly aware that he'd been awake half the night with their eight-month-old son, Ollie, who was, depending on which website you read, either in the midst of a sleep regression or suffering demonic possession.

'Pants!' she said. 'I need actual proper pants. Preferably a top too.'

'You've got plenty of pants,' Aaron groaned.

'But you put them somewhere weird!'

'I put them in your drawer. That's not weird, it's tidy.'

She opened the drawer with too much force, pulling the whole thing out of the unit. 'This is all activewear. I can't wear activewear to a crime scene.'

Finally she located a pair of black pants that almost accommodated her postpartum figure, and a white shirt she'd bought because it did not require ironing. She poured herself into them, studying herself in the wardrobe mirror.

I look like such a mum.

She stifled the thought, pulled the pillow off Aaron's face and kissed his forehead. 'I'll call you when I know what's going on,' she promised.

'Don't call me before eleven,' he warned her, replacing the pillow with a scowl, eyes still stubbornly closed. 'Or I'll be angry.'

He's dreaming if he thinks he'll get to sleep until eleven.

Jillian unplugged her phone, put on her watch, found a pair of shoes under the bed, and stuffed her Victoria Police lanyard into her bag. She flicked the lamp off, walked to the door and turned the overhead light off.

'Take an umbrella!' Aaron called, his voice no longer muffled. 'And don't forget to –'

She closed the door on his words.

On a normal morning, lying in bed with Aaron's long body next to hers and the cat rolled into a tidy ball at her feet, the rain would have been comforting. She would have slid back into a nourishing sleep and dreamed of Ubud in the rainy season. Rain was God's white noise, she had once told Aaron, because she loved white noise and he hated it. But as she stood on the front porch waiting for a gap in the deluge in which to sprint to the car, her hair already reacting to the humidity, it felt like Aaron might have been right. It was a sign.

There was the briefest of abatements and she made a run for it, the puddled paving drenching her shoes and ankles. In the car she stopped to confirm that she had her phone and make-up bag. A crack of thunder boomed directly overhead.

A sign. He was just saying that because he doesn't want me to go back yet.

The roads, almost indistinguishable from the world around them, were empty. It was too early for school traffic and too miserable for cyclists and joggers. The only other sign of life on the way into the city was a solitary silhouette hunched under an umbrella outside the Footscray Road Costco store.

On Dudley Street, which looked as though it might be mere minutes away from flash-flooding, the traffic thickened. The city beyond was a blurry canvas of dark blues and darker greys. She was at the corner of La Trobe Street before she realised she hadn't brought an umbrella after all. 'Shit,' she said aloud to the rain and the windscreen wipers. While waiting for the light to change at William Street she did a quick frisk under the front seats and located amongst the tissues and coffee-cup lids an old Chanel lipstick, two pieces of unused chewing gum and a large paper bag.

Well, not quite an umbrella, but sure.

Her destination was marked out by the red and blue flashing of police lights. She U-turned into a designated police parking space near the corner of Lonsdale Street and checked the make-up she had applied in intervals on the way. At some time during the postpartum period she had decided that changing her hair colour from its natural ashy brown to a darker, sultry tone would make her feel like a new woman, but in the half-light of the car it made her look washed out, used up. She climbed out into the rain.

The paper-bag umbrella was already capitulating to the weight of the downpour as she ran across Little Lonsdale Street. Two uniformed officers stood hard against the wall of an underground carpark, absently watching the gutters swell with water as they chatted. They did not see her. She was at the front of the Commonwealth Law Courts building before she realised that the officers must have been at the back entrance and she could have saved herself a few additional metres of saturation. Thunder boomed again.

The staff entrance was to the side of the main entrance, its glass door tucked behind a cafe whose neon peppermint slice and garish blueberry cheesecake were illuminated by the light of a refrigerator cabinet. Another uniformed officer was stationed at this door and admitted her swiftly. As the thick glass closed behind her the rain was silenced. Jillian was ushered through an atrium that ran the entire length of the building and into a lift, up to level twelve and back into her old life.

'I need you on it,' Des had told her. 'I know we said Monday but this case is big.' Jillian was already feeling for the lamp switch at that point, ignoring Aaron's protestations. 'Some judge has been killed, a family law judge. If this ends up being Warwick 2.0 then we're in for a real mess.' The detective inspector was referring to Leonard Warwick, suspected Family Court bomber who had only recently been arrested and was yet to stand trial for terrorising the Sydney family law judiciary in the 1980s. 'McClintock and his crew were meant to be on call but one's down with gastro and the other's on family leave so I'd really appreciate it if you'd –'

'I'm on my way,' she'd said, understanding that however he might phrase it, Des just wanted her, his most trusted subordinate, to be there.

On level twelve, the uniformed officer showed her through a glass security door and with a curt nod returned to his station. Jillian found herself at the junction of two identical-looking corridors positioned in an L-shape. The passage in front of her was dark and quiet. From the passage to her right comforting sounds emanated – low voices, a telephone ringing, gentle rustling. She followed them past framed photographs of robed men and women, and doors that gaped open like ugly smiles. In one room she caught sight of a red-faced young woman who sat staring blankly with something grey wrapped around her shoulders, a paramedic and a police officer in attendance. In the next, a man of thirty or so paced back and forth wringing his hands like Lady Macbeth under the supervision of another uniformed officer.

From the farthermost office, something large and round and blue wobbled into view. It looked like an enormous blueberry.

'Jilly! Hi!' The blueberry was Meg Hassler, one of the crime scene examiners, wearing a full PPE kit distorted into dark blue by a trick of the light. Meg was extremely pregnant.

Jillian felt her stomach lurch and thought irrationally that perhaps she could duck into one of the offices and hide until Meg left. Instead, with great effort, she forced her face into an enthusiastic smile.

'Congratulations!' she beamed, her cheeks aching with the intensity of it. 'Des told me. How much longer before you go on leave?'

'I'm done next week,' Meg said. Her cheerful face was very pink and her happy eyes had the glaze of third-trimester exhaustion that Jillian remembered.

'And when are you due?'

'Not for another month but I'm booked in for a C-section anyway.'

'So exciting,' Jillian trilled, worried that she sounded too excited, although Meg did not seem to notice.

'It is. It really is.' Meg nodded emphatically. 'What about you? You look amazing, not like you've got a baby at home at all. Must be so tough having to leave the little man?'

'Oh, he's in good hands,' Jillian said, 'Aaron's taking some time off now.' And to change the subject she asked, 'Is Mick around?'

'I think he popped downstairs for something, not sure exactly what.' Meg gave a knowing chuckle and leaned forward conspiratorially. Jillian could smell a sickly sweet perfume, something adolescent and overbearing, as Meg whispered, 'I knew Des would want you on it. He's always so pissy with Mick, I feel sorry for the poor bloke.'

Jillian smiled but did not concur. She had an on-principle objection to ever feeling sorry for Sergeant John McClintock. 'Show me where the action is?'

The judge's office consisted of two rooms, separated by a thin plaster wall and a frosted-glass door. 'They call it chambers, not an office, makes it sound so fancy,' Meg said as she led Jillian into the outer room, whose light turned on at their movements. Two desktop computers were positioned at two desks, one next to the door and the other facing out towards Flagstaff Gardens. The telephone on each desk was alight with flashing red lights, and the hum of the overworked monitors and hypnotic swirling of their screensavers gave the place an air of the recently abandoned. Jillian detected the burning scent of freshly printed paper mixed with something acidic and tangy. The entire breadth of the internal wall had bookshelves built into it. They seemed to be a physical calendar for the coming days and weeks. 'Thursday, 19 April' read a typed label on the top right shelf, on which sat one very thick file. 'Friday, 20 April' read the next, on which there were another seven or so files.

'I don't have all the details,' Meg told her, 'but her name is Kaye Bailey. She's a judge, obviously. Her associate,' Meg gestured towards the two empty desks, 'one of the people who sit here, found her first thing this morning. Mentioned there was a party here last night. A judge retiring, I think she said. The doc said time of death was likely between midnight and two am.'

Jillian's eyes flicked across the two associates' desks. There were small signs of outside life there – a picture of a blond man holding a chocolate Labrador puppy was pinned to the wall closest to the door, and under the desk were three different pairs of black high-heeled shoes; the desk facing the window had running shoes and a gym bag sitting on the chair, and beside the phone was a picture of two men wearing university robes while proudly holding certificates at a graduation ceremony.

'She's in here.' Meg pushed the internal door open and gestured for Jillian to follow her into the second office. This room had evidence of an older presence, of someone with the time and financial resources to procure the artwork on the walls, the extensive book collection and the bronze bust of Ruth Bader Ginsburg whose shrewd eyes surveyed them.

The person to whom these items belonged lay on the floor, unseeing eyes looking towards the ceiling, a series of evidence markers surrounding her like a full-body halo. She was a middle-aged woman with dark hair, greyed at the roots, wearing a brown suit skirt and a white shirt. She was not wearing shoes or stockings and her legs were positioned at an awkward angle, both turned in slightly. The cause of death was immediately obvious, although they would need to wait for a post-mortem to confirm this. Her lips were a pale blue, her neck had several deep indentations, and a large bruise was visible on her right cheek. She had been strangled and beaten.

Jillian inhaled sharply. She had worked in law enforcement for over ten years and had been a detective for six. In that time she had developed a strong stomach but there was something grotesque about seeing a dead body in such a sterile environment. Murders of women almost always took place at home, typically their own home and mainly in the bedroom or kitchen. They were invariably committed by their current or ex-partners. It made their deaths seem private, domestic. Knowing that a woman had been murdered in an office, a real office – not just the front for a money-laundering operation or drug importer or an illegal brothel – was unsettling in an entirely novel way. It did not fit. It did not belong.

'Undertaker is on the way,' Meg said. 'We've done the prints on the doors, desk, anywhere else Mick wanted. And I've done the pictures and film. That's vomit on the floor, by the way. From the girl down the hall. Careful where you stand.'

From some distance away came the sound of movement and conversation. 'That might be the undertaker now. Back in a min.' Meg bustled out of the room.

Jillian sighed and allowed her painfully exaggerated smile to fall. She wanted to hate Meg, to indulge in spiteful and cruel thoughts about her and her pregnancy and her baby. She knew that Meg had undergone multiple rounds of IVF and had a number of miscarriages. And as Aaron always reminded her, they were 'actually really lucky'. It was just that she didn't feel lucky. Ever.

But that doesn't mean you get to become a bitter arsehole.

She began a careful assessment of the room, trying her best to ignore the woman lying on the floor while also affording her a sort of respect. She returned to the door and began to move in a clock-wise direction. To her left, immediately upon entry, was a bookshelf that seemed to be occupied mainly by political biographies; beyond that was the window – thick glass, thicker windowsill and several days' worth of dust. She could see La Trobe Street, now filled with rainy-day traffic, and Flagstaff Gardens rendered imprecise by low clouds. Next was a small coffee table in an ugly veneer and two desk chairs positioned to take in what must have been, on a sunlit day, a relaxing view. The judge's desk sat facing the door.

Jillian moved over to the desk, and once satisfied that it would not compromise anything, sat down in the chair behind it. Her feet connected with a pair of black leather shoes and a handbag. She pulled the bag out, finding a mobile phone, a pack of postage stamps, breath mints and a compact.

Three large files sat open on the desk, their innards removed and post-it notes slapped on them. The notes were in a barely intelligible cursive that reminded Jillian of her own handwriting and sat across pages with important-sounding titles and the bright red stamp of the court. *Amended Initiating Application*; *Affidavit of Evidence in Chief*; *Family Report*.

In the middle of the pile was a document that had been well and truly hacked at with a yellow highlighter. It was titled 'Affidavit of Single Expert' and had been written by a Dr Sheffield, psychiatrist, regarding Rahul Sharma and Lisa Nettle.

Rahul Sharma. The name rang a bell deep down in the mines of her memory, and she picked the report up and began to read.

The husband is forty-one years of age and is self-employed as a cosmetic surgeon. He admits at various hospitals in the greater Melbourne vicinity in addition to running his own successful chain of clinics. He was well groomed. His affect was normal. He presented as thoughtful and reflective as he responded to my questions. He stated that he had had two previous long-term relationships, both of which had ended on mutual terms. 'I wasn't ready for marrying and both of them, at those times, wanted to settle down,' he said. Mr Sharma denied that he was violent towards his wife. 'Ask anyone that we socialise with,' he said. 'It was her always coming in with all guns blazing. By the end I was exhausted.'

Jillian searched her memory again but came up empty. Maybe she'd seen Sharma's name on the wall during one of her hospital visits. Or dealt with an allegation against him, perhaps.

She continued reading.

Ms Nettle is a woman of approximately thirty-two years of age. She was neatly and stylishly presented. She generally confirmed Mr Sharma's account of their relationship – that is, that they met on his program where she was employed as a hair and make-up artist and commenced a relationship shortly thereafter. She reported that at the time they commenced a relationship he was going through a 'nasty' separation and reflected that she 'should have heard the warning bells'.

Jillian realised with a start that she knew exactly why the name was familiar. Rahul Sharma was a celebrity surgeon; the type that appeared on charity specials and performed cosmetic surgery on burn victims for free. She looked for the next page but the rest of the report was missing.

She opened the top drawer of the desk, the place where most people kept those vices they were willing to risk bringing into the office. There were approximately seven reusable supermarket bags in various conditions. The next drawer had two opened blocks of Haigh's chocolate that made Jillian's stomach ache with envy, and a post-it note reading 'Kim, 1 pm, DJ'. The third drawer contained three old mobile phones, a number of receipts and a packet of paracetamol.

Well, that's disappointing.

She pressed a button on the computer keyboard and the screen came alight. A blank email was open on one side of the screen; on the other, the judge's calendar.

Jillian stood up and stretched. Her neck clicked. She felt as if she had aged fifty years over the course of bringing Ollie into the world. She could still remember a time when she had been fit and healthy, when her skin had been firm. She had never been model material but she had liked her body. When Ollie had been inside her she had initially enjoyed her expanding stomach, her fuller face, but there came a point when she stopped being the woman she thought she was and became something feeble, needy, pathetic.

There were sounds at the outer door, and a moment later two undertakers came in with Meg and began the undignified process of packing the victim's body onto a trolley.

'Do you guys know what the wait time is for post-mortems?' Jillian asked.

The more senior of the two whistled between his teeth as he considered. 'This'll get priority,' he said. 'I know Sandy'll get onto it quick, but as to exactly when . . .' He shrugged.

They left efficiently, Meg following.

Jillian's neck clicked again as she walked the length of the room, studying the contents of the bookshelf on which Ruth Bader Ginsburg's bust sat. There were legal texts, more political biographies

and a thin layer of dust. To the left of the door was a coat cupboard –
taller than the average man and exceedingly narrow.

I wonder.

She knew she should go and find McClintock and listen politely
as he told her his theory of the case, which would inevitably involve a
large dollop of self-congratulation, but this would only take a second.
Her phone began to vibrate as she opened the cupboard door.

'You there?' Des's voice was rusty and tired.

'I am indeed. Where are you?'

'In the office.' Des yawned loudly. 'Just putting out the usual fires,
you know. You spoken to McClintock yet?'

'Nope. Just looking at the judge's room.'

'What do you reckon?'

'Strangled, beaten too. Meg Hassler said something about a party
here last night. Someone there maybe? The place is a fortress – you
need security to get into the building, then to get to the right level of
the building, and to get inside the right section from there.'

'So no obvious Family Court Killer Part II indicators?'

'No bombs as yet,' Jillian confirmed.

As Des talked, Jillian looked through the items hanging in the
cupboard – a black judicial robe, a brown suit jacket, an old raincoat.
She began to work her way through the jacket pockets, finding only
an ATM withdrawal stub and a bobby pin.

'Do us a favour and make sure you solve it before Mick gets back
from wherever he's gone,' Des was saying.

'Nothing would make me happier.' She tried and failed to wedge
herself into the cupboard, wondering if the killer might have hidden
there. 'Maybe a skinnier person?' she said aloud.

'What was that, love?'

'Nothing.'

Something small and metallic flashed in the bottom right corner of the cupboard. She bent down but the space was deceptively deep and she couldn't reach it without squeezing her shoulders through the door. 'Hang on, I'm putting you on speaker phone, just checking something,' she said. Getting down on hands and knees she tried various positions, finally manoeuvring herself into a yoga pose, backside high in the air and right arm reaching as far into the cupboard as it could go.

'Anyway,' Des continued, oblivious to her contortions, 'there are plenty of nutters with a grudge against family law. That's basically how Pauline Hanson got back into the senate. You know they only arrested Warwick recently? Fucking crazy.'

She laughed. 'Well, if it's another crazy, Mick will be happy. He'll get his face all over the telly.' Her finger finally connected with the mystery object.

'You and I know it. Alright, talk to you later.'

'Bye.' The object, whatever it was, was stuck. Jillian reached in with both hands, her body at an even more undignified angle, and grunted as she pulled with all her might.

'It's just a loose screw.'

She bumped her head on the side of the cupboard in her hurry to turn around. There was McClintock, all six foot three of him, trying to suppress a laugh. 'Des mentioned you'd be coming in,' he said.

CHAPTER 2

Sergeant John McClintock had a winning smile that cracked slightly at the edges. Referred to as Mick by everyone aside from Des, he had begun the detective training program at the same time as Jillian. In their first encounters he had struck her as a jock, blokey, one of the guys. His plain clothes were always meticulously fitted and emphasised his superior physique and height. He kept his sunglasses tucked into the neck of his white shirt and anyone who spoke to him was greeted by that smile and a hand to his hair. That had been enough to earn Jillian's ire. She was deeply suspicious of charming men.

It was even worse that he was sporty. Mick was a mad Essendon supporter and would talk about their woeful season with good humour to anyone and everyone. But he knew just as much about every other type of sport and seemed to follow them all with as much intensity – Premier League, rugby, tennis, snooker . . . He cycled every morning, played in a futsal team with a bunch of other cops, and did weights sessions in the gym at the end of each day. The only people who had time to do that were single men, Jillian thought contemptuously.

The other men in the training program gravitated towards him, became a little too loud, a little too boisterous as they vied for his attention. The women noticed him from a more sedate distance, waiting to be acknowledged. In the formal lectures McClintock would answer questions easily, leaning back in his seat with one arm stretched around the back of the chair next to him, occupied or not. 'Oh to pick the right seat,' one woman had said to Jillian after a lecture.

Jillian thought that the way McClintock sat was indicative of a flawed personality. He was too comfortable with himself, with his right to occupy space in the world. It reeked of male entitlement. Really, it was just another version of manspreading, but because he was handsome people didn't mind.

She had picked him for a coaster, someone who had realised early in life that they could rely on their physicality, their presence and their charm to get by, and they were just fine with that. Finding out that he was bright too had come as a nasty shock.

After training, Jillian had moved to Des's crew at Homicide and McClintock had done a stint in Vice and a secondment at the Australian Federal Police. She thought that would be the last she saw of him – no one ever returned from a secondment to a better equipped, better funded area – and yet there he was, two years later, in the lift, a head taller than everyone else and shaking hands and high-fiving like a celebrity.

He had moved onto her team while she was on maternity leave, backfilling her position as acting senior sergeant, something Des had complained about on a visit to her in hospital. Des was one of the few higher-ups impervious to McClintock's magnetism. 'I'm not interested in Mr Hair using us to charm his way up to the big boys,' Des had snarled. This was one of the things she liked most about Des: his assessment and appreciation of character.

'How you been, mate?' McClintock asked now, from the doorway of Judge Bailey's office. 'How's the baby?'

At detective training there had been a joke among the girls that you could tell if you had a shot with Mick by whether or not he called you mate.

Clearly I'm still out of the running.

'Baby's good. I'm good too,' she lied.

Did he hear Des and me bitching about him?

'You're looking well rested,' he said, still smiling down, running a hand through that hair. 'Wouldn't guess you'd just had a kid.' His height loomed over her, making her very aware of her physical vulnerabilities. She instinctively took a step backwards, but she found herself momentarily thawing under his flattery. What she wanted, in her most private thoughts, was for no one to be aware that she'd even had a child.

'She must be a good sleeper?' McClintock continued.

'I had a boy.'

'Ah. My mistake.' His face remained impassively polite.

Give me a hint. Did you hear us bitching?

'Look, about what I –' she began, but he interrupted quickly.

'Yeah, I had a poke around in that cupboard too,' he said, peering into it. 'I saw that screw, got excited. Don't know what I thought it was but it seemed interesting.' He gave a stretch and rotated his shoulders. 'She was strangled, awful way to go.' He shook his head in overplayed sadness and any thawing of her attitude towards him disappeared. 'Anyway, the ambos have finished with the girl who found her. She passed out just when I arrived but apparently she's good to chat with us now. Shall we?'

'Sure.'

They both moved towards the door at the same time and Jillian sensed a single beat in which he considered whether or not to let her leave the room first, before chivalrously standing to the side.

As though to compensate, he walked half a step in front of her on their way back up the corridor. They passed Meg who was in close conversation with another member of crime services, her gloved hands orbiting her huge belly. She winked at Jillian.

The doors she had walked past on her way in were now closed – presumably to protect the judge's employees from the sight of their boss being wheeled out on a stretcher. McClintock raised his hand to knock on the door where the female associate was when the sound of raised voices, two younger and insistent, one older and demanding, began at the internal liftwell further down the corridor. Jillian saw two uniformed officers, one of whom she recognised as the man who had escorted her upstairs, attempting to prevent another man from exiting the lift. 'I require the officer in charge,' the older man said, trying to manoeuvre around the police. 'I want to speak to him this instant. You there,' he said, catching sight of McClintock behind the police. 'What is going on? I demand you tell me what's happening immediately or I'll phone the attorney-general.'

'Acting Senior Sergeant John McClintock,' McClintock began. 'I'm the officer in charge . . .'

Actually, I think that's me, mate. Of course, he was acting in her role. *Bet he doesn't want to leave . . .*

'I've been trying to get into my chambers for over twenty minutes,' the man said, not soothed by McClintock's introduction, his mouth an indignant pout. 'This is outrageous. We do extremely important work here, people depend on us. I mean, really, have you never heard of communication? I'm the chief judge, you'd think . . .'

'You're the chief judge?' McClintock repeated.

'Chief Judge Meyers,' the shorter man spat.

Over the judge's shoulder Jillian could see the open door of what looked like a conference room. She caught McClintock's eye and gestured for the judge to be directed into that room. 'Let's go in here,' she suggested with an apologetic smile. 'So that we can tell you exactly what's been going on.'

Jillian's approach to witnesses had always been pragmatic. She was not the type to lean into the toughness that so many of her colleagues preferred – to shake recollections or incriminating information through threats or bullying. She preferred to assess the person she was talking to and assume the role she thought was most likely to produce results with the least verbal and physical resistance, whatever that might require of her. There was no vanity in policing, at least the way she did it.

His Honour Saul Meyers was directed to a table in the vacant room. He sat at its head with an air of stern dignity that was undermined by the boxes of empty wine bottles and bins of leftovers slumped against the kitchenette wall in the corner. It was clear that the room had recently hosted some type of function.

Meyers had a pug-dog face with glorious jowls that Jillian thought might have been exaggerated by tiredness and a tendency to breathe through his mouth. His hands, large and meaty, were clasped before him on the table as though in prayer. She could smell aftershave, a hint of hand soap, and on his breath old wine, coffee and sleep.

Jillian took a seat adjacent to the chief judge and gave him a smile. 'I'm Jillian,' she said, but did not offer him her hand or her rank. She sensed McClintock watching her curiously. 'We appreciate your patience, Your Honour,' she added, even though it was he who had somehow bluffed his way through the uniformed officers guarding the entrances to the court. 'Obviously it's an enormous privilege to be speaking to you.' She stifled a feeling of sickness at her own obsequi-ousness – this was a man who needed to believe he owned whichever room he sat in.

'Yes, well, of course, of course,' Meyers said, softening immediately and directing his focus to her. 'But really,' he added, remembering himself, 'I must be kept informed of what's going on. This is my court, you know. There are judges, registrars, other people waiting to come into work. The wheels of justice need to turn.'

'Kaye Bailey's been found dead,' McClintock said brusquely, sitting down with, Jillian thought, a slightly sulky look. 'She was found early this morning by one of her associates. It appears she passed away several hours ago.'

The chief judge sat back in his seat, his pink cheeks losing some of their sheen. 'Dead? Kaye? And last night you say? Oh goodness me.' He unclasped his hands and ran one through his hair, drumming the table with the other. 'How? What happened exactly?'

'We've only been here slightly longer than you,' Jillian said.

He nodded. 'I'll need to get Angela in, we need to figure out what to do. Without Kaye they'll probably need me to stay on . . .'

'Stay on?' Jillian repeated blankly.

'Kaye, she was my replacement. Announced it last night at the party.' Meyers looked as though he might vomit.

'So the party last night was for her? Is that what all of this was about?' She gestured towards the celebratory debris around the room.

'It was my retirement party,' the judge said, looking slightly offended. 'Good heavens, dead. I really must get Angela up here.'

'Judge, if we could just obtain some information from you quickly first,' said Jillian. 'We know there are logistics to consider but you're probably the most knowledgeable person we'll talk to in this investigation. It would mean a great deal to have you give us some background.' Jillian again sensed McClintock studying her, perhaps confused or even disgusted by her tone.

Honestly, why not just offer him a massage too?

Meyers seemed mollified. 'What do you need to know?' he asked.

'We need a list of everyone who was at the party,' Jillian said, producing her daybook. 'Can you write the attendees down for us please? Full names.'

The chief judge took the pen she offered and began making notes in an elegant cursive that did not match his physical presence. When he was done he squinted as he perused his list before handing the book back to Jillian. There were twenty-two names. 'That's everyone, as far as I can recall, at least. We were expecting more but a number of judges were on circuit. I said to Ginny we should make it next week but she said –'

'And what time did the party start?' McClintock interrupted.

'Oh, about five-thirty. I think everyone was there by sixish. We stuck around until . . .' He paused, scratched his cheek. 'Actually, come to think of it, I'm not sure I remember exactly when we left. Before midnight, but, ah, well, anyway, it was a lovely night. Just tragic that it's ended up like this. Everyone's going to be so shocked. And of course, her family. I'll –'

'What can you tell us about her family?' McClintock asked. Again, he sounded irritable, even aggressive.

Just annoyed that I'm taking the lead.

'She has a daughter, not sure how old. Ange will know.' He looked intently at his hands before returning Jillian's gaze. 'I think the ex-husband lives overseas somewhere but I'm not certain.'

'Did she have a partner?'

'Screwy – Michael O'Neil. He's a barrister. Thought he might have turned up last night, actually. He was invited. But he didn't show.'

'Michael O'Neil?' McClintock leaned forward. 'Didn't he do Archbishop Carrigan's defence?'

Meyers nodded. 'That would be him, although he doesn't do crim anymore. He's mainly family now, I believe. Carrigan's what he's famous for though, no doubt about it. They all said he wasn't the same after that case, although Screwy's whole life is a succession of tragedies. The man just attracts misery.' He sighed. 'I'd met Carrigan a few times over the years, sort of ran in similar circles, you know. Lovely bloke when I met him.'

A lovely, child-molesting bloke?

'So this Screwy, he's Kaye's partner, and he didn't attend the party even though he was expected?' Jillian clarified.

'That's right. Probably wanted to avoid Ginny. Fair enough, I would too if I was him.'

'Ginny?'

'Judge Virginia Maiden. She and Screwy aren't on the best of terms.'

'How did Kaye seem at the party? Did you get the impression she was worried about anything? That anything was bothering her?'

'She was her usual self,' Meyers said with a small shrug. 'Professional. Kaye's not one to let her guard down – wasn't one, I suppose I should say.' Jillian sensed that the chief judge had more to say, but that it might require gentle encouragement.

'Your Honour,' she said carefully, 'if there was anything about Judge Bailey's character or personality that might lead her to, say, offend or upset people ...'

Meyers gave an appreciative grunt, as though Jillian had grasped a fundamental truth. 'Kaye was very hardworking, but she fell into a trap that a lot of lady judges seem to – professional martyrdom. They lose their sense of fun. Although in all honesty I think even at the bar she was a bit like that – so I heard, anyway. People said she was difficult, wouldn't settle. You know, it's these younger women who don't want to settle, want to prove themselves. Have to make things hard for everyone.'

Yep, how right I was.

'So you've known her a while?'

'I suppose I have. Kaye was appointed, what, around seven years ago perhaps. Maybe less, but she was at the bar for a good ten before that. Reputation preceded her. When she was appointed I tried to be supportive, told her she didn't need to take everything so seriously, she was allowed to enjoy herself. Well,' he shook his head, 'that conversation did not go very well. She called me sexist. Can you believe it? Sexist! I have two daughters!'

'Were people expecting you to announce your successor at the party?'

'I doubt it. Not really the done thing, is it? Grant forced my hand. He loves stirring the pot.'

'Grant is?'

'Judge Grant Phillips. Good friend of Kaye's, actually. Goaded me into it. All in good fun, though.'

'And how was the news of her appointment taken generally?' Jillian asked.

Meyers considered his hands a moment. 'Well, she was very honoured, of course. She told me she thought she had very big shoes to fill. I assured her she'd be fine. Told her I was only ever a phone call away if she needed anything.' He smiled, looking pleased with himself.

This is the same woman who you just told us called you sexist? Right.

'But what about the other guests?' Jillian prompted. 'Was every-one happy with her appointment?'

Meyers laughed.

'They weren't, then?'

He licked his lips. 'It wouldn't have been a huge surprise. She would have been regarded as a strong contender amongst her colleagues. But she's put noses out of shape over the years, that's for sure.'

'Did anyone seem particularly upset?'

'Not particularly. No.'

'And just for our records,' McClintock said, 'can you tell us what your movements were at the party?'

Again Meyers contemplated his hands. 'We had speeches at I think around seven-thirty or so, and then I sat down to eat with Ginny.' He gestured towards a corner of the room. 'Over there. I sat there most of the night; people came to pay their respects. We went on to the Danish Club for a nightcap. I went home.'

'How did you get home?' McClintock asked.

'I took a taxi.'

'And do you remember the last time you saw Judge Bailey at the party?' asked Jillian.

'Well, she didn't bother coming to say goodbye, which I thought was quite rude.' He looked at Jillian. 'What were you asking again?'

'The last time you saw her?'

Meyers blinked at her. 'The last time? Well, just after the speeches, I think. She was flitting around . . .'

'You said she put some noses out of joint, could you tell us a bit more about that?'

The judge shook his large head. 'Oh, she wanted everyone to do supervision, family violence training, things like that. Very touchy-feely in the way she approached it all. Said she was worried about the impact of the threats. In all honesty, she was considered a bit of a whinger.'

'Threats? She received threats?'

'We all did occasionally. Never anything to worry about. It's part of the job, making people unhappy. Judges have to toughen up. Associates too. You don't go into the law expecting everyone to be nice to you.'

'So threats weren't taken particularly seriously then?'

Saul Meyers puffed his chest out. 'We have the best security of any court buildings in the entire country here,' he said huffily. 'So it wasn't like anyone could actually do anything, even if they wanted to.'

Except that someone did.

CHAPTER 3

They left Saul Meyers alone in the conference room with instructions to the two uniformed officers that they should stand firm against any attempts by the older man to leave or make telephone calls. The last thing Jillian wanted was for the crime scene to somehow be compromised or for another seven judges to arrive on the floor making demands. The detectives then walked the short distance back to the office housing the dead judge's associate.

Jillian rapped lightly on the frosted glass. A motherly looking uniformed officer opened the door, gave McClintock an appreciative look then said over her shoulder, 'I'll leave you to the detectives, honey.' She showed herself out, revealing a slight woman sitting at a desk, arms held protectively over her upper body, eyes red. Her dark hair stuck to her still wet, hollowed-out cheeks. Christianne D'Santo, deputy associate to Judge Kaye Bailey, was an emaciated picture of agony and despair, an Edvard Munch painting come to life.

'I'm Senior Sergeant Jillian Basset,' Jillian said, holding out a hand.

'Acting Senior Sergeant John McClintock,' her colleague offered.

Christianne looked up at them blankly, as though not entirely sure what was happening.

'I'm Jillian, this is John,' Jillian repeated as McClintock pulled up chairs for each of them. 'We'll be investigating what happened to your boss. How are you feeling?'

'I'm fine,' Christianne said, 'just shocked. I think I fainted or something. I can't stop thinking about her face. Her lips were blue, and her neck, the marks . . .' She began to shake, her legs bumping against the underside of the desk. 'Is she, is she still here?'

'No,' Jillian explained gently, 'she's on her way to the coroner. They'll do a post-mortem, liaise with the family regarding releasing her for a funeral, all that side of things.'

'Okay, that's good.' Christianne took a deep, long breath. 'I didn't like the idea of her being there like that, she just seemed so exposed.'

'So,' Jillian began, but McClintock was ahead of her.

'Tell us about this morning, what time did you arrive? What did you see, what did you touch?' he said.

'Sure.' Christianne took another deep breath and made an effort to stop shaking. 'Um, well, I guess I got in at around six, maybe a bit after. I was first in. That is, none of the lights were on so I thought I was first. I don't normally start that early but Kaye was going to leave the judgement on my desk to photocopy and I wanted to get it all done then go to yoga at seven-thirty and come back. But then the judgement wasn't on my desk, so I opened the door to her room and there she was. I was so confused, I just . . .' She shook her head. 'It didn't make sense. I'd just seen her, like, I don't know, ten hours ago, and now there she was on the floor. Matt arrived just as I was trying to figure out what to do. We called an ambulance, I don't know why now; I mean, she was cold. And we asked for police too.' She shook her head again.

'So you worked quite late then? Or were you at the party?'

'We did pop in to the party, Matt and I. But only for a little while.

We were trying to get this judgement proofed. A big one. She's been working on it for ages. I think Kaye sent us home around nine, maybe nine-thirty, I'm not entirely sure. I messaged my boyfriend when I was waiting for the train so I can check if you want.'

'In a minute that would be wonderful.'

'And when you left, where was Judge Bailey?' McClintock asked.

'She was in chambers,' Christianne said, wiping fresh tears from her eyes. 'She said she was going to read through it one more time and then sign the orders I'd drafted. She was sitting at her desk when we said goodbye.'

'And you and your colleague left together?'

'That's right. We walked down to Flagstaff Station. Our trains both leave from the same platform so we waited together. It was just, I don't know, we were in such good moods – Sharma was going out, which was this massive relief. We'd all been really stressed about it, especially Kaye. Everyone was talking about it, speculating about it, so to have it done was just huge. And then when she got announced it was so exciting. We were going to go out for lunch today to celebrate.' Christianne broke down in sobs.

'Sharma's the judgement you were working on, is that right?' Jillian asked, conjuring a vision of Rahul Sharma in his designer scrubs, a bright white smile as he looked earnestly into the eyes of some victim of a car accident or botched surgery.

'Yes,' said Christianne. 'It was very complicated and Kaye knew that regardless of what she did one of them would appeal, so it had to be perfect. And I think it was, you know? I mean, I'm obviously not a judge but the work she put in –'

'We understand they announced she was getting a promotion last night. What was the reaction to that?'

'Oh, good I think,' the associate confirmed. 'I mean, everyone clapped and came and congratulated her and all that. Kaye seemed a bit surprised, as though she wasn't expecting it to be announced like that but I suppose it was a party, they all had their hair down, you know? That was when Matt and I went back to chambers.'

Jillian produced her daybook. 'We've been given this list of people who were there last night. Is there anyone missing?'

Christianne studied the chief judge's writing carefully. 'I think that's everyone,' she said after a few minutes, 'but Matt and I were in and out. It was mainly the judges and some barristers.'

'How did Judge Bailey seem yesterday?' McClintock asked. 'Before the party?'

'Well, normal, I think. We didn't really chat much, we were all busy. There was court in the morning. Not very many matters on, just four from memory. Court finished at twelve-thirty then Kaye went out to lunch.' Christianne paused. 'Actually, I suppose that was a bit unusual, she normally gets one of us to pick her up a sandwich from downstairs but she said she was having lunch out and then going to run some errands. Typically, if she was really busy she'd just focus on what needed to be done, make everything else wait.'

'Was she meeting someone for lunch?' Jillian asked.

'She didn't say.' The associate furrowed her brow briefly.

'Did she mention anyone called Kim?'

McClintock raised an eye and looked curiously at Jillian.

So he didn't check the desk drawers then.

'Kim?' The associate shook her head. 'No, not that I can remember.'

'And how was she after lunch?'

'She seemed fine. Nothing stands out. But we didn't really get a chance to talk, we had to go straight back to court at two-fifteen for another mention and then we kept working on Sharma. We all had our heads down.'

'What about at the party?' Jillian said. 'Was she acting unusual at all? Was anything bothering her?'

'Not really, I don't know.' Christianne looked confused. 'I think she was a bit stressed by that time because she had to put in an appearance, obviously, but she just wanted to keep working. And then after she was announced she basically went straight back to work. I knew she was going to stay late last night.'

'Righto,' McClintock said, getting to his feet. 'That's great, thank you.' He did this without asking Jillian if there was anything else she wanted to ask, or anything else Christianne thought might be relevant. This arrogance was the reason Jillian did not like John McClintock. Irritated, she remained seated as he moved to the door.

'What can you tell me about Judge Bailey more generally?' Jillian asked, in part because understanding the victim of a crime was often instrumental to solving it, and in part to irritate McClintock. She would have otherwise left the question for a later interview, when Christianne was less overwrought. She sensed rather than saw McClintock sit back down again.

'She was lovely,' Christianne said. 'I hadn't worked with her long, I came over last year. I'd been in another chambers but when this opportunity came up I jumped at it. Kaye worked *really* hard, harder than anyone I've ever met in my life, and she had really high standards. She wanted things to be perfect, and exhaustive – no stone left unturned. She also did some controversial things that bothered a whole lot of people, but she didn't care at all. Like she made it known publicly that she thought it was possible in family law matters to order damages in property settlements where there had been family violence, even though some of the other judges said she was crazy. Well actually, a lot of people said she was crazy. You should see some of the emails we get.'

'What type of emails?'

'Just from angry litigants and stuff. I think every chambers gets them from time to time, but Kaye got more than most. Well, that's what I was told anyway. I'm not sure why. The court didn't really do anything about it so Matt and I just kept a record in case. We called it the Black Book. I guess it was like, black humour, you know? Trying to keep it a bit light. It wasn't really juicy, just horrible emails and pictures of, well, dicks.'

'You mean actual dicks? People were sending her pictures of penises?'

'Yes, that's right. She'd get sent one every few weeks, to her email or ours. You can ask Matt where the book is.'

Again, McClintock got to his feet, and again, Jillian refused to be rushed.

'Is there anything else you'd like to tell us, Christianne?' she said, not looking at her colleague. 'Anything you think we should know that we haven't asked about?'

The associate looked down at her lap for a moment. 'This may be nothing,' she said, 'in fact I'm sure it is. But I think Kaye and the CJ had a bit of a fight last night. I didn't hear it myself, I only heard people talking about it. We had the door to chambers open and the bathrooms are just facing us. I suppose I was eavesdropping. It sounded like things got a bit heated.'

'A bit heated? What exactly did you hear?' Jillian asked.

'I couldn't even say for sure who it was, only that it was a woman, saying that she thought Saul – the chief judge – calling Kaye a bitch just pretty much summed him up. And then whoever she was talking to said she could understand now why people said Kaye had a sharp tongue, that she'd never seen it before but the rumours were true, or something like that.' Christianne's eyes welled with tears again. 'I'm sure it's nothing, just, well, I can't believe she's gone.'

They released Christianne, under the protective wing of the uniformed officer, to the outside world. 'She'll get you home and make sure you're okay, and we'll be in touch if we need to talk to you further,' Jillian explained as the young woman was led down the corridor.

McClintock stretched. 'Interesting that Meyers didn't mention any tiff with our victim last night.'

'Very interesting,' Jillian agreed. 'Although he seemed pretty boozy to me; suppose it's possible he doesn't remember it.' She looked towards the door behind which the chief judge was sitting amongst the mess of the previous night. 'I wonder if it's normal for him to get to work this early?'

They interviewed Christianne's senior colleague, Matthew Coulter, in yet another judge's chambers, this one a mirror image of Judge Bailey's. He was a short, thin young man with red cheeks and the deliberate diction and clipped vowels of the privately educated.

'Chris and I left together at around nine-thirty, I'm pretty sure,' he said, thoughtfully. 'It had been a day, we were exhausted.'

'You've worked with Judge Bailey a long time?'

'Since she was appointed, so eight years January next year. I got the job straight out of law school.'

'You must have got to know her really well.'

'Yes,' he confirmed. 'I did. We worked really well together.

Although chambers is a pretty intimate environment, if you don't get along with your judge you don't last.'

'What was she like?'

'Oh, great! Very funny, very hardworking. She'd read every file, take them all home and read through every single thing before a hearing. A lot of them don't do that, you know? They treat every family like they're interchangeable. Kaye didn't believe in that. She actually,' the associate leaned forward conspiratorially, 'referred to it in a judgement. A decision someone else had made got sent back by the full court and Kaye had to hear it all again, the whole trial. She said in her judgement that she felt if reading through the file was required, the errors by the other judge wouldn't have happened. She did not take that well.'

'Who didn't take it well?' asked Jillian, momentarily lost.

'Oh, the judge, the original one.'

'Who was it?'

'Um,' he looked towards the door as though worried he might be overheard. 'Judge Maiden,' he said quietly. 'I think Kaye liked pushing her buttons every so often.'

'We understand there might have been an altercation between your boss and Judge Meyers last night. Do you know anything about that?'

'Only what Chris told me as we were waiting for the train. But it doesn't surprise me. He's a bully and he's not even smart.' The younger man said this with malicious delight, allowing the word 'smart' to sit on his tongue slightly too long.

'You felt that he bullied Judge Bailey?'

'Not just Kaye, everyone who made his life difficult, who asked him to do his job. He's lazy and likes to throw his weight around. And so inappropriate. You know he once told me he thinks all Indian people are liars? He said when he has a case where the family are Indian he just ignores their evidence. Creep. I was glad he was going. Kaye was too. And her being his replacement. I'm sure he would have been pissed off about it.'

'Christianne mentioned something called the Black Book?'

'Oh that! He didn't like that either! Meyers, I mean,' he clarified. 'Yeah, that's right, ages ago, he told Ange we shouldn't do it. This was before Christianne had started working with us, actually. But we didn't listen. I reckon he was just worried about a paper trail.'

'Interesting chat,' Jillian said thoughtfully as Matthew was escorted down the corridor by another uniformed chaperone. 'We've already got competing stories about what happened between Meyers and Bailey last night, along with a book of threats and abuse to track down.'

She looked down the corridor towards Judge Bailey's chambers. That end of the building was now quiet, waiting for the commercial cleaners who would remove the stains and odours that inevitably accompanied murders. 'We need a plan,' she said, glancing at her watch. 'It's nine-thirty. People will be waiting downstairs to get into the building, and as His Highness told us, all the judges and support staff will be confused too. We need to triage the twenty-odd people at the party, figure out who's important, who we can leave for later. Let's get the registry manager on the phone – Angela, he said her name was.'

McClintock reached into his jacket pocket and pulled out his phone. Jillian held up her daybook on which she'd written the number as provided by the chief judge, and heard confirmation that the registry manager was waiting downstairs for entry, along with every other employee in the complex. Jillian arranged for a uniformed officer to escort Angela inside and she and McClintock went to meet her at the liftwell, each lost in thought. A few minutes later, they were greeting a broad-cheeked, dark-haired woman of perhaps forty.

'I'm Angela Hui,' she said smoothly, extending a hand to McClintock and then Jillian.

She was dressed like the quintessential HR employee – pleated grey pants, crisply ironed shirt, a bulbous engagement ring and carefully applied make-up. Jillian had always held this type of woman in awe. She could not comprehend how they found the time to maintain such rigorous grooming practices, with or without kids. Even before Ollie, Jillian had always applied her make-up in the car, left her nails to their own devices, and had never in her adult life ironed a shirt.

They broke the news to her as they walked the short distance to the conference room where they had left Saul Meyers. Angela paled but did not speak. The relief of the chief judge when she followed them into the room was palpable.

'Chief Judge,' Angela said smoothly. 'I'm so dreadfully sorry, such awful news.'

The pair exchanged commiserations that seemed to Jillian not entirely sincere, before quickly getting to practicalities. Meyers was more than content for Angela to make all the arrangements.

'I'm going to need to tell Canberra,' she said, 'and we'll need to notify all the staff here. Obviously there are major security issues to contend with. As for the court matters listed today, I don't know how on earth we should deal with that . . .'

'Our team will deal with the security issues and liaising with those higher up,' Jillian said. 'On all of the immediate information at least. What I need from you now is to arrange a space where we can meet with all of the judges at once, somewhere not on this floor. I'd also like a separate interview room. We'll need the contact details for Judge Bailey's family too.'

Angela produced her phone from a monogrammed Louis Vuitton handbag, tapped on it efficiently for the briefest moment and then handed it to Jillian. 'Those are the contact details for her daughter,' she said.

'Thanks. Now, can I ask you to text all the judges and tell them we need to see them. They'll need to park outside the building and present themselves at the staff entrance. We'll arrange for them to be escorted in.' As she spoke she was aware of McClintock in her peripheral vision. *Bet he doesn't like that I've taken control.*

Angela nodded and typed intently on her phone. 'There,' she said after a few minutes, 'every judge notified. I suggest we use one of the courtrooms for the meeting.' She looked at Saul Meyers. 'If that's alright? Perhaps 2A, it's the biggest.'

The chief judge nodded his agreement.

'Good,' Jillian said. 'Why don't I go with the chief judge,' she said to McClintock, 'and perhaps Angela can take you to deal with security. We'll need all the CCTV, any logs of what time people came and left last night. Whatever there is. We'll also need to liaise with the coroner –'

'I called Sandy already,' McClintock said breezily. 'They'll do it in the next forty-eight, top priority. I told them I'll go.' This was not a request, but Jillian bit her tongue.

Better to have him out of the way.

'There'll be a press conference later too,' he added.

Of course, you wouldn't want to deprive the public of your precious mug.

She suppressed a smile as she followed Angela out of the conference room.

The registry manager led them away from the public liftwell and into an alcove off an adjacent corridor where another pair of lifts waited. 'These will take us down to the courtroom,' Angela told Jillian as she pressed the button. 'I'll get you set up and then I can take you,' she addressed McClintock, 'to liaise with Tomir. He's the head of security.'

At level two the lift opened onto a narrow, blue-carpeted corridor that ran the length of the building. To the left, windows looked out onto small balcony gardens and beyond those, into the office building on the other side of a lane. The rain, as vigorous as ever, fell silently. They followed Angela to the right, passing numbered doors with red lights above them, all turned off; presumably because no court was in session. At the end of the corridor, Angela opened the heavy door with some effort and Jillian found herself behind the judge's bench in a large courtroom whose entire far wall looked out on the deluge on La Trobe Street. From the internal wall three large portraits of stern, judicial figures surveyed the space. Several long rows of slightly tatty seats faced the judge's vacant chair which was perfectly positioned under a bronze seal of the Commonwealth.

'I'll just get some water,' Angela said, and disappeared back down the corridor. She returned a moment later with two jugs, some plastic cups and a couple of boxes of tissues. Having confirmed that the chief judge required nothing else, she ushered McClintock out of the room.

Ignoring Jillian, Meyers sat down at the judge's bench as though he were hearing a case, and began to write in a green book that had been placed there in wait. The old man grumbled to himself as he wrote, crossing something out and muttering its replacement.

As she waited for the other judges to arrive, Jillian wondered what Des was intending to do with McClintock. Surely now that she'd returned to work his acting contract would expire and he would need to be moved on. Or would Des keep him on, noting that this was likely to be a feeding frenzy of a case and that he was a well-regarded officer?

He's part of the crew for this one now.

A pretty top-heavy crew.

There was a knock at the door and three people entered, all looking curious and slightly irritated.

'If it please the court,' a tall thin man said to Saul Meyers with a mock bow.

The chief judge gestured for him to sit down at the bar table. 'Got some bad news unfortunately, Grant,' he said. 'I'll tell you more when everyone arrives.'

So this is Grant Phillips?

He sat down at the end of the table, his long legs sticking out to one side and his elongated fingers pressed down onto the shining wood.

A stocky woman with thick brown curls sat next to him. 'I'll be glad when they finally let us bring the cars in,' she said. 'I was doing laps of La Trobe Street for almost an hour and had to go and park at the Market.'

'I think I was right behind you,' said the third judge, a man whose face was lined and pockmarked. 'Listening to Jon Faine fawn over the premier. Bloody ridiculous.'

'Never listen to talkback radio on an empty stomach, Angus,' Grant Phillips advised. 'Especially if it's Jon Faine.' He turned his attention to Jillian. 'What is it then? You're police, I assume? Has a bomb been found somewhere in the building? Give me one wink for yes, two for no.'

'Oh for heaven's sake,' said Angus. 'They aren't going to bring us into the building if there's a bomb, are they?'

'I thought Minister Cash might have read my treatise on the definition of a casual worker and decided she was better off without us,' Phillips responded.

Three more judges entered, all over fifty, all white. 'Well, this is all very interesting, Saul,' said a severe-looking woman wearing a drenched trench coat and a put-upon grimace. 'What's going on?'

'He's going to tell us when everyone arrives, Ginny,' Phillips said. 'But just before you came in he did mention that Attorney-General Porter has confirmed they're definitely getting rid of the court and that we're all going to become justices.'

'Don't be ridiculous,' she frowned.

There were twelve judges in total when Meyers cleared his throat. 'That's everyone, I think.'

'What about Kaye?' Grant Phillips interrupted. 'She's got her judgement on, she's definitely in today, unless she's too hungover from last night's celebrations.'

'Well, as it happens, that's what I'm here to talk to you about.' Meyers stood up awkwardly and came down from behind the bench, as though realising that delivering the news from the pulpit might not be appropriate. He leaned on the back of a vacant chair on the opposite side of the bar table and drew a ragged breath.

'Colleagues, I have some distressing news. Judge Kaye Bailey was found dead this morning – in chambers. My understanding is that it is being treated as a suspicious death.'

Jillian watched the faces of the judges as Meyers passed on the limited information he had been provided with. All of them appeared shocked, although Jillian thought she saw a hint of satisfaction on Virginia Maiden's austere face. Grant Phillips looked as though he might faint.

'This is one of the detectives investigating Kaye's . . .' the chief judge struggled with the word, 'murder. She's going to talk to each of you this morning. We'll also need to talk about the logistics for the next few days but I don't have anything else to tell you at this point. We'll obviously be dealing with the security issues. Angela will be in touch.'

As Meyers responded inadequately to his judges' questions, Jillian compiled a mental list of the order in which she wanted to question the men and women present.

Grant Phillips.

Virginia Maiden.

Bearded man.

Curly-haired woman.

Angela knocked and entered and Meyers sat down again, obviously pleased to be relieved of his duty to manage the crisis. McClintock stood in the doorway and Jillian went to meet him outside the room. 'How'd you get on?' she asked.

'Tomir is still on his way in, he was apparently meant to start late today, medical appointment. They're going to do the presser at five-thirty. Des is dealing with the A-G department at the moment, AFP too, in case it turns out to be terrorism.'

'Alright, great. I'm going to talk to the judges one by one. Could you hang in here, just make sure no one is getting too chatty before they speak to me? I think they'll mainly be hassling Angela, in all honesty.'

'Yup.' He ran a hand through his hair.

Already thinking about his press conference.

Angela had arranged a small room directly opposite the courtroom for the interviews. It contained three chairs, a table, a poster promoting family violence services and the strong smell of disinfectant.

'I'm sorry,' Grant Phillips said when he and Jillian were ensconced within. 'I feel like I've been hit over the head or something. I'm still in a state of complete shock. I mean, I saw her last night, she was just so well, glowing as usual. I just can't imagine how this has happened.'

Jillian observed him for a moment. The judge had a thin face, greying brown hair, and grey-brown eyes that wrinkled slightly as he talked. It gave him a wry, friendly appearance despite his obvious shock.

'I understand you and Judge Bailey were friends?' she said.

'We are. Were,' he corrected himself. 'I've known her since she was a solicitor, she used to brief me back when I'd just started in family. Good god!' He looked stricken. 'Has someone told Ama? And Bruce? Jesus, and poor old Screwy.'

'We're making all those arrangements. Bruce, that's her ex-husband?'

'That's right, he's based in Singapore, but over here a fair bit, they were still close. Screwy – that's Michael O'Neil, her partner – well, on and off.' He put a hand to his anguished brow. 'Sorry, I'm just, just staggered. She'd just been appointed CJ, has anyone told you that? Just yesterday they told everyone, at the party.'

'We did hear about that, yes.'

'I mean, not a huge surprise in a lot of ways, I'd tipped it, teased her about it yesterday morning, actually . . .'

'We've been told there was some tension at the party, did you witness that?'

The judge looked surprised. 'Word got out fast then. I believe there was some tension between Kaye and Saul. I don't know what over, but she looked a bit upset when she left to go back to chambers. I didn't get to ask her about it . . .'

Jillian had him take her through the evening before and unlike his boss, he willingly obliged. 'Let me see, I visited Saul in his chambers, we had a drink around five then walked to the conference room together. I popped out shortly after six; my wife had arrived and I went down to fetch her, we came back up together. I'm not sure exactly what time Kaye got there but it wasn't long after Harriet, my wife. Christianne and Matthew were with her. Hari and I chatted to Kaye for a while, she was in great spirits, she was finishing off this nasty judgement that had been dragging on, causing her a lot of grief. She said she was getting the thing done tonight even if it –' He stopped. 'Well, she said even if it killed her.'

He poured himself a glass of water from the jug on the table. 'Anyway, she was in and out of the party as best as I recall. Harriet gets anxiety so we sort of stuck to ourselves for the most part. Had a chat with Saul fairly late in the piece, which I suspect he wouldn't remember – he was a few bottles deep at that stage. Then we popped in and said goodnight to Kaye on the way out. I suppose that was around ten-thirty or so. She seemed fine.'

'Who else was still at the party when you left?'

'Saul and Ginny – both of them the worse for wear, I'll say that. Saul's face was practically falling off his body. And two blokes from their bar days that they kick around with, Greg Eaves and Graham Norman, also pretty shabby.'

'Anyone else?'

'Don't think so. Saul was a bit disappointed it wasn't a bigger celebration.'

'I understand that Judge Bailey's promotion to chief judge was somewhat controversial.'

'Well yes, sure. But I mean, these things are always controversial, there's always someone who feels hard done by, thinks it was their turn. Kaye was never like that, probably why she was appointed. In all honesty, aside from the obvious I should think most people were happy for her.' He looked down at his hands and sniffed.

'The obvious being?' Jillian probed gently.

'Ginny, Saul, some of the older lot. Ginny's always fancied herself CJ-in-waiting – delusional. They weren't going to appoint her at sixty-nine when she'd have to leave within the year. And Saul's never forgiven Kaye for an appeal she ran against one of his terrible judgements when she was at the bar. They're old school, these folk. That's another reason they weren't fans of Kaye. They were brought in to do industrial relations, bankruptcy, that type of thing, back when family law was just meant to be a tiny part of the workload. Neither of them is particularly well regarded in family law whereas Kaye is. Was. And that's despite some pretty adventurous jurisprudence. I suppose they're less tolerant of human frailty, which is the nub of family law really, when you get down to it. Two people groping around for each other's weaknesses.' He looked at her. 'You married?'

'I am.'

'Well, may you never have to set foot in this place for legal reasons. You seem like a sensible person. Is your husband sensible?'

'He likes to think so.' She smiled at the thought of Aaron, likely still curled in a ball and trying to sleep off the fatigue of the full-time parent.

'Then you'll probably be alright.' Grant Phillips gave a smile of his own, a sad one.

Jillian found this exchange somehow reassuring, as though it were a guarantee that she and Aaron would always be content.

'What can you tell us about Michael O'Neil – Screwy?' she asked.

'Oh, Michael's harmless,' Grant said. 'I mean, on an interpersonal level. He's awful in court, just brutal. I used to be opposed to him, back when we both did criminal law. He was defence, I was a prosecutor. Whenever I knew he was defending I'd tell the police we had to settle or we were screwed. I think I might have invented the nickname, actually. Everyone was devastated when he started taking family law briefs.'

'How long had he been seeing Kaye for?'

'I'm not really sure, maybe a year or so. It was very low-key. I'd been expecting to see him last night but he didn't show. Not that there's much love lost between him and Saul, but I ran into him outside court earlier in the day and he said he'd be there.'

'Do you know where he lives?'

'Well, mainly at chambers, in Owen Dixon. They say he goes in at five am and stays until midnight. But I believe he's got a place in Fitzroy.'

'We'd like to talk to your wife too, if you could give us her details.'

Grant Phillips looked fleetingly concerned. 'Of course, but Harriet is in very delicate mental health. Would it be alright if I broke the news to her first? I'm a bit worried about how she's going to take this.'

Jillian agreed and the judge got to his feet. 'I'll do it right now, before she hears about it from anyone else. I'll let her know you'll be over – when?'

'We'll be in contact within the next twenty-four hours.'

'Alright.' He smiled sadly again. 'Let me know what else I can do.'

Jillian returned to the courtroom. McClintock was nowhere to be seen, and the various judges were talking with panicked excitement between themselves while Angela was simultaneously on the phone and typing on a computer behind what Jillian assumed was the associates' desk.

'He's just popped out to take a call,' Angela said on seeing Jillian.

'Okay, I'll talk to Judge Maiden next.'

'Judge Maiden indicated that she needed to return home for an emergency,' Angela said, sounding slightly embarrassed. 'Said it couldn't possibly wait.'

CHAPTER 4

Three hours later Jillian emerged into the early afternoon. The sky was still grey but the rain had stopped and the air was cool, the last hints of early autumnal warmth washed away. The crowds she'd glimpsed waiting to enter the building as she moved between court-room and interview room had now dispersed, and she could see uniformed officers stationed at the public and private entrances to direct people away. She yawned luxuriously, the type of yawn that would earn her a mock rebuke at home, because it was she who slept soundly all night while Aaron dealt with the baby. 'Don't tell me you're tired,' he would say, and even though he was joking she would feel ashamed.

This yawn was not from tiredness, though, but from the emotion of the morning. She felt invigorated to be back at work but she had forgotten what it was like to be thrown into the midst of other people's grief, and to be responsible for offering them some hope of resolution.

'Coffee?' McClintock asked from behind her. 'Regroup? My shout.' They had not spoken since he'd allowed Virginia Maiden to leave the building while he was on his phone call and he clearly sensed that she was irritated.

'Yes, good plan.'

'Bit cheeky of Maiden to bugger off like that when she was told to wait,' he said as they walked along William Street in search of 'decent coffee', as McClintock put it. 'I did make it clear no one was to leave.'

You should have been there watching her.

'But it's not her, so she won't be galivanting off into the sunset. Still, pretty rude.'

'What makes you think it isn't her? Every other judge I spoke to indicated there was no love lost between her and Kaye Bailey.'

'She's pretty old, she wouldn't have the physical strength to strangle and beat a younger woman.' McClintock said this as though it were completely obvious.

They ordered drinks from a smart cafe next to the Magistrate's Court. Its slick surfaces and exposed copper piping were in stark contrast to the two figures sitting with their heads down on cardboard beds just outside the door, takeaway cups extended in the hope of donations.

What awful weather to be sleeping rough in.

'So,' McClintock said as they waited for their orders. 'I saw Meg Hassler heading out earlier. She said there are hardly any fingerprints in Kaye's chambers, someone did a big clean-up last night. She reckons the only ones they found will belong to the associates and Kaye. Our murderer must have wiped down whatever he touched.'

'What did you make of the associates? Christianne and Matthew?'

'I don't like them for it,' McClintock said decisively. 'They alibi each other, they both seem genuinely broken up, and she's tiny, she couldn't strangle anyone.'

'I tentatively agree,' Jillian said. 'What about the chief judge?'

'He's a dickhead,' McClintock sneered. 'I'd like it to be him. Wouldn't be surprised.'

'He is a dickhead,' Jillian agreed. 'And I get the impression that he really didn't like Judge Bailey. We need to talk to Maiden and those barristers they were with, try to confirm whether they did all leave together.'

'Soy latte and a skinny cap for Mick,' a young woman called. As she handed McClintock the coffees, Jillian noted that the barista had drawn golden hearts on his cup. She rolled her eyes.

'So get this,' he added as they left. 'The CCTV for the building – the whole building – was shut down last night for routine maintenance.'

'You're joking?'

'Nope. Pretty convenient, right?'

'Didn't they know there was a party on?'

'Apparently they did, but the judge didn't want to reschedule and they had to do the maintenance that night. I thought it sounded weird but Tomir still hadn't come by the time I left and I'm told he was in charge of the whole thing. I asked the bloke I spoke to about proximity cards too. He said there's a way of seeing who came and went and when, but he doesn't know how to work it. We need to wait for this Tomir fellow. I rang him; he was at some medical appointment. Said he'd be in later.'

'Maybe one of our guys can get on it.'

'Yeah, I'll check it out. What about you? How'd you go with all the old folk?'

She laughed despite herself. 'They're not that old, some of them are only in their fifties. But it's a tricky one. We've got a few people who fairly openly didn't like Kaye Bailey, and a few more who say they did, although none of them have volunteered anything much about words exchanged between her and Meyers, which is a bit irritating. Closing ranks, I guess. And that's just the judges. I'm told she pissed off one or two of the barristers who were there. The good thing is that unless we have some sort of genius assassin, or she let someone up into chambers herself, it must have been someone at the party. You'd need access to the building and you'd need to know where to go. Right?'

'Yup, agreed.' They had walked back to the court building and now took damp seats at the side of a fountain that ran the length of the entrance. The smell of wet grass wafted across from the gardens, mingling with the stench of fuel and overflowing gutters.

McClintock took a large sip of his latte and turned to her. 'Look, you can head off if you want,' he said. 'Back to your bub. I'll go back to base, prepare for the presser. We've already spoken to so many people and I know you weren't meant to be back until next week.'

'Are you trying to get rid of me?' Rage was rising up from the pit of her stomach faster than she could control it. She felt incredulous. This was her job. This was her case. How dare he?

'What? No!' He looked surprised. 'I just assumed you'd want to –'

'Mick, do me a favour and don't ever make assumptions about what I might want or not want.' Her heart was beating fast and loud. She wanted to punch him.

'I'm sorry, I didn't mean to –'

'Okay, let's drop it.'

Already her anger at him was dissipating, to be replaced by anger with herself. *What the hell was that about? Why did I react like that?*

Her phone beeped and she fished it out of her bag. It was the first time she'd looked at it since speaking to Des hours earlier. It was a message from Aaron. She realised that she had not given her family more than a passing thought in the momentum of the morning. Was that normal? Shouldn't she be missing them?

She opened the text. *You forgot your meds. Remember to take ASAP when you get home. X*

CHAPTER 5

Jillian arrived at the St Kilda Road offices of the Homicide Squad late in the afternoon. She had not been in the building since going on maternity leave at thirty-six weeks, naively imagining a glorious period of rest and relaxation before her baby boy was expelled into the world. On her last workday she had earnestly sworn that she would bring her new charge in to meet her colleagues as soon as she could and bombard them with photographs in the interim. She had not kept either promise.

She took the lift from the damp warmth of the subterranean carpark, a mixture of excitement and nervousness in her belly. She was aware that people would ask about Ollie and her new life. She was also aware that she would likely lie in response, and then feel guilty about it. But she was returning to her spiritual home, and would shortly be inundated with the smells of instant coffee and reheated leftovers and sweat and perfume and detergent, and these would be so very welcome, even beautiful.

She saw Des before he saw her, the familiar outline of his upper body protruding from his desk as though they were two parts of the one organism. He was on the phone, eyes gazing into the middle distance.

'Hello stranger,' Detective Constable Paula Mossman said warmly as Jillian made her way to her old desk. Mossman had started the year before Jillian went on maternity leave, and while they'd never had an opportunity to forge a close relationship, Jillian had respect for the junior detective. 'So glad you're back,' Mossman said, beaming at her. 'It was beginning to feel like a bit of a boys' club.'

She gestured to Jillian's desk, which sat closest to Des's office. 'Poor old Mick wanted to sit there but Des was adamant that no one else touch it, so he's your new cubicle buddy, where Jim used to sit. Did you hear Jim retired?'

Jillian made small talk with Mossman as she settled the items she'd carried up from the car. Her desk was indeed almost exactly as she'd left it – passwords written on post-it notes, notepads with to-do lists, a picture of her and Aaron and their cat stuck to the edge of her monitor.

She cast an eye over McClintock's desk. Several neat piles labelled according to case, a biography of Roger Federer, and protein snacks in a Tupperware container. There was no sign of the detective.

'Has Mick made it back yet?' she asked Mossman.

'Yeah, he said he was off to deal with the press conference. I assume he's gone up to talk to the big brass.'

'Right.'

'Des has asked me to chase up the CCTV from a few places on Little Lonsdale that might overlook the carpark entrance. He's sent someone out to the victim's house too, get any personal items, all that jazz.'

'Ta.'

Jillian turned to wave to Des, who remained on his phone, looking bored. 'Two minutes,' he mouthed to her.

Having collated the items she'd removed from the crime scene, Jillian reread her notes from the morning, made photocopies of the Black Book that Matthew had located for her, which was in reality a blue folder, and called Angela requesting access to the email accounts of Judge Bailey and her associates. She would need to have IT try to trace the ISPs for the threatening emails. The judge's iPhone, which had been in her handbag, was flat and, she assumed, passcode protected. She plugged it into her own phone charger, hoping they could obtain the passcode later. She then liaised with forensics and began making a list of tasks according to urgency.

She requested that a Fitzroy panda car drive to Michael O'Neil's house and confirm whether or not he was at home. When she received confirmation that he was not, she then tried the mobile telephone number they had been provided with by one of the judges at the court. He did not answer. This was troubling. She knew that statistically, as the judge's current partner, O'Neil was the most likely perpetrator, even though there was no evidence that he'd attended the party.

She googled his name and found a photo of him on the Victorian Bar website. His appearance was not what she'd expected. The barrister was wearing a maroon shirt with large lapels, the top two buttons open to expose voluminous chest hair. The hair on his head was dark brown and equally abundant. He looked, Jillian thought, like an aged relative of the actor Heath Ledger. His written profile was somewhat more conventional but revealed little of interest: *Admitted to practice in 1990, called to the bar in 1991; worked in criminal law from 1990 to 2010 before moving to family law. Clerk McDougall.*

Jillian phoned the barrister's clerk and learned that O'Neil was having a few weeks off. When she asked where he had gone, the older man, who spoke with the rasp of a committed smoker, could not be drawn. 'Finished as of yesterday. Said he's not taking his phone. Said he wants to get back in touch with nature.'

'Any way of getting in contact with him? I'm with the police. This is extremely important.'

'Carrier pigeon?' the man suggested with a laugh, seemingly unperturbed that the police were trying to contact one of his barristers, although, she reflected, that was probably not that remarkable. 'He'll pop up soon enough.'

Bugger.

She conducted searches on each of the judges through the Law and Enforcement Assistance Program database without optimism. As she had expected, LEAP merely confirmed that those with a criminal record were unlikely to be considered fit and proper people to preside over the wrongdoings – criminal or matrimonial – of others. A person with the same name as Christianne, whose last known address was in Queenscliff, had been arrested for trespassing as a teenager, but it was not clear from the records what had come of this. There was no Matthew Coulter in the system at all. A Michael O'Neil with a date of birth that put him in the lapelled barrister's vintage had been arrested twice for drink driving, in 1999 and in 2007, although she doubted that this was the same man that a well-known judge would be in a relationship with.

Next she called Virginia Maiden. The judge's clipped voicemail told her to leave a message. She then phoned Grant Phillips, who said that his wife was in a dreadful state but could talk to the police tomorrow. 'She's an absolute mess,' he said. 'Harriet doesn't have many friends, and Kaye was one of the few she saw regularly.' He sounded as though he might burst into tears.

She was trying to make contact with the two barristers who the chief judge had apparently remained at the party with when she was interrupted by Des.

'Alright, rock star, let's catch up,' he called from his office door.

Detective Inspector Des Maldon was a small-boned man with a whiskered face and thinning light brown hair. He was partial in the summer months to short-sleeved collared shirts that displayed his bony arms, and in winter, to home-knitted jumpers. He was almost always found with a cup of instant coffee, half drunk, in his vicinity. He was not immediately impressive or charismatic, but behind a daggy veneer was brutal intellect and aching compassion. There was no one at St Kilda Road who Jillian admired more.

'You good?' he asked as she sat down. A casual question full of implied meaning.

'I'm better.'

'And Aaron? Ollie?'

'They're good too.'

He studied her a moment. 'Happy to be back?'

'So happy.'

'That's the way. How'd Captain Hair go?'

'Fine. As expected. How long is he sticking around for now I'm back?' *Please say he's finishing tomorrow.*

'Knew you'd ask that. He was contracted until the end of the month but with Jim gone, there's a spot free and he's expressed interest in it. Only catch is that he couldn't be acting as a senior now that you're back. I think he's mulling it over.'

'Right.'

'So what's the scoop anyway?'

She talked him through the morning's events, finishing with the disappearance of the icy Judge Maiden.

Des whistled. 'What a doozy.'

There was a knock on the office door and McClintock entered. 'Hey,' he said, taking the seat next to Jillian, 'didn't realise we were having a meeting now, my bad.'

'We were just catching up,' Des said. 'When's the post-mortem? Is one of you going?'

'I am,' McClintock said immediately. 'Sandy said hopefully tomorrow. Said she'd give it priority.'

'Good,' said Des.

'And the press conference is scheduled for five-thirty today; they said they want you there,' McClintock told his boss.

'Do they just?' Des smiled. 'Best tidy myself up a bit then.' He leaned back in his seat. 'How'd the family take it?'

McClintock looked towards Jillian expectantly. 'I thought you were doing that?'

'What? We didn't discuss that. I thought . . .'

'You're the officer in charge, right? But that's fine, I'm happy to do it.'

With great effort she restrained herself from reminding him that he had insisted he was the officer in charge with Saul Meyers. 'No, that's fine. I can do it. I'll do it right now.'

'Actually, I'll take care of it,' said Des.

Jillian began to protest but her boss raised his hand, silencing her while simultaneously shooting an irritated look at McClintock.

'Not on your first day back. Send me the details, I'll need to speak to them before the press conference. Family first, always.' Des gave a decisive clapping of his hands. 'Okay then, on with the show.'

CHAPTER 6

It was ten-fifteen pm when Jillian pulled up outside the half-renovated Yarraville weatherboard she and Aaron had lived in for the past four years. She had been out of the house for over fourteen hours. Her clothes smelled of dampness and sweat, and her body, drunk with exhaustion, had ceased normal communication with her mind. It instead responded to commands with a sluggish befuddlement. And yet she had not felt this alive, this happy, in a long time.

Her key jammed in the front door and she jiggled the lock clumsily, waiting for the familiar click. The door had been out of kilter ever since they'd had the house restumped, a year or so after moving in. On three occasions, she and Aaron had been locked out. It was one of many problems that needed fixing. The trouble was that neither of them was particularly handy, and other things had demanded more urgent attention – rewiring, replumbing, removing disturbing amounts of asbestos. In the last weeks of her pregnancy, when she was driving herself mad with waiting, Jillian had finally tried to fix the front door herself, using an Ikea toolkit purchased three rental houses ago. She had managed to unscrew the hinges easily enough, and to lower the door onto the ground. She had sanded the edges for an hour and a half in a swirl of wood dust. Then

Aaron came home and, on seeing his heavily pregnant wife struggling under the weight of a hardwood door, threw the closest thing to a tantrum she'd ever seen him have. He had managed to reattach the door himself, but it was no better. *One day . . .*

'I'm home!' she stage-whispered into the hallway. Light came from the kitchen and she heard the comforting sounds of domesticity – the murmur of the television, the running of water in the dishwater, the washing machine charging through one of the many daily loads that had become necessary with the addition of Ollie.

'Hello,' Aaron called from the couch, and she found him lying on his back, his face half illuminated by the television screen, an empty bowl of what might have been pesto pasta on the coffee table. His T-shirt was stained in two places and his shorts looked to have baby vomit across the left leg. He flashed a sleepy grin. 'You were ages.'

'I know, right – did you see the presser?'

'And the highlight reel.'

'Big news then?'

He laughed softly. 'You mean this?' He changed channels on the remote and the exterior of the Commonwealth Law Court building flashed onto the screen, running on a loop with photos of Judge Bailey. 'I think people are actually half hoping it will be like that Warwick bloke again.'

Jillian lay down on top of Aaron and pushed her face into his chest. She sighed as she breathed in the smells of him – soap and wine and nappy cream.

'Seems like she was an incredible woman,' he said, pulling Jillian close.

'I don't actually know much about her yet.'

'You know who the bad guy is?'

'Early days.'

She turned onto her side so that she could see the screen. 'Spoke to that bloke,' Jillian said as Saul Meyers' round pink face appeared. 'He was her boss. Turn it up?'

'We're all completely devastated, the whole court,' Saul Meyers was saying solemnly to an unseen journalist in his plummy voice. 'She was quite an extraordinary woman, very intelligent, very kind, very passionate, particularly about issues relating to family violence.' His eyes looked ever so slightly bloodshot.

'Have I missed Des?' she asked. 'I didn't get to see him do his questions at the station, I was on the phone.'

'Yeah, he popped up earlier.' Aaron shifted his weight. 'They'll show it again any minute. He was looking a bit rough, poor bloke. Like a sad old dog. Didn't help that they put him next to some model.'

Three guesses who that was.

'Des isn't sad,' Jillian said. 'He's just got sad eyes. How'd he do?'

'He was fine. So was the other one. You want to eat something? There's pasta in the saucepan still.'

'In a minute, I'm all comfy.'

On the screen the chief judge's head was replaced by that of another man. Younger, thinner, with the sharp eyes of an opportunist. 'This bloke's mad,' Aaron said, reaching for the remote. 'I'll mute him.'

'No, leave it on, I want to hear what he says.'

The man's name flashed across the television: Roger Barlow – President, Save Australia's Children.

'Obviously this is a dreadful tragedy,' Roger Barlow said, his mouth faking a sympathetic smile. 'Just dreadful, but as our organisation has been saying for years, the Family Law Courts, the family law system, has been responsible for countless deaths of men, women and children, and has perpetuated the abuse of more. Should we be surprised that a tragedy like this unfolded, given the circumstances?'

'So just to be clear, you're saying this violence is understandable, are you?' an incredulous male voice asked off camera.

'Told you,' Aaron said. 'Real class act.'

'No,' Barlow replied smoothly. 'Not understandable, but also not unexpected. People are being driven to breaking point. They're going bankrupt trying to see their children. And without systemic reforms, we might expect things like this to keep happening. As I've said previously, Kaye Bailey wasn't just a judge, she was an activist, at times with an anti-family agenda. There's a reason she's referred to as the Australian Ruth Bader Ginsburg.'

'I suspect a lot of people would think that was a compliment, mate,' Aaron sneered at the television. Aaron had always been a true bleeding heart. When Jillian first met him, at a wedding eight years ago, his reaction on learning she was a police officer was to physically recoil. It had taken her three dates to convince him that not all police were representatives of what he called 'the fascist state'.

'That reminds me,' Jillian said, 'she had a bust of Ruth in her office.'

'Chambers,' Aaron said, readjusting his body so he could look at her. 'Judges and barristers have chambers, not offices.'

'Right, I knew that.' She yawned deeply.

'Did you say hello to Ollie?'

'I didn't want to wake him.'

Aaron didn't respond but she felt his body tense slightly beneath her.

'Alright, I'll do it now,' she said, a little impatiently. She eased herself up and let herself into Ollie's bedroom as quietly as she could. With a sliver of light from the door for guidance, she tiptoed towards the expensive Scandinavian cot she had purchased in those joyful, anticipatory months prior to her son's birth. He lay on his back, arms above his head and sleep suit dishevelled, breathing deeply.

'Hey you,' she whispered. 'I'm home from work. Hope you and Dad had a nice fun day.'

Part of her wanted to reach out and touch him, to run a finger along that plump cheek, but she knew that she wouldn't, that she couldn't. She knew that the risk was too great that she would wake him up and that then he would want something from her that she wasn't able to give – comfort, reassurance, love.

She had always assumed that she would be an excellent mother, that the exacting, meticulous work ethic she had brought to every other element of her life would prepare her for bringing a child into the world. She had read every book, attended every course and followed every recommendation of the doctors and midwives who had seen her through the pregnancy and the birth, and then discovered in the aftermath that it wasn't enough. That she would never be enough.

'Alright, goodnight,' she whispered stiffly.

Some women just aren't designed for this.

Aaron was returning to the couch from the kitchen as she closed the door. 'Still out?'

'Dead to the world.'

She sat down heavily and a moment later he put a bowl of pasta, a glass of water and her medication down on the coffee table in front of her.

'You forgot this morning,' he said gently.

Too tired to argue, she put the pills in her mouth and pretended to swallow, only spitting them out when Ollie let out a cry a moment later and Aaron disappeared.

CHAPTER 7

Aaron was still asleep when she left for work the next morning. He had gone in to Ollie sometime after two-thirty and was cuddled in next to him in the double bed that had once been reserved for friends after a big night out. The two of them looked so complete lying there together that she resisted the urge to wake Aaron and warn him of the dangers of co-sleeping, knowing in her gut that she was motivated more by jealousy than any genuine concerns for Ollie's safety. She knew that their son was fine, that Aaron was in the lightest stage of sleep and would wake at the smallest indication that something was wrong. Her husband was a natural father, a man from whom love and patience seemed to flow in abundance. He had trained as a social worker before returning to university to study psychology and had spent the previous few years assisting those in recovery from drug addiction. Now he spent his days with Ollie going between playgroups and parenting catch-ups and baby-related appointments.

So much better at it than you.

Yesterday's rain had given way to blue skies and tepid sunlight. McClintock was already at his desk when she arrived at St Kilda Road, his too-long body crouched over his monitor as he typed intently. It was a little after seven-thirty and he looked irritatingly buoyant.

'Just putting through a request for her phone data,' he said by way of greeting.

'I already did that yesterday,' she said. 'I copied you in.'

He looked up, surprised. 'Did you? Sorry, missed it. Oh well, this will just make clear how urgent it is.'

She turned her computer on and went to make a coffee in the kitchen. 'Did Des tell you he spoke to the daughter and the husband?' she asked when she came back. 'Both are alibied, obviously – they were in London and Singapore respectively. Both pretty devastated.'

'Oh. I wasn't informed.' McClintock sounded a little put out. He stretched and said, 'I faxed through a warrant request for Michael O'Neil's place.'

Jillian thought this was premature. 'And you didn't think to check with me first? As the officer in charge of the investigation?'

He shrugged, oblivious to her tone. 'I'm not saying we need to use it, I just thought it would be helpful.'

He returned to his typing and Jillian began on the emails she hadn't been able to get to or had only skimmed the day before. Some of the CCTV footage from the businesses surrounding the court had already arrived and she opened file after file, searching through the often grainy, always low-quality video for number plates or the glimpse of a face. A restaurant called Salvatore's provided the most useful angles. Although it did not show her the carpark entrance itself, she was offered clear vision of each driver and each vehicle as they turned left onto Little Lonsdale which was, mercifully, a one-way street. Between seven and nine pm a single taxi idled in designated taxi parking directly outside the restaurant. Shortly after the cab departed, she registered the first judge leaving – the surly Angus from the day before – in his court-issued car. As the minutes ticked over she made out most of the judges she had met. At ten thirty-five Grant Phillips' long face was clearly visible from the driver's side of his car. At eleven-fifteen, the same footage showed four people huddled together as they made their way towards William Street, their faces obscured by darkness. 'Meyers and his cronies?' she said to herself. The footage thereafter was uneventful, the legal end of town unsurprisingly quiet in the early hours of a Thursday morning.

As she had anticipated, footage from Flagstaff Station showed Judge Bailey's two associates waiting together on platform three for their trains. At nine thirty-two pm Christianne boarded a South Morang line. Ten minutes later, Matthew took the Hurstbridge. 'They check out, then.'

Little could be gleaned from the other CCTV they had received so far. A chemist that faced onto the front of the court showed nothing but a couple sleeping rough in the doorway. A convenience store on Latrobe Street showed an obviously drunk man urinating onto a parking meter.

Jillian turned her attention to the belongings that had been removed from Judge Bailey's East Melbourne flat on Des's instruction the day before. Several boxes had been placed in the meeting room and she went in and began to open them, one after another. There were a number of court files that Bailey seemed to have been working on, and whose content had been as brutally dissected as the Sharma and Nettle folder on her work desk. There were a series of notebooks, most of which seemed to relate to judgements she had been working on, as well as bills, cards and the occasional handwritten letter.

'Any joy?' McClintock called.

'Nothing that interesting.'

At midday she got to her feet and returned to the cubicle she now shared with McClintock. 'I reckon I might go to O'Neil's house, see if we can find some friendly neighbours to chat to.'

'Yeah right,' McClintock agreed, also getting to his feet. 'Let's go. I just asked for his bank records, actually. Thought they might help.'

For the second day in a row, the traffic flowed easily. They drove through the city, past jacketed workers and comedy festival posters, both moved by the slight breeze. McClintock tapped out a chirpy rhythm on the steering wheel. She had wanted to drive but he'd peered suspiciously through her front passenger window and declared that he wasn't willing to risk his work clothes on her stained upholstery.

At a red light, McClintock leaned across and opened the glove box. Jillian pushed back into her seat to avoid contact, irritated that he was so oblivious to the physical space he claimed.

He retrieved a packet of mints and took one for himself before offering them to her.

'I'm good, thanks.'

'You and Des are pretty tight, hey?' he ventured as the light changed.

Jillian was unsure how to answer this. She was close to Des, that was true, but it was a peculiar type of closeness. Each of them knew things about the other they would never mention to another living soul. She trusted him totally and unconditionally. And yet she would never socialise with Des, never call him for a casual chat or invite him over for a barbecue. He had visited her in hospital, but that didn't count. Eventually she said, 'We work well together, we just gel, I guess.'

'Nah,' said McClintock, 'it's more than that. I can tell. Wish I could get him back onside. He's always pissed off with me.'

I don't think you were ever onside . . .

'I think the trick with Des is to just play it straight,' she offered. It wasn't as though she could tell him that Des didn't like entitled jocks who he suspected of using Homicide as a step up to Command.

'Play it straight, hey?' McClintock said. 'I thought I did.'

Try being less smug. Less smarmy.

And less you.

Michael O'Neil lived in the gentrified wedge of Fitzroy between Brunswick Street and the Royal Exhibition Building. It was an area Jillian knew well from her time at the University of Melbourne, when Fitzroy had been the type of place where six students could cram into an unrenovated Victorian terrace for $50 a week each. Morton Street, where O'Neil lived, sat adjacent to the housing commission towers, but from the vantage point of the securely middle-class.

These houses, like the share houses of Jillian's youth, were mainly Victorian, although there were a few modernist incursions. European SUVs and hybrid sedans lined either side of the street. A large cafe on the Brunswick Street corner was overflowing with young professionals enjoying coffees and perfectly poached eggs. Jillian eyed the window piled high with fresh croissants and her stomach rumbled audibly. 'I'll need to pop in there before we head.'

Michael O'Neil lived at number 47, which, at least from the outside, was the sole surviving relic of the earlier, grungier Fitzroy Jillian had enjoyed. A badly maintained front garden overwhelmed the small path that ran from a sloping brick fence to a front door whose yellow paint was chipping off. Old catalogues had been piled unceremoniously on the narrow porch, next to an outdoor seat on which a black and white cat was curled. On the ground was an ashtray overflowing with cigarette butts. Jillian thought of the photograph on the Victorian Bar website.

I suppose this fits.

'Surely not?' McClintock said, assessing the house over his sunglasses like a real estate agent. 'He's a bloody barrister.'

The cat jumped down from the seat, arched its back and began rubbing its body against McClintock's suit pants in a luxurious figure eight. He bent down to pat it.

Jillian knocked. 'Michael O'Neil, are you in there? It's the police.'

There was no response, and no noise from within. The door itself had an old-fashioned letterbox slot and Jillian pushed it open. 'Mr O'Neil,' she called again as she peered into it. 'Can you open up, please?' In the half-light of the house she could make out nothing save for a grey-blue carpet and an abandoned shoe. She slid a business card through the slot.

They spent some time trying his neighbours but the only person who answered was an older woman with limited English, who seemed to be trying to convey that she thought McClintock would make an excellent husband for her granddaughter. They returned to the car, dejected. 'We'll try his chambers,' Jillian said. 'Just in case.'

McClintock flicked the radio on and allowed talkback radio to fill the car as they drove back to the city. An AFL player's manager was being interviewed about rates of pay. 'You've got to understand,' he told the interviewer, 'that these boys put themselves under shocking stress. They can effectively give up their entire bodies for the game and they should be compensated accordingly. It's always possible that they'll never work again.'

'Right on,' McClintock said, thumping the steering wheel.

They parked on Lonsdale Street, near the corner of the Owen Dixon Building where the vast majority of the city's barristers worked. Men and women wheeling black briefcases were returning from the various courts. In their black gowns and white collars, they looked as if they were from a different time.

'Don't they wear wigs anymore?' Jillian asked absently.

'Don't think so. Maybe in the County Court, but nowhere else.'

'Huh.'

The building's innards were as removed from the present day as its occupants. Serious faces peered down from photographs and oil paintings; boards with long lists of names announced honours, appointments, ceremonies; printed posters advertised spit roasts and trivia nights. A central artery connected the eastern and western wings, and numerous corridors led in every direction. Jillian and McClintock passed a clerks' office where people sat barking lists of names into phones, a conference room and a pigeonholed wall stuffed with documents tied in maroon ribbon.

'This way.' McClintock ushered her into a lift.

'Do you actually know where you're going?' she asked, wondering if he was like Aaron, who would head decisively in any direction when he was lost, just to keep moving.

'Yup. I've been here before.'

At level five, they got out and followed plush carpet to a large window overlooking the domed roof of the Supreme Court. A directory board pointed them to the left.

As they walked, Jillian caught glimpses of figures at desks, talking on phones, reading from white folders. There were scraps of conversation too, tantalising in their apparent importance. 'Tell Don if he wants me I want the money in trust now, I'm not risking it again,' a woman groaned into her receiver. 'Five a day, non-negotiable.'

'I see what you're saying,' said a young woman looming over a suited older man, who was sitting at attention in an upright chair. 'But I can't sell her on that. She says she's scared shitless, and regardless of what you or I might think about that, we know Sally will err on the side of caution.'

Michael O'Neil's office was the last door on the left-hand side. It was closed and there was no thin strip of light or sound of movement within that hinted it was occupied. Indeed, it had the same abandoned air as his home. Jillian knocked, then gently tested the handle. 'Locked,' she said. McClintock tried the door himself.

Just in case I didn't do it right.

'You looking for Screwy?' In a room across the corridor, a man of perhaps seventy with several chins was sitting at his desk with a mess of papers spread out before him, his neck craned forward to see what they were doing.

'We are,' Jillian said. 'You know where he's got to?'

'He was gonna take some time off so I'm not really expecting him in,' the man replied. 'You spoken to his clerk?'

'We're police,' Jillian said.

'Are you just? This about poor old Judge Kaye then, is it? Bloody dreadful.' He shook his head. 'Just unbelievable.'

'You knew her, did you?' said McClintock, joining Jillian at the office door.

'Only through Screwy.' He took a slurp from a thick mug. 'Come in if you want.' He gestured to the chairs facing his desk.

His office reminded Jillian of her long-deceased uncle Bob's study – equal parts serious-looking dark wooden furniture, sporting memorabilia and old framed photographs.

'Buxton's my name, by the way. Tim Buxton. What did you say you lot were called?' He had a deliberately colloquial manner that grated on Jillian – a blokishness that reminded her of a politician visiting with factory workers.

'I'm Detective Basset. This is McClintock.' Jillian sat while McClintock walked casually to a bookshelf housing several framed photographs. 'Homicide Squad.'

'So it's definitely murder then, is it? Well, that's a damned shame. You hear things, you sort of hope, but . . .' He shook his head again. 'So goes it.'

'You've heard things, you say?'

'I just meant there's been a few judicial suicides in recent years, that's all. Obviously you don't want it to be that either, but the thought of someone . . . Well, that's even worse.' He dunked a sugary biscuit in his tea.

Behind her, McClintock said, 'Is this Daniel Modhi?'

Jillian turned to see him holding a framed photo. Tim Buxton got laboriously to his feet and walked over to join McClintock. 'Sure is, that's at my daughter's christening. Back in 1985. You know him? Wouldn't have thought he'd be your vintage.'

'I've never met him. My old man knew him, though. He was in Organised Crime back in the day. Used to point out Modhi in the paper. Always said he was a slippery bastard.'

Tim Buxton laughed wheezily. 'Well, that's about right. I reckon he would have been offended if anyone said otherwise. Who's your old man then?'

'Ron McClintock.'

The barrister's face lit up. 'Is he? Well, there you go. Real pain in the arse your old man was. Didn't miss a trick. And you're following in his footsteps.' He stood back to survey McClintock. 'He must be really proud.'

A look passed across McClintock's face, too quick for Jillian to interpret, and he replaced the photograph.

'He still around then? Your dad?' Tim Buxton asked.

'Retired maybe five years ago, passed away soon after that.'

'Ah. My sympathies. That's why lawyers never retire, you know. They say sharks have to keep swimming because they'll sink if they don't, and it's the same for us lot. If you stop working, things start to go. I retired a few years ago. Had a stroke straightaway. So I came back.' He smiled, revealing pale yellow teeth.

'I think Dad always regretted stopping,' McClintock conceded, and the unreadable look returned – a tenseness at the jaw and at the edge of his eyes.

'Well that sounds right. A cop like that, real dogged, what's he gonna do in retirement except drive your mum nuts and piss off the neighbours.'

'That's pretty much how it played out.'

The men shared a silence and Jillian felt very aware of her femaleness.

'Do you happen to know if Mr O'Neil knows what's happened?' she said.

'Not sure, love,' said Buxton. 'Last I saw of him was on Wednesday night. He came back from court around four-thirty and we took a breather together, popped down for a bite at the club. We came back here. He had a conference. He was still going when I left, which was well after ten.'

'Just to be clear, this was Wednesday this week, the day before yesterday?'

Buxton nodded.

'Conference with who?'

'I can't remember the name, younger woman, red hair. Annoying voice. They had a client with them too. Some young bloke.'

'Did he happen to mention his plans for the rest of the night?'

'Nope. Heard him on the phone at one stage telling his lady love he might not make it any time soon.'

'You heard him talking to Judge Bailey?'

'Well, I assume it was her, ño guarantees. But it was a really quick call, he might have just been leaving her a message. I wasn't really paying attention.'

'What time was this?'

'I was packing up, so late. Maybe quarter to ten?'

He returned to sit at his desk and looked at the detectives carefully, his old eyes shrewd. 'Now make no mistake, Screwy wouldn't have had anything to do with it. He worshipped that woman, absolutely doted on her.'

'You seem very certain of that?'

'Of course I'm bloody certain, I've known him since he came to the bar. He doesn't have a bad bone in his body. That's why he always gets himself into bother – doesn't get paid and the like. Plus, he's endured his own hardships, he'd never inflict that on another person. I'm sure of it.'

The barrister raised his left wrist, looked at his watch and whistled. 'I've got to go, I've got a date with Modhi's son-in-law in the cells.'

Jillian and McClintock looked at each other. McClintock shrugged ever so slightly.

'Thanks,' said Jillian, standing up. 'You've been very helpful.'

At the door she turned back as an idea occurred to her. 'Would you know where Greg Eaves and Graham Norman have their chambers? They nearby?'

Tim Buxton gave a little snort. 'They're both on level four, but if they don't have briefs or they're done for the day I'd bet my firstborn that they're at the Essiong. Just go down to level one. You'll find it easy enough.'

'What did you make of that?' McClintock asked as they took the lift down to the first floor. 'Seemed like a ripper bloke.'

You only think that because he liked your dad.

'He sure was a character.' Jillian wasn't sure 'ripper' would have been the first word that came to her mind. She'd always found lawyers who dealt in organised crime uncomfortable to deal with. It wasn't that they were particularly unpleasant people, in fact those she had encountered were generally quite the opposite, but she was wary of the type of person who was able to bat for the bad guy, the really bad guy, with no apparent crisis of conscience. To her mind, the crime families, those who ran the drugs and the protection rackets and the illegal brothels, were in some respects more culpable than the average rapist or murderer. Their entire business model depended upon the unalloyed exploitation of others. She did not understand how a man like Tim Buxton, who apparently attended family functions with Daniel Modhi, could maintain a clear moral compass.

'He's famous, did you know?' McClintock said.

'I didn't.'

'My old man used to hate him. He got cross-examined by him once, in a murder trial, I think. Dad must have fucked up a bit because he was spitting chips when he came home afterwards.'

'I didn't know your dad was a cop. You've kept that quiet.'

McClintock shrugged. 'We weren't close.'

The Essiong Club was little more than a cafeteria looking out onto William Street. While a small sign indicated that it was for members only, no one prevented the detectives from walking right in. Greg Eaves and Graham Norman were immediately identifiable because they were sitting in the far right corner with Chief Judge Saul Meyers.

'Getting their story straight?' McClintock whispered as they made their way over.

'Afternoon,' he said to the group with a slightly threatening under-tone. 'Chief Judge? And is this Greg Eaves and Graham Norman of Counsel?'

The three men looked up at the detectives, the two barristers blank-faced. 'Who are you then?' said one. 'Have we met?'

'These are the detectives investigating Judge Bailey's murder,' Saul Meyers explained to his friends with apparent irritation. 'Look, with the greatest respect, you can't just waltz in here demanding to speak to me. You need to make an appointment.'

'We weren't actually looking for you, Chief Judge,' Jillian explained. 'It's these two gentlemen we're after.'

'Lucky us, hey,' said the second man, nudging his friend in the ribs. He had a leering glint in his eyes. 'What can we help you with, dear lady?'

'We'd like a word,' she said. 'Perhaps we might move to another table? Your name?'

'Eaves. Anything for you,' he said with a wink to the other men, and got to his feet. 'Over here alright?'

In a low voice to McClintock, Jillian said, 'We'll take them separately, okay? You do Norman?'

Jillian had dealt with many a lecherous man, and not just during her time in the police force. After thirty-six years of interacting with the other sex, there were few male behaviours that surprised her, although Greg Eaves had to be given credit for a concerted effort. Her simplest questions – what time he had gone to and left the party, where he had gone afterwards, whether he remembered what time Saul Meyers and Virginia Maiden had left – were met with every conceivable double entendre, a dinner invitation, and the insight that 'Ginny had great tits when she was younger too.'

Jillian looked across at McClintock, who was talking to Graham Norman at the other end of the room. The two of them had their heads close and seemed to be sharing a joke.

Of course.

She turned back to Eaves and said, 'What can you tell me about Judge Bailey's interaction with the chief judge at the party?'

'Kaye bit his head off, so he was in a mood after that. God, she could be a bitch. I know you're not meant to speak ill of the dead but she could be. It was Saul's night and she bloody had a go at him in front of everybody. Graham was joking that it must have been her time of the month and then Saul said she must have been bleeding since 1990 in that case.' Eaves stopped to let out a loud bellow at this. 'Anyway, Ginny had organised some bloody decent wine so we stuck around until that was gone. I reckon we left about eleven. Then we buggered off to the Danish Club, stayed there for an hour or so, chucked Saul in a cab and went home. You married?'

The second time I've been asked that already in this case. Although at least Grant Phillips wasn't hitting on me.

'So Judge Bailey got stuck into him, did she?'

'Bloody oath, should have heard her.' He adopted a prissy voice to imitate the dead judge. '"You were a terrible lawyer, a worse judge and a fundamentally appalling human being. Your retirement is a blessing for this court, for the employees, the litigants and the jurisprudence. I cannot wait to eradicate your memory, and to ensure that all of the rubbish you have presided over is never repeated again." She'd always been power hungry, one of those who want to get in and meddle. Going to the bench is meant to be service, you do it to ensure stability. Saul, Virginia, most of the others, they all got it. Bailey never did.'

Jillian wondered if this was the 'sharp-tongued' comment that Christianne had overheard being referred to outside chambers. She had assumed that Bailey had told the older judge to 'piss off' or something of that ilk. If Eaves' report was accurate, this was closer to a complete take-down. 'How did the chief judge react to the earbashing?'

'He was bloody devastated,' the barrister replied indignantly, his cheeks becoming blotchy as anger overwhelmed him. 'Awful things to say, and at his retirement party.'

'And what happened then?'

'Well, she left I think, stormed out. We told Saul not to worry about her, but he was pretty shaken. Everyone had a turn at talking him down; even the Bailey apologists like Phillips were trying.'

'And how did he seem for the rest of the night?'

'Oh, he got over it after another drink or so. We all told him, "Now everyone's seen her true colours anyway." Reckon that cheered him up a bit.'

Jillian stood up and with some effort, interrupted McClintock's conversation. 'You good?' she asked.

'Yup.' He got to his feet.

'She keeps you on a tight leash, doesn't she, mate?' Graham Norman said with a laugh. 'You look after yourself. Nice to chat.'

'Well?' Jillian asked as they walked back to McClintock's pathologically neat car. 'My guy says Bailey gave as good as she got in their little argument. Had some pretty sharp comments for Meyers.'

'My guy said that too, although he also said he can hardly remember anything but he knows they were leaving the Danish Club by around midnight because his credit card statement told him as much. And he's positive they put the chief judge in a cab around twelve-fifteen and he was plastered.'

'So,' Jillian said thoughtfully. 'The question is, where did Meyers tell the cab to go? Home or back to the court?'

CHAPTER 8

They had planned, depending on whether or not Michael O'Neil could be located, to meet with Judge Grant Phillips' wife, Harriet, at their home in Hawthorn before trying to catch the elusive Judge Maiden who lived the next suburb over. However as McClintock entered Phillips' address into his GPS, his mobile began to vibrate. He answered it without checking the number, something Jillian found bizarrely uninhibited.

Who just answers their phone? It could be anyone! A telemarketer, a scammer.

Or a psychologist wondering whether you're coming to your appointment today.

'Angela, yes of course,' McClintock crooned. 'How are you?' There was a pause. 'No, that's okay, we're actually close by. We can pop in now if that suits?' He signed off, looking mildly excited.

'Angela Hui. Says she forgot to mention something yesterday that might be important. Guess we can try and catch the security guy at the same time?'

*

Three film crews were stationed outside the Commonwealth Law Courts, all in various stages of preparation for live crosses – the journalists coated in thick pancake make-up, the crews toying with equipment. There was still an obvious uniformed police presence at the building, although they didn't seem to be doing much aside from 'instilling a sense of safety in the public', as Des would put it.

Printed signs had been posted on the doors of both entrances and Jillian read one with interest: *Due to unforeseen circumstances the Commonwealth Law Courts will be closed until further notice. All documents can be filed online or by post. Please contact the relevant chambers for all matters currently before the court.*

'Good way to create chaos,' she mused aloud as they waited for Angela to fetch them at the staff entrance. 'Kill a judge, the whole system practically shuts down.'

Angela stepped out of the lift and waved to them through the window as she flicked her security pass in front of the sensor. The building was even quieter than the day before and their feet echoed loudly on the polished floor as they followed her to the lifts.

'They've said we can all return to our offices tomorrow,' Angela said. 'Aside from Kaye's chambers, obviously, which are still waiting on the cleaners, but almost everyone is home until we confirm new security arrangements. Most of the judges are concerned it's going to be another Family Court Murders scenario.'

At level twelve she guided them out of the lift, through the security doors and to the other wing of the L-shaped building from that in which Judge Bailey had been murdered. Her office was the first door on this side, a large space that seemed to be part sitting room, part storage facility and, in the far corner, her workspace. 'Not quite as grand as chambers,' she said. 'Apologies for the mess.'

She led them to her desk and indicated for them to sit. The wall next to her was peppered with inspirational quotes and photos of people holding cocktails on beaches and by swimming pools.

Just as I would have predicted.

'I feel terrible for not mentioning this yesterday,' Angela said, 'I just, well, we weren't thinking clearly, any of us. There was so much going on trying to deal with all the staff, the listings, everything else. I clean forgot.' She looked from McClintock to Jillian. 'The thing is, last year, there were two security breaches involving Judge Bailey.'

'Two?' Jillian repeated.

'That's right. Now, the first one wasn't particularly serious in and of itself. It was a litigant, a woman called Rosa Mastromonica – she rushed Kaye in court, threw a jug at her. This woman was self-represented, clearly disturbed. She got herself over the associates' desk while Christianne was to the side of the room talking to someone. Kaye pressed her panic button, security came and removed her.'

'Do we know where she is now?' McClintock asked.

Angela gave a little cough. 'She actually suicided shortly after that hearing. I know Kaye was quite distressed when she found out about it. But then later last year, November, I think, there was a more serious incident. I've got the footage here. I wanted to email it but I couldn't figure out how.' She pressed her keyboard and frowned. 'Sorry, computer has just updated. I'll just need to restart it.' The three of them grimaced as a series of crunching noises reverberated from deep within the machine. 'This will take a moment,' she said apologetically.

'While we've got you,' Jillian said, 'can you tell us how Judge Bailey got along with her colleagues? The other judges, I mean. We understand there was some tension between her and the chief judge. And Judge Maiden too.'

Angela looked uncomfortable. 'Is this confidential? It's just . . .'

'If you know something that's relevant you need to tell us,' Jillian said.

'Well,' Angela said, 'yes, there were some issues between Judge Bailey and the CJ. I think there'd been bad blood before Kaye was appointed; they're very different people, you understand. Saul is old school, Kaye had a very different approach to the job. But the CJ was very upset about her being his replacement. He asked me to write a letter.' She leaned forward and lowered her voice. 'To the attorney-general's department, to raise concerns about her selection. I told him I couldn't, that it was inappropriate, and, well, I didn't say this to him but I thought Kaye was a good choice. He was quite annoyed with me after that.'

'When was this?'

'Last week.'

'But we understood Judge Bailey only found out she'd been appointed on the night she was killed.'

Angela again looked uncomfortable. 'I'm not sure what happened exactly. I mean, it's possible the chief judge sat on it. I knew she was going to be offered the role but I didn't mention it to her, of course – it wasn't my place.'

The detectives looked at each other.

'How did you know?'

'I sat in on the selection committee – they have a representative from the courts, a senior judge and representatives from the attorney-general's department. Saul was on the panel too.'

'Did she have run-ins with any of the other judges?'

'I don't think she and Judge Maiden liked each other particularly, but that's not surprising – again, Virginia is very old school. But aside from that she got along well with most of them as far as

I know. That said, the judges wouldn't come to me if there were issues. They'd go to the chief judge. They aren't subject to the APS Code of Conduct or anything like the rest of us, and they tend to manage themselves, really.'

'And close ranks?' Jillian suggested.

'Well, yes.'

'How did Judge Bailey get along with the support staff?' Jillian asked as the computer entered the next stage of its tortured rebirth.

'Oh, she was one of the few who never had any issues. Some of the other chambers basically have a revolving door; she had a very low turnover. Matt's been with her since she was appointed, Christianne came last year when Kaye's old deputy went to the bar. The few people who have left have done so amicably. Plus we had requests from other associates to move to Kaye's chambers if a position became available, which tells you something. The associates like to talk between themselves.'

'We're still waiting to hear from your security manager,' McClintock said. 'Don't suppose you could give him a call?'

'I'll text him right now,' Angela said, and did so. 'There, I've told him to call you as soon as possible. I think he's doing the rounds with the uniformed officers today, explaining all the entrances to them, and I know Saul's keeping him busy trying to deal with new security procedures before he properly finishes up.'

Her computer emitted a dinging noise. 'Ah, here we go.' Angela clicked her keyboard and spun the screen around so that the detectives could see it.

The CCTV footage was in the same blurry black and white as that salvaged from the surrounding premises. 'Thought the court would spring for better CCTV,' she said, squinting hard. 'Our techies might be able to work some magic . . .'

The video showed a figure in a dark hooded windcheater entering the corridor behind a courtroom that looked identical to the one they'd seen the morning before. The man – Jillian was sure it was a man – walked quickly but casually. At the liftwell that connected the courtrooms to chambers he pressed a button before looking around. A moment later he held something to the sensor pad and pressed the button again. The view changed to the camera inside the lift. The man's identity remained concealed, just the suggestion of a nose. The view then changed to the public lift that Jillian had first used to access chambers the day before.

'He got out here on level twelve,' Angela said. 'Then we don't see anything for almost forty minutes, until he gets back into the public lift, goes to the ground floor and leaves. The scary thing is, no one would even have noticed if Tomir hadn't been running through the whole system later in the week. There were three judges sitting that day so it was blind luck that he didn't run into anyone. The security guards on duty didn't notice anything amiss at the time either.'

'How do you know this related to Judge Bailey?' said Jillian.

'Her wallet was stolen,' Angela said, 'and she was one of the three judges sitting in court that day. But we think we know how the breach happened. Court wasn't sitting at that point. I think Kaye had taken a bathroom break or something. Christianne was in the courtroom by herself. She had taken her lanyard off and left it there while she went down to the registry, which is in the basement. Not a long walk, but she would have been gone at least a full minute. We think he ducked in, grabbed it and went straight behind the judge's bench. Pretty game. It's a wonder he didn't run into Kaye as she returned to court.'

'Do you know who he is?' McClintock asked.

'We couldn't identify him on the footage, obviously,' Angela said. 'But Kaye was one hundred per cent certain it was a litigant called Brian Shanahan. He's been in and out of the court system for years. She had him for a few of his matters, he was trouble the whole time, and very unhappy with her decisions. She was sure he held a grudge and she was sure he was at court that day – not before her; he had another matter at the time before a different judge. But the court hearings are open to the public so apparently he just let himself in, took a seat at the back of the room, stared daggers at her for a while and then left.'

'And this was never investigated, either internally or through the police?'

'No.' Angela shifted uncomfortably. 'A decision was made not to escalate things. We cancelled the card he used, and that was it. I held on to the footage only because something like this, well, it's always at the back of my mind.' She pursed her lips and Jillian saw fleeting evidence of real feeling behind the matte foundation and discreetly botoxed forehead.

'And it was Kaye's decision that it wouldn't go any further?'

'No,' said Angela. 'That was the chief judge's call.'

CHAPTER 9

Brian Shanahan had a hard compact face, piercing grey eyes and a robust internet presence. A brief perusal of his publicly available Facebook information, his various websites and the LEAP records available allowed Jillian to piece together a detailed life story.

Shanahan had been a secondary school teacher in Geelong for over a decade, until the breakdown of his relationship with his first wife – a breakdown that had culminated in accusations against him of harassment and stalking, and a guilty plea to one charge of breaching an Intervention Order. On his own telling, he had been left so violated and so traumatised by the family law system and the decision to take his house from under him, that he had lapsed into a three-year depression during which he had been unable to work. Thereafter he completed a Masters of Education and secured a job at an international school. Within six months of resuming his career he 'fell victim' to the advances of a Year 12 student. The girl, a Chinese national, moved into his home, and at eighteen was pregnant with his child. When she sought to return to China with the child, Brian Shanahan returned to the family law system in an effort to stop her. The years since had seen him wage wars on many fronts – against the mother of his child; subsequent wives; the teaching regulator; and, for reasons Jillian did not understand, Workcover. All of this was documented in agonising detail on his personal website.

All Shanahan's subsequent relationships appeared to have ended with mutual Intervention Orders. His last known address was in Lara, a small town in the dead zone between Werribee and Geelong.

'We really need to check him out straightaway,' Jillian told Des on the phone as McClintock navigated the car through the thickening mid-afternoon traffic. 'If this is the Family Court Murders all over again it'll be someone like him. Plus he's probably got form for getting into chambers. Angela is going to send through all the judgements relating to his cases, said it will give us some context, whatever that means. We'll push the Phillips interview until tomorrow and go straight out to meet the family from here.'

'If I can stick my two cents in,' McClintock interrupted, 'I'm liking the chief judge. He had means and motive.'

'We're trying to track down the cabbie who picked him up from the Danish Club, that should prove it one way or the other,' Jillian said. 'But while we're waiting on that, I think we need to check Shanahan out.'

'I'm with you,' Des said. 'We can't sit on this. I'll touch base with the daughter and the ex-husband when they land. I think we got told they were getting in around five but that seems too optimistic to me. We've organised a hotel in East Melbourne, so you can do your poking around and then go see them.'

'Yup, sounds good.'

While McClintock navigated them to the Geelong freeway Jillian called Grant Phillips to make alternative arrangements. 'By the way,' she said, 'did Kaye ever mention a Brian Shanahan to you?'

'Oh yes,' the judge said with a humourless laugh. 'I'm well aware of Mr Shanahan's dealings with Kaye. She had the misfortune of handling a few of his matters. I've had him myself one or two times, an awful parenting case. Pretty much everyone has a Mr Shanahan story. He's a nasty piece of work, a really vile man. I remember he spat on his wife in court once, and stole a bunch of exhibits from his court file. He's the type you know you're going to see on the news one day for killing their ex-partner. Or, you know, running for parliament. You don't think . . .'

'We don't think anything at the moment,' Jillian said quickly. 'We're just asking questions.'

'Of course,' the judge agreed. 'Harriet will be relieved to have another day to absorb the news,' he added. 'Just call me when you're ready. I've cancelled everything for the next week. We'll just be at home.'

Jillian continued to study Brian Shanahan's internet presence, reading items of interest aloud as the freeway took them west with the slowly dipping sun, past aspirational estates protected from the traffic by huge panes of brightly coloured glass.

Half an hour later McClintock took the Lara exit and they drove through a town filled with new developments, the front yards littered with children's toys, trampolines and freshly landscaped gardens. Soon, Jillian thought, Brian Shanahan would find his scrap of land surrounded by places like these, taunted by the squeals of children that didn't belong to him.

The only dwelling on Shanahan's several acres of unfarmed land was an old caravan, docked to the ground and devoid of signs of life, as well as a small prefabricated garden shed. There was no evidence of the 2003 Ford Falcon registered in his name, or of the three Jack Russell terriers registered with the local council.

Jillian rapped on the caravan door anyway, while McClintock walked the perimeter of the central paddock of the property, beyond which the owner had clearly let the land run to a ruin of stinging nettle and rabbit burrows.

Peering through the curtained windows of the caravan, she could just make out a laminate table with a vase of artificial flowers. She could not decide whether this was poignant or unsettling.

'This place gives me the creeps,' McClintock said when he came back.

'Me too. No one in here.'

From the gate came the rumble of an old car wheezing into the place. A man got out, opened the letterbox and, noticing the detectives, extended an arm in greeting. He drove up the makeshift driveway and pulled to a stop next to them.

'Youse looking for Brian?' he asked through his window. His sunburned face and Akubra marked him as a farmer.

'We are,' Jillian said. 'You know where he's got to?'

The man yawned widely, displaying tobacco-stained teeth. 'Yeah mate, he's out for another week or so. I'm just checking the mail.'

'You know where he's gone?'

'Who's asking?'

'We are,' said McClintock, proffering his badge. 'We need to talk to him.'

'Cops eh?' the man said, not sounding particularly surprised. 'He doesn't like cops.'

'He ever mention the family court to you? We're told he's not too keen on that either,' McClintock said.

'He mighta, but I probably didn't listen. He gets bees in his bonnet real quick, old Brian. I just run me sheep out there sometimes,' he gestured towards the wasteland beyond the caravan, 'and get his mail when he's away. Think they're visiting family.'

'They?'

'Him and the new missus. They're on their honeymoon.'

'Can't believe that bloke found someone to marry him again,' McClintock said when they were back on the freeway. 'Where to next? East Melbourne?'

'Yeah, we'll have a poke around before we meet with the daughter and the ex. If nothing else pops up, we'll do Phillips and Maiden first thing tomorrow. I'm not expecting anything. You heard anything about the post-mortem?'

'I just emailed again before we got back in the car. No updates. Nothing on the O'Neil bank records either. Or phone for that matter.' He scowled up at the slowly darkening sky. 'I hate this time of year, starts to get dark too early.'

'Oh, I like it.'

'Where do you live?' he asked.

'Yarraville. You?'

'City. We'll practically be driving past home for you. How's your husband going with the babysitting?'

'He's not babysitting, he's parenting.'

'You know what I mean ...'

'He's fine, loves it,' Jillian said, not mentioning that Aaron had actually been doing it for months. To change the subject she said, 'Any word from Tomir, the security bloke, yet?'

'Nope.'

'That's really bizarre. Normally they love helping cops.'

'I agree. I did a LEAP, he's clean, although given he has a security licence that isn't surprising. No dodgy connections as far as I can see.'

'Very strange.'

They reached Kaye Bailey's East Melbourne home a little after five-thirty, having stopped at St Kilda Road to update Des and retrieve the set of keys from the judge's belongings. Jillian was slowly getting used to time passing differently now that she'd been released from the confines of home and the shackles of Ollie. It moved with purpose. She moved with purpose.

Judge Bailey's home was in an elegant art deco complex in a sedate street behind the Catholic Archdiocese of Melbourne. Jillian, who at the insistence of her grandmother had been raised Catholic and educated at Catholic schools, always experienced an intensely visceral reaction to the presence of the Church – a mixture of guilt and defiance. On the one hand she was reminded of how many years it had been since she'd attended mass or gone to confession, on the other hand was the fact that she didn't believe in it anyway.

'Weird place to want to live,' McClintock noted as they got out of the car. 'Not exactly a happening area, unless you like hospitals or priests.'

'It's close to the city,' Jillian said, 'and it's safe. If you're a woman living by yourself you want to feel secure.'

McClintock shrugged. 'Fair enough.'

The judge's building was dark brown with pale green accents and curved balconies running the length of the first floor. A security door had been retrofitted under an archway at the front. Beyond the glass door a shining lobby waited, its two curved staircases leading upstairs in opposite directions. There was nothing outside Judge Bailey's door aside from an old pair of working boots that Jillian suspected had been put there as a decoy in case an intruder ever made it this far.

The door opened without resistance and the detectives found themselves in a large open-plan space that served as dining room and lounge. As Jillian turned to close the door she noted that two additional locks had been installed – a deadlock and a bolt. She gestured to McClintock who raised his eyebrows in surprise.

There was a kitchen to their immediate right and beyond that another doorway which led to a bathroom and laundry. On the opposite wall were two doors, one of which was wide open revealing a room that bore the signs of recent and regular occupation – shoes on the floor, a half-full laundry basket, a mug on the bedside table. Bailey's desk, empty of laptop or papers, looked back towards the city. Jillian noted that new lockable windows had recently been installed.

The desk drawers had been emptied, their contents now sitting in the conference room at St Kilda Road. Jillian looked briefly through the judge's clothing drawers, bedside table and wardrobe. 'Nothing interesting here,' she called to McClintock who she could hear moving around in the next room.

'Same,' he responded.

She turned towards the door, noting as she did that a light jacket was hanging from a hook that had been nailed inexpertly into the wood. She checked one pocket and then the other, which produced a stray piece of notebook paper on which a few bullet points had been written.

- *La Roy & Connor – draft?*
- *Speak to JE*
- *Resign? Letter?*

CHAPTER 10

With the assistance of the consulate, Ama Singh, Kaye Bailey's daughter, had flown back to Australia from the United Kingdom within hours of learning of her mother's death. Her father, the judge's ex-husband, Bruce Singh, had been contacted in Singapore and also stated that he would be returning to the jurisdiction as soon as a flight could be obtained. Confirmation was provided that the pair had safely arrived at the Park Hyatt Hotel a little after six-thirty that evening, and at seven-fifteen, Jillian and McClintock were shown to a room on the third floor. By Jillian's calculations, Ama would now have been in Melbourne just long enough for the dreadful reality of her situation to have begun sinking in.

They were greeted at the hotel room by a police liaison officer who introduced the detectives to the judge's daughter and ex-husband. Both stood to greet the detectives. Bruce Singh was a slight man, not much taller than his daughter, with the hint of a shadow on his cheeks and a gentle smile that seemed to strain under the weight of the current circumstances. The daughter was athletic and sturdy looking. Her eyes, red and swollen as they were, projected a calm, intelligent strength.

'I'll nip down and see where those meals are,' the liaison officer said, squeezing Ama's shoulder as she moved past her. 'If they can't do the pasta, any other requests?'

'Anything vegetarian,' Ama said, 'for both of us, thanks.'

The young woman directed her gaze towards the detectives. Jillian introduced herself and McClintock and the four of them sat together at a circular table that looked out, through thin curtains, onto a balcony.

'It's only just sinking in now that I'm here,' Ama said abruptly, her voice quick and nervous. 'I just can't stop crying, and I'm jetlagged too.' She reached into her pocket and produced a handful of tissues which she wiped aggressively at each eye. 'Water, I need water. Can I get you some?'

'I'll get it,' her father said, pushing his chair back and locating a kitchenette hidden behind a cupboard door. 'You talk.'

'We've always been very close, so close,' Ama said as her father returned to the table and placed glasses and a jug of water in front of them. 'Dad moved to Singapore after he and Mum broke up, so it's been Mum and me since, like, high school. This semester in the UK was going to be the longest we'd ever spent away from each other. She said it would be good for me, but I knew she didn't really want me to go, didn't want to be apart from me.'

'What are you studying?' Jillian asked.

'Law. Like Mum. I want to get into politics. Mum was always saying if you want to change the system you need to know the rule book the system uses first. Sorry, I'm babbling, I know.'

'She must have been extremely proud of you,' McClintock said gently.

'She was. She really was. It was embarrassing, actually. Everyone we met, it was like, "This is Ama, she's going to change the world."' Ama sniffed.

Bruce Singh reached for his daughter's hand. His eyes too looked raw.

Jillian offered condolences on behalf of the police and gave a basic overview of the circumstances in which the judge had been found, what the detectives had done so far and what they still needed to do, and the information they were waiting on. 'We want to be clear that at this stage there's no one person we're particularly pursuing. For the moment we're casting a very broad net. We're going to ask you some questions that might seem a bit odd. Please don't read too much into them. Alright?'

Ama took a deep breath. 'Alright,' she promised.

'Yes,' Bruce Singh agreed.

Before Jillian could put her first question, McClintock asked Ama, 'What can you tell us about your mother's relationship with Chief Judge Meyers?'

Ama made a sound halfway between a laugh and a cry. 'Well, she didn't like him, that's for sure. She thought he was pretty useless, lazy. She told me he didn't like to do anything inconvenient. I remember her saying that. He definitely stressed her out a lot. She reckoned he came in just before ten every morning and left as soon as court was done, whereas sometimes Mum wouldn't be home until after midnight.' She took a sip of water. 'Also,' indignation became clear in her voice, 'he didn't protect her. I remember last year she was getting some pretty awful emails or something. She was really upset and he basically told her to suck it up. That's why we moved to the new place, in December. After Smokey went missing, Mum said we were done.'

'Smokey?'

'Our cat. It really freaked her out. I mean, it was probably nothing, he was really old and he'd been sick and I remember thinking she was overreacting. I guess I didn't realise quite how serious it was.' Ama shivered.

'So you're saying you moved here because of the threats your mother was getting? And she thought someone might have hurt your cat?'

'Yeah. Initially she got CCTV put in at our old place but we were always forgetting to turn it on and off and, yeah, with Smokey gone . . . So we moved to the new apartment. Quieter area, good security, neighbours who are always around, that type of thing.'

'And your mum had those new windows and locks put in?'

'Yeah,' Ama agreed, 'before we even moved in. It was a big deal, getting those windows, because of the heritage overlay or something. She spent a fortune.'

'Did she ever say who she thought was responsible for the threats?' McClintock asked.

'Not that I can remember, but I'm sure it would have been someone who didn't like a decision she'd made.'

'Did she ever mention a man called Brian Shanahan?' said Jillian.

Ama nodded slowly. 'Yes, I remember that name. She said if a man called Brian ever called me or, like, added me on Facebook or anything, I had to tell her straightaway.'

Jillian and McClintock exchanged looks.

'And did that ever happen? Did he ever try to make contact with you?'

'No.' She shook her head.

'And did she mention an incident last year when it was discovered that a litigant had entered the secure area of the court?'

'No. Not to me.'

'Was there anyone your mother confided in?' McClintock asked. 'Close friends? A psychologist? Family members? Michael?'

'She told me about that incident,' Bruce Singh said. 'Her wallet was stolen, she had to cancel all her cards. We still have a joint account we top up for Ama. I was the one who told her she should move, because he'd know her address from her licence.'

Ama looked aghast. 'One of you should have told me!'

'Your mother didn't want you worrying or deciding not to go to London,' Bruce said gently.

'But I could have been here . . .' Ama began to cry anew.

'Were her stolen credit cards ever used?' Jillian asked.

'Not that I'm aware. And the joint account was never accessed.'

'What can you tell us about your mother's relationship with Michael?' Jillian asked Ama.

'Oh, he's nice, bit eccentric but in a fun way. They go to dinner, listen to jazz, that type of thing. They've been seeing each other for a year or so, but, like, only when they have time. He travels to Sydney a bit and of course Mum's hours are crazy.'

'Did you have the impression they were serious?'

Ama laughed even as fresh tears began to stream down her face. 'No! I mean, it wasn't something I talked about with her but he never stayed over here or anything. They would just go to things together, sometimes take a trip. I think it was mainly good companionship.'

Bruce said, 'I think Michael had been sweet on Kaye for years. She always had her fans. Grant Phillips was really struck with her too, although he'd never leave his wife.'

'Grant, ew!' Ama threw her father a disgusted look. 'Really?'

'You know the Phillipses then?' McClintock asked Bruce.

'Sure, Kaye and Grant met soon after she started practising. He was at our wedding if I recall correctly. His wife too.'

'She's weird,' Ama said. 'She gives me the creeps.' Ama seemed suddenly to remember something. 'The account! I meant to tell you straightaway. I have access to Mum's bank account, like, just in case. I checked it at the airport and there was something strange. Mum transferred forty thousand dollars out of the account the day that she . . . that it happened.'

'Forty thousand dollars?' Jillian repeated incredulously.

'Yes, here, I'll show you.'

Ama produced her phone and opened an internet banking app. She pushed the phone across the table. 'There, see,' she said, pointing at the screen.

Jillian looked at the transfer. There was a long reference number and a BSB. She clicked on the transaction details. 'FarrugiaPerriam Trust Account.'

'I should have done that,' Ama said. 'But who are they?'

'They're a Sydney-based law firm,' McClintock said, after a moment of searching on his own phone. 'Specialising in family law and employment law. So your mum never mentioned getting a lawyer?'

'No.' Ama shook her head emphatically.

'Not to me either,' confirmed Bruce.

'What if,' Ama said suddenly, 'what if she was trying to get work to do something about her safety? What if she was going to sue the court or something? Can we find out?'

'We'll contact them as soon as possible,' Jillian said. 'Best that you leave that to us.' She did not want the grief-stricken family finding out potentially significant information before she did.

'Back to Harriet Phillips – you say she gave you the creeps, why was that?'

'Oh, I'm probably being a bit nasty. She's just always so awkward, won't make eye contact with me. I think Mum found her hard work too. I never understood what Grant saw in her.'

'We found a note in your mum's jacket that indicates she might have been thinking about resigning. Did she ever mention that to either of you?'

'Mum would never resign!' Ama insisted, red spots appearing on either cheek. 'It was her dream to get appointed.'

'She never said anything about that to me either,' Bruce agreed.

'Do the initials JE mean anything to either of you?' Jillian asked, thinking of the note in the dead judge's pocket. 'Or the name Kim?'

They stared at her blankly.

Ama's phone, sitting in front of her on the table, began to rattle as a call came in. She silenced it before showing the screen to Jillian. 'That's me and Mum at my high school graduation,' she said. The picture showed a smiling Ama of seventeen or so with her mother, both of them dressed elegantly, their arms around each other in a show of deepest pride and affection. Ama began to cry again and Bruce edged his seat closer to his daughter, wrapping her in a one-armed embrace.

Jillian looked away. She found this type of grief the hardest thing to deal with in a murder case. The grief you witnessed immediately following a death was a different beast from the grief at a funeral. At funerals there was a plan, an understanding of roles and responsibilities, an order of proceedings. In relatives who'd just been informed that a loved one had died there was just raw shock and pain, manifested in unpredictable but intimate ways.

She let Ama and her father have a moment, her attention turning back to the picture Ama had shown her. This was the type of love that only existed between children and their parents. Jillian's whole body ached with envy.

I want that.

Or at least I want to want that.

CHAPTER 11

The sky was clear and dark when McClintock and Jillian left the hotel. Despite herself, Jillian yawned. 'Look, I don't want to piss you off or anything,' Mick said, 'but you could head off when we get back to the office. We're not getting out to see anyone else today so it's just going to be phone calls and chasing up phone data.'

'Nah, I'm good.'

They got into the car, their doors slamming in unison.

'Is your hubby going back to work? Or he going to do the dad duties long-term?'

'I'm not sure, actually,' Jillian said. This was true. She and Aaron had not discussed long-term arrangements, or, she was ashamed to admit, what his professional desires might be. He had taken extended leave to assist in caring for Ollie and she had responded by booking in her return to work.

'You missing him?'

'No,' Jillian said, mildly surprised. 'We've been together for a long time. It takes a while to miss him these days.'

'I meant your baby.'

'Oh. Sure. I mean, of course.'

But not really.

To avoid further discussion, she phoned the law firm that Judge Bailey had transferred forty thousand dollars to again, even though she knew no one would answer her call at that hour. She left a second voicemail message.

'Probably won't get back to us until Monday,' McClintock said.

'The timing's a bit much, isn't it?' she said. 'Transferring that type of cash to a law firm the same day you get promoted and killed. Her suing the court does seem like a real possibility. And you can understand why she might engage a firm up in Sydney if she was worried about gossip.'

'Maybe Meyers got wind that she was going to escalate things?' McClintock suggested.

The office was quiet by the time they returned. Jillian turned her computer on and conducted a brief search for any unhealthy snacks she may have hidden in her desk in those last days before maternity leave. Nothing. She remembered the box of fundraiser chocolates in the kitchen that she had promised herself she would not buy.

She bought two, put one in her pocket and ate the other as she returned to her desk. Her phone was flashing ominously and she realised when she picked it up that it hadn't been diverting to her mobile all day. There were seventeen messages.

The first was confirming that the phone data on Michael O'Neil's movements the night of the murder would be emailed to her that afternoon. She took the second chocolate bar out of her pocket and began to eat as she listened to the second message, from forensics, a third from Virginia Maiden's husband saying she was too distressed to talk, and a fourth and fifth from unknown numbers, each offering only silence.

'Did you just eat two chocolate bars?' McClintock demanded from his adjacent desk.

'I was hungry,' she said defensively, caught off guard.

'Well, don't eat that shit. Here.' He held out two Tupperware containers he'd produced from his drawer. 'Protein balls and cashews.'

Of course he has fucking protein and nuts.

She took some with a grunted thank you as she continued to note down numbers.

'Oh fuck off,' McClintock said to his own phone. 'That bloody security guy is messing with me.'

'We can go and see him tomorrow,' she said.

'I've got the post-mortem first thing.'

'On a Saturday?'

'Yeah, I was surprised, they're squeezing it in as a favour.'

Of course they are.

Attending post-mortems was not strictly necessary. Some detectives considered it a matter of respect, attending to confirm exactly what the victim had experienced, acknowledging both their dreadful passing and their humanity. Jillian took a more practical position – the best way to ensure she gave a victim due respect was to find the person responsible for their death as soon as possible.

'You expecting any surprises?' she asked, wondering whether McClintock's desire to attend was based on respect or an expectation that he would be first to receive some spectacular clue.

'Nah,' he said. 'Strangled, right. But I want to be there.'

Ah, so this is about putting in face time with the forensic pathologist?

She turned to her emails, one ear still pressed to her phone. Michael O'Neil's phone data had come in. 'Emailing you something,' she told McClintock once she'd read it through. 'O'Neil pinged near the court at eleven-thirty Wednesday night. I'm pretty sure that's just the nearest phone tower for his chambers, but still, interesting.'

'Huh.' McClintock didn't sound particularly interested. 'We should get Shanahan's too. I'll do it.' He got up and stretched, a whole-body stretch that seemed overdone, and came with much exhalation.

'You right there?' she couldn't help saying.

'Just got a dodgy hammy.'

He returned to his seat where he phoned the cab company, putting the phone on speaker so that hold music assaulted her ears.

Jillian gave up trying to listen to her voicemails, thinking she'd try again when he left. Checking her mobile, she saw that Aaron had sent her five text messages, primarily pictures of Ollie over the course of the day.

Very cute, she replied. *Another few hours for me. Don't wait up. Love you.*

'Right, see you tomorrow,' McClintock said after another fifteen minutes of waiting on hold. 'May as well do this from home.'

She returned to her voicemail messages. 'Hello, this is Lisa Nettle,' said a woman's voice, nervous and insistent.

Lisa Nettle!

'I have some information about the murder of the judge. It's just, well, I'm sure, one hundred per cent sure, my husband is responsible. He's a sociopath, he lies, and he hates her. He's capable of it. I know you probably think I'm crazy but I'm not. You should look into him.'

Jillian dialled the number the woman had called from but it went straight to voicemail.

She thought back to Judge Bailey's desk, the assortment of documentation, the psychiatric assessments she had read. She thought about the court security, and the likelihood of a celebrity surgeon somehow sneaking into chambers and killing the judge the day before his judgement was to be handed down. Kaye Bailey had been strangled and beaten, the work of someone who must have genuinely hated her, must have had an intensely personal and visceral reaction to her. Would a celebrity doctor risk everything to kill a judge before he even knew the results of his case?

CHAPTER 12

Jillian woke in the morning to the sounds of Aaron noisily making coffee. 'Make one for me?' she called out as she searched for further work clothes.

'You starting early again?' Aaron said when she came into the kitchen, tying her hair back. 'I was going to bring you brekky in bed, Ollie's still out to it.'

'I can't wait,' she said, 'today's gonna be big.' This wasn't strictly true but the idea of waiting around at home, potentially doing nothing, was intolerable. In the real world she could be productive, could contribute. 'Can I have that in a keep cup?'

'It's Saturday,' Aaron protested.

'I know. I'll try and be home early.'

'Just remember we've got dinner tonight,' he said as he poured her coffee and kissed her goodbye.

'I'll be there,' she said, trying to remember who they were meant to be seeing.

'And remember you've got Ursula booked in for Monday, tell Des before you forget.'

Ursula was the psychologist Jillian had been meant to engage with. She was a nice enough woman, brisk and maternal and with a deep voice and a no-nonsense insistence on accountability, but Jillian detested what she represented.

'Alright,' she said, knowing that she had no intention of following through.

There were very few people in the office. Jillian had asked Ama if she knew her mother's phone passcode and been provided with two different options. 'It should either be my full birthday or just the days and months.' However when she tried one and then the other, neither worked. 'Damn.' She put the phone in an envelope, labelled it and shot an advanced warning email to the team who would be responsible for trying to unlock it. 'Extremely urgent' was the heading.

Although it was still early, she called Lisa Nettle again, and again got her voicemail. She located an address for her in Carnegie and sent McClintock a text asking him to drop in on her after the post-mortem.

She then scrolled the FarrugiaPerriam website looking for personal contact details for the two partners listed. She located mobile telephone numbers and left voicemail messages for both, wishing she had thought to do that the night before. She knew McClintock was following up on the cab company but she called them anyway. She was finally put through to a shift manager who told her they were still trying to confirm whether anyone had made such a fare. 'We'll let you know when we can,' the woman said with an air of finality, and ended the call.

Shortly after nine her phone rang and a woman introducing herself as Jane Harley, the 'on duty' partner from FarrugiaPerriam, asked how the firm could assist the police. Jillian thanked the solicitor for returning her call so promptly and explained about Judge Bailey's murder and the bank transfer. There was a pause when she finished talking.

'Are you there?' Jillian asked.

'Look, I understand where you're coming from, I'm as shocked as anyone that a judge was murdered, but regardless of the circumstances we aren't able to give out any information about people who may or may not have utilised our services.'

'We know she utilised your services, or intended to. She's put a large sum of money in trust,' Jillian responded, feeling frustrated. 'Surely given this is a murder investigation you can talk to me?'

'As I said, I can't even confirm whether or not we were acting for her,' the partner said opaquely. 'Best of luck.' She hung up before Jillian could push the point further.

Jillian tried Virginia Maiden again, and when the judge again didn't answer, she called Angela Hui.

'Look, I'm sorry to call you on the weekend, but we're having a hard time reaching Judge Maiden. Has she been in touch with you?' she asked when the registry manager answered. 'And your security manager too? He's not returning any of our calls.'

'Judge Maiden hasn't been in since the Thursday morning, but she sent a text asking when we were expecting everything to start opening up again and whether she was allowed back in chambers. So I'm assuming she'll be back in on Monday. Tomir's been around but really busy, I know he and the CJ, well, almost-retired CJ, spent most of Friday afternoon trying to come up with some new security protocols. I'll message him again now and remind him.'

'Just send me his address please.'

A few minutes later she was in her car, following the soothing tones of her GPS to an address in Tullamarine. Tomir Staniak's house was a large, recently built brick construction with no front fence and several cars parked in its generous driveway. When Jillian pressed the doorbell she heard immediately the barks of a dog, the profuse swearing of a male teenager, a woman yelling something in what Jillian thought might be Polish, and a television being turned down.

A tall, broad-shouldered man with white hair and a protruding belly answered the door, his wife directly behind him with a confused look on her face. As Jillian introduced herself and explained the purpose of her visit, the television began to blare again. Tomir said something to his wife that Jillian could not understand before indicating to Jillian that he would join her in the front yard. 'My son,' he said, gesturing back towards the source of the now reduced noise. 'Teenage boys, they're fucking horrible. The things he says to his mother and everything always so loud.'

She explained that they had been trying to contact the security manager for days.

'It's been a fucking shit show,' he told her with no hint of an apology. 'We don't know whether or not it is safe to have court open, whether they need to all stay home and do it all by phone or the computer.' He sighed heavily. 'The last two days, just nonstop questions from everyone, phone calls at all hours.'

'Tell me why the CCTV was down?'

'Oh, that was for a system upgrade. Totally routine, one hundred per cent. We do it once a year mostly, always after hours.'

'And who knew about it?'

'Everyone. We sent a whole-court email. We have to.'

'It seems kind of risky for an environment like the court to shut down all the CCTV, doesn't it?'

His jaw tensed slightly. 'I don't make the rules. And if I didn't do the upgrade, maybe something terrible happens and I get the blame for that.'

'What about getting upstairs, is the only way to do that with a proximity card?'

'Yes. You need a card, and to know where to go. None of those floors are marked anywhere – to protect the judges. No one could get up there unless they knew where they were going.'

'But it happened once before, didn't it? Someone got up to Judge Bailey?'

'Yes,' he agreed, reluctantly, 'but since then, we've changed our processes, we cancelled the card he used, gave everyone new training about security, everything. No one would get through that now.'

'Have you ever dealt with a bloke called Brian Shanahan?'

He shrugged. 'When he's in court they call one of us in to keep an eye on him. He behaves himself when we're there.'

'Have there been any other incidents involving Judge Bailey that you're aware of? I know someone threw something at her last year. Anything else?'

'That woman always had problems.'

'I'm sorry?'

'Always something or other, to be honest with you. Personally, I think she brought it on herself – very rude, very snobby.'

'Right,' Jillian said, surprised. 'Was there something in particular that she did?'

He shook his head. 'She's just always walking around with . . .' He put his nose in the air in a gesture of unearned superiority.

'I see.'

Clearly concerned that he may not look sufficiently sympathetic,

Tomir added, 'I'm not saying she deserved it or anything, just that, yeah, she could be a bit of a snob.'

'Look, we need all the information about who was in the building that night, all the proximity card data.'

'Yes, yes,' Tomir responded, 'yes of course, just give me a few days. A few days, alright? I'm onto it, you have my word.'

When Jillian returned to the office McClintock was at his desk, reading intently. He looked over as she sat down. 'Where were you?'

'I paid the security manager a visit at home.'

'I thought I was doing that?'

'You were, but he was giving you the run-around. Besides, you were at the post-mortem. Anything interesting?'

McClintock looked slightly wounded. 'Nah. She was strangled, as we knew, hit a few times across the face, kicked too – probably just for fun, after she died. No DNA anywhere.'

'What about Lisa Nettle?'

He shook his head. 'Nice house, really nice. No one home though. I left a card. Neighbours said she left early Friday morning in the car with the kids. Didn't know where she was going.'

'Pretty weird to call us and then not answer.'

'Maybe she's a nutter.' He leaned forward slightly as an email notification pinged. 'Bailey's phone records have come in.'

While McClintock identified each and every call the judge had made or received since the start of the year, Jillian reviewed her personal email account, finding unexpected poignancy in the older woman's attempts to unsubscribe from all manner of services she no longer required. She had hoped that they could meet with Harriet Phillips later in the afternoon but when she phoned Judge Phillips he answered from the outpatient section of the Melbourne Clinic where he told them, with evident distress, that his wife was seeking treatment. 'At this stage Monday is looking like the go.'

At five o'clock, McClintock got to his feet. 'I'm gonna work from home tomorrow,' he told her as he stretched one hamstring, then the other. 'Keep going through the records there.'

'Fair enough.'

'Alright. See you Monday? You wanna meet here?'

'Let's meet at court. Try and catch Maiden and pick up the proximity card stuff.'

'Right.' He gave her a joking salute as he left. 'Catch ya.'

'Bye.'

Her desk phone rang. 'I knew you'd pick this one up,' said Aaron's voice, exasperated but amused.

'Sorry, what's up?'

'Just reminding you, dinner, half an hour.'

'Right, who with again?'

'You're hopeless,' he laughed. 'Andy and Veronica. Pho 84.'

Andy and Veronica were Aaron's university mates, and their only remaining friends who had not succumbed to the biological and social pressure to reproduce. Jillian and Aaron would be able to enjoy adult conversation, discuss movies and which television to binge-watch, which new cafe was worth a look-in. How she had come to dread the 'play dates' that now seemed to be their only regular source of social interaction. These ill-fated excursions seemed entirely pointless to her – babies were too young to interact with each other in any meaningful way. Instead, they were just opportunities for the adults to compare developmental milestones while the children tried to bang into each other on a lounge-room floor. At play dates, she and Aaron would talk to friends they had known for years and Jillian would leave feeling as though everyone had had a lobotomy except for her. She packed her bag and left swiftly.

There had been an afternoon footy match at the Docklands stadium and the after-game traffic heading west was as thick and unyielding as wet cement. As Jillian waited for the lights to change, her mind went back to Ollie's birth. The euphoric, ethereal moments when she and Aaron took turns to hold him to their chests, run fingers along his puffy cheeks and tell him they loved him. She had phoned her mother and they had somehow had a good conversation, a nice conversation that hadn't turned into a therapy session. Aaron's mother had cried when they had FaceTimed her. Then they were led out of the birthing suite and into a hospital room with tiny Ollie in his plastic cot, swaddled tight and fast asleep, and Jillian had felt so proud of herself and her body for what had been made, and for making so many people happy in the process. Aaron had returned home to feed the cat and it was while he was gone that the thought had come, like a whisper, quiet and insidious.

You are going to ruin Ollie's life.

When Aaron came back an hour later with a huge bundle of flowers and a pizza, she'd pretended everything was alright. But she felt as though her heart had turned to marble. She told herself that things would improve when they got home, and then that they would improve when Ollie turned one month. And then suddenly he was three months old and things were not better, they were worse. It was no longer just about how she might ruin his life but how she might accidentally do something terrible to that perfect little body. That she might even purposefully do something. She had decided then that the best way to make sure she didn't ruin his life was to keep her distance.

She parked on Victoria Street twenty minutes late. Next to the Pho 84 restaurant a greengrocer was moving the last of his wares inside. Bunches of coriander lay in limp surrender in the remaining wooden display crates. The air smelled of pork fat, lime and engine oil. She could see Aaron and Ollie through the front window of the restaurant, Ollie playing with a chopstick while Aaron talked to Andy and Veronica, his face animated. Jillian experienced the same sensations she had when she saw the two of them asleep together – exclusion and jealousy mingled with a distant tenderness.

Veronica turned towards the window, caught sight of her and waved. Jillian fixed her smile and pushed the restaurant door open.

'Hello all,' she said, kissing Aaron on the forehead and running a hand along Ollie's face.

'If it isn't our celebrity friend,' Veronica said with laughing eyes. 'We were just telling Aaron we saw you on TV the other night looking extremely important.'

'Was I?' This happened from time to time. In her early years in Homicide she'd been self-conscious whenever she saw signs of waiting media. She would walk through crime scenes awkwardly. But these days she didn't notice the cameras and paid the journalists no attention.

'You and some very handsome man were wandering around in the background while the journo was talking. You want to give us the hot take?'

'Veronica!' Andy scolded her.

'I was just teasing, I know she can't.' Veronica was unabashed. 'I just find it all so exciting. I never get to deal with anything more interesting at work than bureaucratic incompetence. Jillian's life is like a true-crime podcast.'

'Well, it is true crime,' Andy said. 'Actual real crime.'

'I do love it, you know,' Jillian said. 'Although the handsome man I'm guessing you saw is a total pain in the arse.'

'Oh, tell me,' Veronica begged. 'Is he totally up himself? I don't think someone can be that attractive without being up themselves.'

Jillian considered how best to describe the many things that irked her about McClintock. 'He's really blokey,' she said. 'And a real jock. Plus he's too ambitious. He wants the case to himself.'

'But you're ambitious,' Aaron said, sounding slightly amused.

This surprised her. She looked at her husband, eyebrows raised. 'Am I?' she asked.

'Ah, yeah.' He was smiling, but she felt an accusation just below the surface.

'Anyway, dreadful business with the judge,' Veronica said. 'Killed in her own office.'

Jillian didn't respond.

'Oh, come on,' Veronica implored. 'Just blink once if it's true, it can be our little secret.'

'Ronnie,' Andy warned.

'Alright, alright, I'll talk about something else. Tell me how this little marshmallow has been going?'

I'd much rather talk about work, actually.

'Do you think Ronnie and Andy were okay?' Aaron asked as they lay on the couch later, half-heartedly watching *The Crown*. 'I thought he seemed a bit shitty with her a few times.'

Jillian tried to recall whether she'd detected any discord between their friends. She generally regarded them as one of the happier couples in their group. 'Yeah? When?'

Aaron lifted his head from Jillian's lap and looked at her. 'You didn't pick it up? When he was having a go at her for asking you about work.'

'I thought that was all in good fun.'

'Nah, he was needling, I think. He can be a bit like that. I'm sure I've told you before – he was actually pretty gross to her at uni when they first started going out.'

'Sweet old Andy?' Jillian was surprised. 'Surely not. He worships her.'

'It's true. I'm sure I've told you. He had counselling back then, tried to work through it. Seemed a lot better afterwards, but now I wonder if he's slipped again.'

'Well, I guess everyone is different with their partner than they are with other people.'

'Not you,' Aaron said, pulling her face towards him to kiss her. 'You're a ball-breaker with everyone.'

Jillian awoke to her mobile vibrating against her head. It was a little after six and the room was empty. Aaron had slept with Ollie again. He had also moved his favourite pillow into the spare bed in Ollie's room. She held her phone up and squinted into the screen, waiting for her eyes to adjust. It was an automated text message from her psychologist's office.

To confirm your appointment on Monday, 23 April 2018 at 9.30 am please respond Y. To cancel, please respond N.

She did not respond.

She got up and dressed. She could just fit back into her pre-pregnancy clothes, the things she had worn in the days when she and Aaron still went places. She checked herself in the mirror and for the briefest of moments she was her old self again, not the person who was happiest when she was working and who struggled to look her husband in the eye.

She took her work bag into the kitchen. Aaron and Ollie had not yet risen and the house was luxuriously quiet – she could hear nothing but her own breathing, the gentle creaks and moans of the house, the squawk of birds outside. She flicked the coffee machine on and bit into an apple.

That's my scurvy risk taken care of at least.

Coffee made, she set herself up on the lounge-room floor, spreading out her notes, the copies of LEAP documents she'd made, and Kaye Bailey's so-called Black Book. The lounge-room floor had always been her preferred place to work. She and Aaron had put a great deal of effort into the room, into choosing the right rug, mounting the television at just the right height, choosing the most comfortable yet aesthetically pleasing couch. Now the carefully curated space they had so painstakingly created was disrupted by a baby bouncer that Ollie had already outgrown, plastic toys and a portable change table.

On her laptop she replayed the CCTV footage Angela had provided them. She'd lost count of how many times she had meticulously analysed each frame, hoping for some revelation, but the man's face always remained barely visible under his hooded windcheater. He seemed to be holding his head quite deliberately down as if cognisant of the security cameras. All Jillian could deduce from the blurry image was that he was shorter than average and not particularly heavy set.

It was the brazenness of his actions that intrigued her most. That and the pointlessness of his behaviour. She could not understand why someone would enter that part of the court building, aware that it wasn't open to the public, and then take the lift, all of which presented so many opportunities for detection, only to steal a wallet. Had theft been the point? Or were there other objectives?

She googled Brian Shanahan again and, using a Facebook account she'd created for such occasions, requested access to the various family law pages he ran. A few did not require permission and on them Shanahan demonstrated his lived experience of the *Family Law Act*. 'Property settlements at court – what to say in your affidavit' had six hundred members; 'Everything you need to know about Spousal Maintenance' had a paltry two hundred and ten.

Jillian turned to the Black Book. Someone with a sense of humour, presumably Matthew, had gone to the effort of handwriting an internal cover page in gothic text that read: 'Here be the dissatisfied litigants of Bailey J.'

There was page after page of printed-out emails, most short and succinct. 'Feminazi whore, suck a cock and die' was the first entry, sent from someone called burneyofbyron@zmail.com. 'I will take your children off you, see how you like that slut' was the next entry, also from Burney but sent a month later. 'If I ever see you in the street I will gouge your eyes out with my bare hands and strangle you until your spine snaps,' wrote angryteddy99@shoot.com. The earliest emails dated back several years but the book had been updated regularly, with the most recent being a photograph of a noose with an invitation to 'choke on this, I know where you live' dated only two weeks earlier.

Jesus.

In addition to the emails there were file notes of anonymous phone calls, and an extensive collection of penis photographs. These were for the most part disembodied shots, with no other body parts evident, and no accompanying messages. They had been sent from email addresses clearly crafted with Judge Bailey in mind. Things like stopbaileycorruption@maildrop.com, famlawwhore@zmail.com, and stoptheantimalebailey@shoot.com. Jillian googled the email addresses to see if these same accounts had been used on any websites or social media, but could find nothing.

Guessing that the photos of penises had also been prepared specifically with Judge Bailey in mind, she opened the electronic copy of the Black Book on her laptop. She then copied the images, one after another, into an image search. It did not take her long to confirm that her instincts were spot on – these were indeed bespoke dick pics.

'What on earth are you looking at?'

She turned to see Aaron standing right behind her, fully dressed but still bleary-eyed with sleep.

'It's for work. Obviously.'

'Sure,' Aaron teased. 'Ollie's still down. I thought I might duck up to Anderson and get a loaf and a few croissants. What do you reckon?'

'Yeah okay, sounds good.'

'Keep an ear out for him.'

'I will.'

She got up and stretched. Being alone in the house with Ollie unnerved her. It reminded her of those dreadful months after Aaron had gone back to work, when she had spent every minute of the day worried about what she might do to herself, or to her child. She wished she'd offered to go and get the croissants.

She checked her phone and was surprised to see that a new email had come in containing Michael O'Neil's bank statements. *On a Sunday! And I didn't even need to flirt with anyone.* Unfortunately, the barrister's banking activity reminded her of her grandmother's attitude towards money.

O'Neil takes out $800 cash each Tuesday and lives off that for the week, she told McClintock via text. *Been doing that as far back as I can see.*

She emailed through a request for Saul Meyers' phone records, wondering as she did whether the chief judge's acrimony towards Bailey could have culminated in allowing someone to enter chambers to do away with her. Would a man like that, self-important and satisfied but a servant of the law regardless, really be willing to do that? To risk everything?

Well, he drunkenly abused her in front of colleagues. Would people have guessed him capable of that before they witnessed it?

There was the smallest of cries from Ollie. She got to her feet and tiptoed to his bedroom door.

Please don't wake up now.

She opened the door gingerly and crept to the bed where Aaron had left him. Ollie was still asleep.

Silly Daddy should have put you in your cot.

Silly Daddy's a better mother than I'll ever be.

Remember when you thought . . .

Panic gripped her and she felt her hands become clammy. She left the room and closed the door as quietly as she could, then slumped against the other side of it and hyperventilated.

CHAPTER 13

Jillian had agreed to meet McClintock at the court at nine on Monday morning. When she arrived, it was to find that the building had reopened to the public. Barristers, solicitors and litigants were sitting in the cafe and congregated outside the huge rotating glass doors. McClintock was already waiting for her, bouncing up and down on the balls of his feet as though he needed some immediate outlet for his apparently inexhaustible energy.

They were greeted in the central atrium by Angela who confirmed that both Judge Maiden and Tomir Staniak were at work already. The registry manager reacted with genuine surprise to the news that Judge Bailey might have engaged a lawyer. 'I would have thought if she really wanted to pursue the safety issue she'd have gone through all the internal options first. She never struck me as a litigious woman,' she mused as she took them out of the lift and through the security doors on level twelve. 'Could it have been about reviewing some part of her employment contract? But, no . . .' She shook her head. 'Honestly, I'm mystified.'

'Any tips for dealing with Virginia Maiden?' Jillian asked.

Angela pressed her lips together as she considered the question. 'Make sure you always address her as Judge,' she said finally, although

Jillian had the distinct impression that the registry manager wanted to say more.

Judge Maiden's chambers were staffed by a pale young woman typing furiously on her computer and an equally pale young man scribbling notes on a whiteboard. They each looked up at the detectives' entry.

'Is the boss in?' Jillian asked. 'We're the police.' Both associates looked too confused to question them further and the young man merely gestured towards the closed inner door. Jillian knocked once before opening it.

Judge Maiden looked up from her desk in surprise. She was certainly not a warm presence, Jillian thought immediately. She had high cheekbones, incredulous eyebrows, and thin lips worn straight and closed. A pearl necklace against a cream satin shirt gave her upper body a disarming brilliance that sat in stark contrast to her stare.

'Judge Maiden,' Jillian began. 'We're the detectives investigating Judge Bailey's death. My name is Jillian Basset, I'm a detective senior sergeant with Homicide. This is Detective Sergeant John McClintock. We know you're a busy woman but we'd really appreciate the opportunity to chat with you briefly.' As she spoke she realised that McClintock was not behind her but had remained in the outer office where he was looking intently at the notes the male associate was making on the whiteboard. She proceeded further into the room and, without McClintock or an invitation, took a seat facing the judge.

'I can't just stop what I'm doing,' the judge said icily without looking at Jillian. 'I'm in court at ten.'

'This won't take long...' Jillian began, but even as she spoke she was aware of the older woman's attention leaving her and moving to McClintock, who had joined them. Judge Maiden's change in demeanour was instantaneous and almost comical.

He offered her a hand and she stood to accept it. 'It's very nice to meet you,' she said, looking him straight in the eye. 'I was just explaining to your colleague that I don't think there's much I can do to assist you, unfortunately.'

That's one way of putting it.

'I'm sure you'll be more helpful than you realise,' McClintock said as he sat down, and the judge positively purred.

'Of course,' she said, 'anything, of course. We'll just need to be quick about it.'

They were interrupted by the female associate, who knocked and, following a look of merest acknowledgment from her boss, entered the room. She placed two blue sheets of paper in front of the judge and handed her a pen. Jillian noticed that the younger woman's hands were shaking.

Virginia Maiden looked briefly at the pages and then drew a large cross over each. 'You've made the same mistake again,' she said without looking up. 'Fix it. And add those to your shredding pile. Speaking of which, I noticed this morning that it's getting very large. I suggest you put aside a day in the next few weeks to go through everything in there and reflect on how you might avoid those mistakes in the future.'

'But it's not all my –'

'Close the door,' the judge said, her attention already returning to McClintock. 'Useless,' she added as the blushing young woman obeyed.

Virginia Maiden pulled her seat closer to her desk and leaned forward slightly. Slowly and patiently, McClintock took her through the evening of the murder.

'It was just a little, intimate goodbye. Just for the judges, so we could all pay our dues. Saul's an institution, he's been with the court since it started, back when they called us Federal Magistrates. It was a really lovely night too. Nice for everyone to let their hair down, that's why we said no associates and no support staff. You want to be able to relax.'

'We understood Judge Bailey's associates attended.'

'Oh yes,' the judge sniffed. 'That's right. I'd forgotten about that.'

'Could you tell us what time you left the party?' McClintock asked.

'Oh, around eleven, or thereabouts.'

'And did you talk to Judge Bailey at all that night?'

'Just in passing. She said she was planning to visit her daughter later in the year in London. Just small talk, you know. We were both waiting for the bathroom.'

'And what time was this?'

'Oh gosh, maybe ten? Kaye had left the party much earlier but she was still hanging around, making a big show about finishing that judgement. I remember I was looking at my watch because whoever was in there was taking ages. As it turned out, it was Grant's wife. She's a bit . . .' The judge circled her ear with her index finger. 'Poor thing. And that was awkward because we'd already had that strange interaction earlier.'

'In what way strange?'

Virginia Maiden leaned even further towards McClintock, her eyes bright and conspiratorial as though they were sharing a risqué joke at a cocktail party. 'Harriet dropped a hundred-dollar note on the floor at the buffet. I picked it up and tried to give it back to her. Well, you should have heard her! "No, it isn't mine, couldn't possibly be mine, I never carry cash, never, someone else must have dropped it." Honestly, she seemed to be having a bit of an episode, the way she carried on. It was just bizarre. Anyway, the money turned out to be Kaye's, or at least she swooped in and claimed it, perhaps to get Harriet to calm down.'

'So the last time you saw Judge Bailey was waiting for the bathroom later on?'

'Yes.'

'We understand the chief judge and Kaye Bailey had some unpleasant words. Were you present for that?'

'Oh, that all would have come out in the wash.' Maiden waved her hand dismissively. 'Nothing interesting there. Kaye could just be a bit fiery is all.'

'So as far as you're aware then, Saul Meyers wasn't angry with Judge Bailey afterwards?'

'Not really, no. He was upset, of course, she'd said some nasty things, but we all calmed him down. The boys, me. Even Grant had a go, which is unusual – he doesn't typically try to cool a conflict if it means getting to laugh at someone. Saul was fine within a few minutes. We continued on. Had a lovely night.'

She must be lying.

'Have you ever met a bloke called Brian Shanahan?' McClintock asked, and Jillian felt the same sensation she'd had while talking to Tim Buxton – as though she were merely an observer.

The judge rolled her eyes and sighed dramatically. 'Oh yes,' she said, 'I'm afraid we've all had the pleasure of dealing with Mr Shanahan at one stage or another. He's always on someone's docket. What did you say your name was again?'

'I apologise,' he said, flashing her a smile. 'I didn't introduce myself properly, I'm John McClintock, Jillian's colleague.'

I introduced you!

'McClintock, hey?' The judge narrowed her eyes teasingly. 'You aren't related to the McClintock-Garretts, are you? Out in Brighton?'

'Not me, no.'

'Ah, shame. Lovely family.' She looked at him expectantly, awaiting his next question.

'Were you on bad terms yourself with Judge Bailey?' Jillian asked as civilly as she could.

'Well, Kaye Bailey wasn't on good terms with a lot of people. She could be very snide and difficult.' Virginia Maiden was still looking at McClintock, as though it was he who'd asked the question. She gave a little laugh. 'I know we aren't meant to speak ill of the dead, but she trod on toes, said things.' The judge made a dramatic grimace.

'Was there a particular incident that bothered you?' McClintock asked.

'Incident?' She shook her head and laughed coquettishly. 'No, nothing like that. Kaye was,' she searched for the word, 'not very professional. I think she got her nose out of joint when I reprimanded her associate for using the judicial lift. Kaye knew she'd done the wrong thing, Saul had specifically told her not to let that girl use it. Aside from that, we weren't friends by any means but I certainly didn't wish her any harm. She knew Saul and I were close and she always had it in for him, so . . .' She waved a hand in the air. 'And then of course, Screwy calling Saul that time made things pretty awkward.'

'Michael O'Neil, you mean? He called the chief judge about what exactly?'

'Well,' the judge said, her cheeks reddening. 'About me. He claimed I was rude and arrogant when dealing with a self-represented litigant; he rang Saul about it, told him he should deal with me. As I explained to Saul, it was the last day of the duty list, I'd listened to forty matters, and this fellow comes in wasting my time complaining about paying his wife two hundred and fifty a week spousal. The wife was even worse. Saying she needed more, not less, basically trying to run an interim hearing in the last ten minutes of the day...' Judge Maiden looked to McClintock for understanding. 'As I'm sure you'll appreciate, you don't want to start some new investigation ten minutes before the end of your shift. This was the same. We would have been there until Christmas...'

'Fair enough,' McClintock said with an understanding smile. 'How do you find O'Neil in general? Sounds like he has a bit of a nasty streak?'

'Oh look, Screwy can be a pain in the backside but he is also just a sad old man. I don't let him bother me if I can avoid it.'

'We understand you and the chief judge went on to the Danish Club with some others after the party,' Jillian said. 'Do you recall Saul Meyers getting in a cab?'

'I do recall putting His Honour in a cab,' Virginia Maiden said with firm emphasis, still not bothering to look at Jillian. 'Had to tell them where to take him, too.'

'So you told the cab driver his address?'

'I did,' she confirmed.

'And what about you? Where did you go after that?'

'I went home,' Judge Maiden replied, finally looking at Jillian but only to convey her contempt. 'My husband collected me. You may check with him.'

'What an interesting woman,' Jillian said when Judge Maiden had shown them out. The entire interview had been a masterclass in exclusion and belittlement. If Jillian had not been the recipient of the judge's behaviour she might even have been impressed by it. There was a certain skill in making someone feel that invisible.

'I thought she seemed okay,' McClintock said.

'Ugh, well, that's because she loved you. No, she was nasty.'

'A bit snobby maybe,' he conceded. 'But she's just lost her colleague.'

'A colleague she was more than happy to criticise to us,' she snapped. It was as though for everything Jillian said, McClintock had a rosier, kinder explanation. That wasn't how a homicide detective should operate. Had he not learned anything about the dark side of human nature?

'I guess at least now we know Meyers is probably out of the running,' she said. 'Maiden was adamant she gave the cabby his address. We should know soon enough from the company anyway.'

'Suppose so,' McClintock said, although he sounded disappointed. 'Unless he went back in after.'

They found Angela in her office. The registry manager escorted them to the security office which was located in the basement of the building, looking out onto the underground carpark. Tomir and another, older man, sat together, in front of several television screens, looking intently between different camera positions.

Tomir's face fell as he noticed the detectives. 'I'm still trying to put all the proximity card logs on the disk but we keep having problems even accessing the records. The IT boys are working on it now. Jerome's gonna try doing it a different way if it still doesn't work. I'll call you as soon as it's done.'

'Alright,' Jillian said, trying to suppress her irritation. She turned to McClintock. 'Shall we take a drive to the leafy inner east then?'

CHAPTER 14

'I always forget this part of Melbourne exists,' Jillian said when they pulled into Marnong Avenue, Hawthorn, just before midday. 'All this money, these huge houses.'

She still remembered the first time she had made it 'across the river', for the twenty-first birthday of a university friend over fifteen years earlier. The friend had lived at a residential college but the party was at her childhood home, which was far removed from the aging furniture, comfortable rugs and snoring animals of the house Jillian had grown up in. When she had arrived she'd been shown into what looked like an enormous white box, where waiters – actual waiters – had offered her champagne and canapés and directed her to the pool outside for 'pre-dinner entertainment'. Jillian had locked herself in one of the house's many bathrooms for over an hour, overcome by inadequacy.

Judge Grant Phillips' house was a very different affair, although extremely grand in its way. It was the type of home that would serve as inspiration for a children's story – mock Tudor with white walls and dark brown brickwork and so perfectly precise and angular it could have been replicated in gingerbread. It sat far back from the road on a double block, protected from prying eyes by a high brick wall.

At least he'll be well protected if it turns out we have a serial killer.

'It's like a different world,' she said.

'I went to school near here,' McClintock said. 'Few blocks away. I must have walked past this house a bunch when I was young.'

'Your parents lived around here then?'

He shook his head but did not elaborate. He got out of the car and stretched in his performative way. 'What about you? Where'd you go to school?'

Jillian laughed despite herself. 'God, that's such a Melbourne question.'

'Is it?' McClintock looked genuinely perplexed.

'Oh yeah.'

'Oh. Sorry.' He frowned and she felt a lick of guilt.

'Nah, it's fine. I grew up in Ballarat, so the school thing doesn't mean much to me anyway.'

A discreet intercom speaker was nestled in the side of the wall next to a tall wooden gate. It would be impossible not to feel safe here, Jillian thought, protected by quiet streets, unscalable walls, an intercom system.

'Hello?'

'Judge Phillips? It's Detectives Basset and McClintock.'

'Yes, of course,' he responded in that pleasant, gentle tone. 'Come right in.'

The gate creaked open of its own volition and Jillian and McClintock were permitted an unencumbered view of the carefully manicured front yard. Rosebushes had been planted at precise intervals on either side of a paved pathway, and a marble fountain sat in the centre of the verdant lawn. A white Maltese dog appeared without warning and began a frenzied assault on McClintock's ankles.

'Brasher!' Judge Phillips called from the doorway. 'Come right here this instant.' The little dog cowered at the sound of his master's voice and disappeared around the side of the house.

'I'm so sorry about that,' the judge said, walking towards them. 'My wife's dog. The doctor said an animal would be good for her but I'm not convinced that Brasher is good for anything. Good to see you again, Detective Basset.' He turned to McClintock, right hand extended. 'I'm Grant Phillips.'

'Beautiful house,' McClintock said.

'Thank you, we adore it. It's been in the family for a few generations.'

Despite his warm greeting the judge looked troubled. 'You'll have to excuse Harriet,' he told them as he led them through the front door and into a sitting room that looked out onto the rosebushes. 'She's just not managing, poor thing. Hari's a delicate soul at the best of times, but this has truly thrown her. Her psychiatrist has given her something but it doesn't seem to have kicked in properly yet.' He frowned slightly. 'Anyway, I'll fetch her. Make yourselves comfortable.'

He directed them to a velvet-upholstered settee and left them alone to survey the room. It was furnished in stately fashion – shining wooden surfaces, gilt-framed paintings, thick, opulent rugs. A fireplace had been stacked with pine cones in anticipation of the winter to come. Above it, a number of photographs were displayed. A much younger Grant Phillips standing proudly outside a church with a young blonde woman on their wedding day; the same couple, several years later with a young man in a suit; Kaye Bailey and Grant at some type of formal function, Bruce Singh with a protective arm around his then wife's waist and all of them laughing uproariously. Trophies for various competitions were positioned between the pictures.

'Used to do triathlons and Iron Man events,' Phillips said, appearing silently at Jillian's side and smiling at the memory. 'And that one was at a very fancy dinner we had when Kaye was appointed to the bench. I think there were about twenty of us, friends from the bar, Bruce and Harriet. It was one of those really lovely nights. I still remember little Ama reading a book while the adults ate, totally oblivious to her extraordinary mother. Harriet will be down in a moment, she's just getting changed. I've put the kettle on, do you fancy a tea? Coffee?'

The two officers asked for coffee and he disappeared again and returned a few minutes later with a tray. 'I must apologise for the instant coffee,' he said with a grimace. 'As I'm sure you can imagine, it's been a difficult few days and we're fresh out of beans.' He put the tray on the coffee table and invited them to help themselves.

'It's all just devastating,' he continued. 'I keep thinking how the next time I go into work she won't be there.' His voice choked up and he looked down at his hands, composing himself. 'Sorry,' he said eventually, 'I'm still quite upset. Obviously. Kaye and I go back to the nineties, can you believe it? When I actually looked like that.' He pointed to a wall-mounted photograph behind Jillian's head, showing him emerging from the waves at a beach, his body lean and fit. 'Kaye started briefing me early on. I was the one who told her to go to the bar.'

'Perhaps while we're waiting for your wife we could run a few things that have popped up past you?' Jillian said.

'Yes, of course. Anything.'

'I know we briefly discussed Brian Shanahan the other day,' she said. 'When we spoke to Ama and Bruce they suggested that Kaye might have been really quite afraid of him. That she might have thought he killed her cat.'

'I'd forgotten about that. They're quite right, she was in a real state about it for a while. My recollection is that there was nothing specific to say it was him, save that he knew her address from pinching her wallet. Although, of course, there was the thing with the bird, which was probably front of her mind.'

'What thing with the bird?'

The judge grimaced. 'Brian Shanahan's a very disturbed individual. He sent one of his exes dead birds in the post, as I recall. I think one of them might actually have been a pet. Dismembered it. I remember Kaye telling me about it. He also smeared semen on the same woman's car doors. Poor thing somehow proved it was him too, if my memory serves. But the birds came up in Kaye's second trial with him, I'm quite sure of it. That's why she thought he did the cat.'

'Do you happen to know the history? Why he might have it in for Judge Bailey in particular? Seems like every judge we've spoken to knows him.'

'From what I can recall, Shanahan was one of Kaye's first matters when she was appointed to the bench. It was her first duty list, I think, and he came in with this urgent application. The girlfriend or wife, whatever she was, she was Chinese or something, some country that wasn't a signatory to the Hague Convention, and he came in saying she was planning to flee the country and asking Kaye to put an Airport Watch List Order in place. That's a court order that prevents a child from boarding an international flight – emergency-only scenario. Anyway, Kaye refused it. I think she didn't feel there were sufficient grounds, he hadn't put forward enough evidence. The next day the wife bolted overseas with the child and that was that, Shanahan had no way of getting the kid back.'

'Jesus,' McClintock said.

'It does happen from time to time,' Grant Phillips said. 'And of course, once a person is out of the jurisdiction the only thing you can really do is hope they come back in the future, or try to kidnap the child and bring them home. In Shanahan's case it hasn't kept him out of the court – after all, you can always make more children. It's one of the few things that man is really good at, actually – making new children and going out of his way to ruin their lives.'

'Okay, thanks for that,' Jillian said, furiously making notes. 'On another matter, do you know how serious Judge Bailey and Michael O'Neil were?'

'Not really. I mean, no one's really serious with a bloke like Screwy. We all thought she was mad for going there, but some women do love a Byronic hero.'

'Bit of a tortured soul, is he?' Jillian asked.

'More like tragedy follows him. He lost both his wives in accidents, has a kid in rehab.'

'Lost both his wives?' McClintock said with interest.

'That's right. I don't really know the details of it, we've never been particularly close, and Kaye didn't talk about it. I just hear the gossip that floats around. Anyway, the man is always lurching from one catastrophe to the next, and I suppose Kaye loved saving people.'

There was a sudden, startling beep from near the front door. It took Jillian a moment to realise that it was the intercom system. Grant Phillips did not get up, instead he pulled his mobile from his pocket, held the screen to his face, and after a moment pressed a button.

'Just a parcel,' he said, showing them his phone, where Jillian could see a grainy live stream of his front gate. 'Hello there, that can just be left in the letterbox,' he said into the phone. He turned the screen off and put the phone back in his pocket. 'The joys of modern technology, hey? I had a conversation with Kaye about this very system in fact. She came to see me one morning, asking what type of security she should get. In the end she decided it was easier to just move.'

'Is it possible that Kaye was finding the threats a bit much? That she might have been planning to resign?'

'Not that I'm aware of.' He looked at the detectives carefully. 'That isn't to say much, though. Kaye receded into herself over the last few months – stress, I thought. But she wasn't a quitter.'

'Do you know why Brian Shanahan wasn't reported to the police back when he got into chambers? We've been told the chief judge made the call.'

The judge looked awkward. 'Yes, well, Saul was mid-judgement, you see, and he was worried that if the matter was investigated then his judgement might be compromised.'

'How so?'

'He'd been working on it for over a year, which is really far too long, at risk of being appealable, but Saul hates doing judgements. Anyway, he thought there was a risk Shanahan would say he was biased and try to have the trial reconvened, to adduce more evidence if the police got involved, so he told everyone to just leave it.'

'I thought Judge Bailey was dealing with Mr Shanahan at the time?' said McClintock.

'She was his docketed judge for some things, but there were other kids, other fights to have with other partners. As I said, I've had him too. Everyone has. If it were any other jurisdiction he'd have been declared a vexatious litigant years ago.'

'Do you know how Judge Bailey felt about the break-in going unreported?'

'Well, unhappy, but she couldn't do anything about it except go to the police behind Saul's back and she wouldn't do that.'

'And did everyone think it was Brian Shanahan?'

'Yes. It made sense. He'd been seen at court that day, and when he was at court he liked to go in and bother Kaye – eyeball her while she listened to other matters.'

'Do you know why Kaye might have engaged a law firm?'

Grant Phillips looked surprised at this, but his attention was immediately diverted by the appearance of a spectral creature in the doorway.

'Darling,' he crooned. 'Come and have a cuppa?'

Harriet Phillips took a seat next to her husband and he gripped her hand in his. Jillian thought she might have been around sixty. She was very thin with light hair that hung limply around her face. Where her husband had a vibrancy to him, she was all haggardness and frailty.

'The detectives, darling,' he told her gently. 'Jillian and John.'

'Hello,' she said with a strained smile, not quite making eye contact with either of them.

Then in fits and starts she confirmed her husband's account of events at the party. 'Rupert, that's our driver, he dropped me off. Grant came down and got me from the car, took me up to chambers. I really only talked to Kaye and him; I get a bit,' she gulped, 'nervous. We went in to see Kaye at the end, after that fight she had with Saul Meyers. We thought, well, Grant thought, we should show her our support.'

Jillian looked at Harriet. 'So you went to Kaye's chambers to see her together?'

'Yes,' she said. 'I'd seen her briefly outside the bathrooms, and

I said we'd come and say goodbye before we left.' Harriet looked as though she might burst into tears at any moment. 'Sorry,' she said, and her husband gently rubbed her back.

'What did you talk about outside the bathroom?' Jillian asked.

'Oh.' Harriet looked slightly startled. 'Well, just about our children. Damien, our son, is in London for university, and Ama's over there at the moment too. I think we just talked about Kaye going to see Ama later in the year.'

'Wait,' said Phillips to Jillian. 'What were you saying, before Hari came in? Something about Kaye getting a lawyer?'

'Yes, we're aware she engaged a firm in Sydney the day she was killed, but we're having difficulty confirming for what. A firm called FarrugiaPerriam, they seem to do employment and family law. Do you know them?'

Grant Phillips raised his eyebrows. 'Goodness me. And they won't tell you what it was about? Well, if it was litigation, there's a possibility it will continue after her death. A property issue with Bruce maybe? Although I'm pretty sure they sorted all that out years ago. It's very odd.'

Harriet Phillips was listening with a strange expression on her face. Jillian thought she looked as if she was miles away. 'You don't think,' she said, quietly to her husband, 'maybe it was about the bullying?'

The judge appraised his wife. 'I can't imagine she'd ... you mean with Ginny? No. Why would she go to a Sydney firm about that?'

'Bullying?'

'Oh, just Judge Maiden throwing her weight around with the associates. There was a rumour that she made one of them paint her nails or some such thing. Kaye mentioned it to us last year at some function or other, just a bit of outrageous gossip. She loved a story about one of the old guard behaving badly. But Kaye wouldn't engage a law firm for something like that.'

'Just one more question, Judge, if you don't mind?' Jillian said.

'Call me Grant, please,' he said. 'I'm only Judge within the confines of the justice system.'

Very different from Judge Maiden . . .

'Tomir Staniak, the security manager, do you know much about him?'

'Not really. He's been around the court as long as I have, maybe longer. Why do you ask?'

'He's just taking a while to get the proximity card information to us.'

'Proximity card?' The judge grimaced. 'Ah, so Saul hasn't told you?'

'Told us what?' she prompted after the judge was silent for several seconds.

'The night of the party, Saul instructed security to remove the proximity card requirement for our floor. So that his friends could get in, without him needing to fetch them up.'

'He did what?'

Unfuckingbelievable.

'I know,' Grant said. 'I told him it was a stupid idea . . .' He shook his head. 'And he emailed everyone and told them, thought if any spouses were coming they might like to show themselves in too.'

'He emailed everyone on the floor and told them there was no security?'

Phillips inclined his head ever so slightly in reluctant agreement.

The interview concluded, the Phillipses walked Jillian and McClintock to the door. Harriet remained on the threshold, as though some invisible barrier prevented her moving further, while the judge walked them to the gate.

'I'll get my parcel while I'm here,' he said. Before they left he offered a final apology. 'Harriet's not very talkative at the best of times, but as you probably saw, she's a total mess at the moment. We're going back to the Melbourne Clinic tomorrow, see if she should be readmitted.' He smiled. 'For better or for worse, hey?' And with that he ushered them out onto the street.

CHAPTER 15

'Are you still breastfeeding?' McClintock asked as they waited to order at a slick sandwich shop on Autumn Road.

Did I really just hear that?

'Sorry, what?'

'Are you still breastfeeding?' he repeated, eyes fixed on the chalkboard menu over the counter.

'That's what I thought you said . . . Why on earth would you ask me that?'

'I was just wondering,' he said casually. 'Because when my sister first went back to work after her baby she got mastitis.'

'No, I'm not,' Jillian said tersely. She felt the same anger that she had experienced outside the court rising in her stomach again.

Maybe he wants to explain mastitis to me now. Christ, I'm going to yell at him.

'Order for me, will you?' she barked. 'Whatever you're having.' She raced outside.

In the cool air she breathed deeply to calm herself. To one side of the cafe was an Italian restaurant beginning to set up for its lunch service. She stood watching a waitress of twenty or so fastening white tablecloths to the outside tables with thick plastic clips. How jealous

Jillian felt just then, of this person who had her whole life ahead of her, who could pack up at a moment's notice and move to Chile if she wanted to. This woman was not obligated to listen to idiotic men mansplain the basics of motherhood to her.

She called Aaron, trying to remind herself of the wonderful reasons why she had tethered herself to this life they had. 'You two looked so cute together this morning, I should have taken a picture,' she told him when he picked up. She didn't tell him that sometimes her heart ached so badly for the days when it was just the two of them that she thought there might be something physically wrong with her. As far as Aaron knew, she was better now.

'Yeah, he was tricky to get down in the middle of the night, in the end I just fell asleep while he cried. Little dude's definitely getting more teeth. We've run out of teething gel and Panadol,' he added, half to himself.

In the background Jillian could hear children's music and Ollie babbling.

'Hey listen,' Aaron said, 'my mum just called, she wants to come over on the weekend, says she'll bring lunch. What do you reckon?'

'You didn't tell her I'd gone back to work, did you?'

There was a pause, just long enough for her to deduce that he had indeed. 'But you *are* back,' he said. He sounded almost testy.

Just breathe. One. Two. Three.

'But I don't want her knowing that,' Jillian snapped, despite herself. Aaron's mother had become a sore point of late. It wasn't that Margot was malicious, or even passive aggressive; Jillian knew that in many respects she had won the mother-in-law lottery. But Ollie's birth had brought out nostalgia in Margot, and her rose-coloured recollections of Aaron's childhood reminded Jillian of her own parental shortcomings.

'What, you want me to lie?'

In another life Jillian had found Aaron's inability to lie to his mother endearing. Now she resented it. 'You know what she's like. I'll never hear the end of it. She'll be all "I stayed home until Aaron went to school because being a mum is the best thing in the world." Like she's the bloody mother-of-the-century.'

'I don't think that's fair.'

'Well, it's true, regardless.' Jillian hung up without waiting for a response.

Nice one, Jillian, instead of yelling at your colleague you yell at your husband.

She turned around to find McClintock standing a mere metre away, paper sandwich bag in hand.

'Jesus! You're like a cat,' she said, silently admonishing herself for letting her emotions get the better of her in public.

McClintock at least had the decency to look slightly guilty. He proffered the bag and they sat on a long bench that ran the length of the cafe's front window. She concentrated on the minutiae of eating, the taking of a bite, the tasting, the swallowing, as she tried to push Aaron and his mother from her mind.

Her phone beeped with an email notification. 'A bloke called Ranjith from the cab company just spoke to Des,' she told McClintock, relieved to have a diversion. 'Said he dropped a fat drunk man off at Meyers' address in Kew very early on Thursday. So that's probably him out, unless he killed her before they left for their nightcap. But we know they were all there by midnight, and we think she wasn't killed before then. What do you reckon? I suppose he could still have come back into the city?'

'Seems unlikely,' McClintock conceded reluctantly. 'Probably just passed out. He's a fucking idiot though, Tomir will lose his job, surely. And all because some spoilt old man didn't want to inconvenience his friends.'

'I know. Tomir could have told us though instead of screwing us around for five days,' Jillian said. 'We wouldn't even know now if it wasn't for Phillips. I guess the good thing is that really, our list of other suspects isn't that impacted – I doubt many people outside the court knew about the absence of security. If Meyers emailed the other judges, it can only be one of them, someone they told or someone who accessed their emails.'

'Or, a very lucky stalker.'

'To Hawthorn and back again,' McClintock sighed as they walked into the station. It was late afternoon and the Homicide unit smelled like deodorant, microwave lunches and the portable heater that Des kept running under his desk from the first fall of leaves in autumn until daylight savings began.

'Didn't pick you for a Tolkien fan,' Jillian said, surprised.

'What can I say? I was very uncool at school.'

Jillian was sceptical that McClintock had ever been considered uncool. She thought of Ama, and her mother's view of Saul Meyers: 'a bit of a coaster'. She wondered if this was in part the reason for her antipathy towards McClintock – was she perhaps slightly jealous of the ease with which he was able to move through the world? She foresaw that with moderate effort and a few contacts he would progress to heights she would have to fight tooth and nail to reach.

She could see Des in heated conversation on his phone. He raised an arm in greeting as he saw them before rolling his eyes dramatically.

Jillian switched on her computer, thinking of Tomir Staniak, his lies and his open dislike of Judge Bailey. Next to her, McClintock was reading furiously, his eyes inches away from his computer screen while simultaneously eating raw cashews.

'Have you done any reading on O'Neil?' he asked, without turning to look at her.

'Only checked LEAP, saw there was a guy with that name with a drink driving history. I assumed it wasn't him but seems like it might have been the more we hear about him. Wasn't a Fitzroy address and we didn't have the date of birth.'

'All this stuff about him as the Byronic hero, the kid in rehab, the deaths of both wives sounds really fishy to me. Here, I'm emailing you something.'

'You reckon Kaye Bailey was murder number three?' Jillian asked as she refreshed her emails. McClintock had sent her a link to an article from *The Herald Sun* dated 4 April 2008 with the headline: 'Drunk Barrister's Private Pain'.

Prominent barrister Michael O'Neil has faced court for sentencing in his high-level drink driving case. O'Neil pleaded guilty to two counts of drink driving on two consecutive days in September 2007. In sentencing submissions today, Sonja Marchetti QC for Mr O'Neil told the court that at the time of the offending, Mr O'Neil was suffering a significant depressive episode as a result of the death of his second wife, Andrea O'Neil, who, as reported by this masthead, died in a suspected suicide earlier that year. Mrs O'Neil was well known as the public face of the Tarquinio coffee family. Ms Marchetti further submitted to the court that this trauma was compounded by Mr O'Neil's son being recently admitted to a rehabilitation facility. Mr O'Neil lost his first wife in a bushwalking accident in 1984.

Psychiatric evidence tendered to the court by Mr O'Neil's barrister noted that his offending was the result of a 'significant mental health crisis' from which he has made concerted efforts to recover. The court heard that Mr O'Neil had admitted himself to a private rehabilitation facility. Two stalking charges against Mr O'Neil were dropped.

'That's interesting,' Jillian said when she had finished reading.

'Interesting? Come on, lightning doesn't strike three times. Suspected suicide and bushwalking accident! Not to mention the stalking.'

McClintock's eyes were alight. How quickly he'd forgotten his conviction that the chief judge was responsible.

'Well,' said Jillian, 'we're looking into him. We just need to find him first.'

'Where we at?' Des called from his doorway, beckoning to the detectives. They followed him into his office and McClintock immediately began on his new theory regarding Michael O'Neil.

'We know from Tim Buxton he was mad about her, we now know O'Neil could easily have got up to chambers – Bailey probably told him to just let himself up when he was done with his conference, he didn't need a card. We found that out today from Grant Phillips,' he explained when Des raised an eyebrow in question. 'We also know he was somewhere near chambers at around eleven-thirty that night and that his phone doesn't get used again after that. We're still waiting to unlock Bailey's phone, but maybe he's proposed, she's turned him down and he cracks it. We know he flies a bit fast and loose. Seems obvious.'

Obvious . . .

Jillian hated the way some men did that, declared things to be obvious simply because they believed them to be true.

Well, okay, some women do it too, but not as many . . .

Des was silent for a moment, then he turned to Jillian. 'Thoughts?'

'It's a definite possibility,' Jillian said. 'I'm fairly comfortable ruling Meyers out after your chat with the cabby. But it's also completely possible he conspired with someone to let them get in to her. His phone records should confirm either way. The business with the security passes explains why he was being so evasive, though. I went through Bailey's work emails and I don't remember seeing one from Meyers about the proximity cards. We'd need to know that she knew about it for her to be able to tell O'Neil. I guess we can get a copy of whatever the chief judge sent out fairly easily.'

'Who else are we looking at?' Des asked.

'We've got Virginia Maiden, potentially – there's something I find quite shifty about her. And there was no love lost between her and Judge Bailey – that's for sure.'

'I don't reckon –' McClintock began.

'Nor do I necessarily,' Jillian agreed, 'but she remains a possibility. She and Meyers claim they left the party together at around eleven with two other mates. The mates were both plastered. Maiden says her husband picked her up from the Danish Club, so we should confirm that. There's a rumour that she wanted a tilt at the top job, even though her age is against her, and she's a nasty piece of work . . .' Jillian sighed. 'And of course Brian Shanahan is far from ruled out. Kaye Bailey was worried about her safety – she moved house for that reason. Meyers didn't want to disrupt his own schedule to deal with it, so while she was getting threats we know that he did bugger-all to stop them. We know it was probably Shanahan who let himself into her chambers on a previous occasion. We're trying to get his phone records. He's on his honeymoon at present, if you can believe it.'

Des snorted loudly.

'I know,' Jillian agreed.

'You happy to rule out everyone else at the party?'

Yes, if only to ensure I never have to talk to any mates of Saul Meyers again.

'I think so,' she said carefully.

'Me too,' said McClintock quickly.

Des ignored him. 'You think so, but there's a but?'

'The Phillipses say they went in to see Kaye at ten-fifteen or thereabouts, so at this point they're the last two people to have seen her alive, that we know of, killer aside, of course. They're each other's alibis. I don't think it's likely to be them; the husband adored Bailey, though the wife is definitely a bit weird. Then there are the associates. My gut says no to them.'

'Mine too,' McClintock said, sounding a little desperate.

'Aside from that,' Jillian went on, 'we got that message from the ex-wife in the judgement Kaye was working on – Lisa Nettle. The husband is Rahul Sharma – that TV doctor. No luck getting back on to her yet.'

'I was just about to mention that I took a call from her half an hour ago, saying she was sure her ex-hubby did it,' Des said. 'Sounded a bit frantic and, to be honest, a bit sauced. She couldn't give me any specifics, just said she knew what he was like and what he was capable of. And she refused to come in or say where she was calling from. I got a bit of a fruit loop vibe.'

'Since his face is all over the TV, I don't reckon he's gonna risk waltzing up to chambers –' McClintock said.

Des cut him off again and moved on. 'Where are we otherwise?'

'We're still trying to confirm the source of the death threats Kaye received at chambers. The techies are working on that as we speak. We've also got this business with her payment to the law firm. The firm won't tell us anything at this point. We're gonna talk to Legal about issuing a subpoena, although Legal reckon the firm will fight it tooth and nail.'

'What a doozy.' Des leaned back in his chair and rubbed the back of his head, his habitual movement in moments of intrigue. If things were stressful he would rub his stomach instead. Jillian sometimes contemplated what it might take for him to do both at the same time. 'But we're getting there,' he said. 'Good-o. Don't stay later than you need to tonight. I'll brief upstairs. Okay?'

They returned to their desks and did not speak for the next two and a half hours. As Jillian sent another harassing email to their techies regarding access to the dead judge's phone, she occasionally looked at McClintock's screen. He was consumed with Michael O'Neil. Her colleague's shoulders sat at a tense angle and Jillian wondered if he was sulking.

At seven they took the lift down to the carpark together. 'You doing anything tonight?' McClintock asked, still sounding slightly wounded.

Good for him to be jealous.

She gave a tight smile. 'Nah, just heading home. You?'

'Going to watch the footy training with a mate. I've got a good feeling about this week. We might actually get up.'

'You got a partner?'

He shook his head but didn't elaborate.

They parted when the lift opened. Jillian got into her messy car and looked at her face in the rear-vision mirror. Her skin was dry and her eyes were slightly pink at the edges. She pulled at a strand of the too-dark hair that she now hated and knew looked dreadful. She felt panicked. It was too early to leave. Ollie would still be awake when she got home. She wondered whether Aaron would have forgiven her for their tiff. She wondered what excuse she could come up with not to see her mother-in-law.

As Jillian reversed out of her park, she caught sight of McClintock, not returning to his car but instead letting himself into the bike cage, where he proceeded to change into a riding kit in full view of the carpark.

CHAPTER 16

Judge Bailey's funeral took place on the 1st of May, an appropriately grey and atmospheric morning. It had been a week since their meetings with Judges Phillips and Maiden, a week since the revelations that level twelve had been a free-for-all on the night of the murder, and since McClintock had begun cultivating his Michael O'Neil theory.

They had exercised a search warrant on Michael O'Neil's house that had produced nothing more than a classical guitar, several CDs of guided meditation and some very amateur oil paintings. They had tried Lisa Nettle again without any success and they had confirmed that Brian Shanahan – like Michael O'Neil – had not used an ATM on his honeymoon and that his phone had last been used in rural New South Wales. The local police had been alerted but there had been no sightings of him.

O'Neil had still not surfaced, which Jillian agreed with McClintock could very well be indicative of a man lying low. It was odd, though, she thought, that no one else had sighted him, that they had received no tip-offs. She knew that the legal fraternity, like police, looked after their own, but she doubted that that applied in circumstances as dramatic and serious as the death of a judge.

Her investigation of Tomir Staniak had met a dead end. The security manager and his wife had been at a local club until ten pm on the night of the murder and CCTV from their own system, and that of their equally paranoid neighbours, showed no one leaving the house after they arrived home at ten-thirty until the next morning when Tomir had left at his usual time.

Judge Bailey's mobile had been another source of ongoing frustration. When the phone had been successfully unlocked and its contents downloaded to their computers, it was to find that all the files had been corrupted. Their 'techie', a man of few words and fewer social skills, had told them to leave it with him but not to 'expect a miracle'.

'So Saul Meyers' phone records are possibly the most boring I have ever seen in my life,' Jillian told McClintock in the car on the way to the funeral. The records had arrived after several days and many irate phone calls, just as they were leaving the station, and she had quickly printed them off to read as her colleague drove. 'Looks like sometimes he calls two different golf clubs on the same day, sometimes a restaurant, sometimes one of his daughters or one of his cronies. But that's really it. There's no joy here. Doesn't call Shanahan by the looks of it. He could have another phone? He doesn't really strike me as a burner phone type of bloke. What do you reckon?'

'Well no,' McClintock conceded, 'but he also isn't a total idiot. He got to be chief judge somehow, right?'

'True. Maybe it's a generational thing – his phone records are as boring as O'Neil's bank records.'

'True that.'

McClintock parked on High Street in Northcote. They had ample time before the funeral was to begin.

It was just after nine-thirty and an aggressive southerly flicked Jillian's hair into her eyes, making them smart. McClintock led the way into a cafe that might also have been a tattoo parlour where they ordered coffees from a bald female barista with pierced cheeks. Just as Fitzroy had succumbed to designer prams and vertical gardens, Northcote had clearly also ridden the wave of gentrification.

They walked the block to the funeral parlour slowly. 'Do you reckon Phillips and Bailey might have had something going on?' McClintock asked, draining the last of his coffee and throwing the cup into a bin.

'That thought did occur to me,' Jillian said. 'Everyone says they were very close. And the ex-husband thought Phillips was keen on her.'

'Maybe O'Neil got wind of it.'

'Possible, I suppose. But Ama was living there until pretty recently and didn't mention anything, and Kaye and Grant had been friends a long time. Why now? And everything we hear about Bailey – she doesn't sound like the type for an affair, does she?'

A yellow cab pulled into the kerb beside them, and Ama and her father got out, followed by a skeletal young man in an extremely narrow navy suit. He looked to Jillian a little like Edward Scissorhands' younger sibling, and was introduced to them as Ama's boyfriend, Hugo.

The Ama of today was a very different creature from the woman they'd first met. Her thick hair was piled on top of her head in a loose bun and she was wearing an almost fluorescent scarlet lipstick that clashed with her deep red dress.

'I made a decision,' she told Jillian as they approached the parlour together, 'that I'm not going to let Mum be defined by the way she died. That's a chapter, an utterly terrible one, but it's not going to be anywhere near the whole book.' Ama tilted her chin up a little and breathed in deeply. 'I'm not saying I don't want justice, but if people only think about her as a victim then whoever did this is in charge of her narrative, and I'm not having that.'

While Ama and Hugo went inside, Bruce Singh hung back with a pained expression on his face. 'Is there any news?' he asked. 'Anything at all? Ama's putting on a brave face but she's struggling so much.'

Jillian assured him they were doing everything they could, exploring every avenue as quickly as possible.

'Has Michael turned up?' he asked.

'Not yet, I'm afraid.'

Bruce sighed. 'We've been talking about why she might have transferred all that money to the law firm,' he said. 'Can't figure it out for the life of me. It just doesn't make any sense. One of Kaye's best friends from university does employment law in Sydney, she would have gone to her if she needed advice. But I asked the friend and she said Kaye hadn't mentioned a thing to her. Unless . . .' Bruce Singh's jaw slackened as he considered some private thought. 'Surely not,' he said.

'What's that?' Jillian said.

'I'm just wondering if perhaps she wanted advice about a Binding Financial Agreement.' He looked at each of them and, seeing their blank stares, continued, 'They do them in family law all the time. Kaye and I did one when we split, just to make sure everything was all neat and tidy.'

Jillian felt certain that she was still missing some vital piece of information. 'But she hasn't recently ended a relationship as far as we're aware,' she said, still confused as to where on earth Singh's hypothesis was going.

'No,' he said, 'but they don't just do Binding Financial Agreements when people are separating. They do them when people are about to start living together, or get married – you know, a pre-nuptial agreement.'

A sombre woman in a cream suit beckoned Bruce Singh into the building. 'I never got the impression she was that serious with him, though. Although maybe with Ama leaving she got lonely? Surely she would have said something,' he said as he was guided inside.

Mourners were beginning to congregate on the street as Jillian and McClintock positioned themselves near the doors. Christianne D'Santo arrived wearing a loose-fitting grey dress that could not disguise her protruding hipbones and the top of her rib cage. There had been days when Jillian would have given her right arm to have that lean a physique, but as she looked at the young associate, standing with a good-looking man also in grey, she felt only an aching sympathy. Matthew appeared from across the road, his hand enclosed in that of a smaller man with thick wiry hair and a long beard. The two associates embraced a moment before greeting the detectives.

'Hello again,' Christianne said. Her face looked tired and a thin layer of downy hair was illuminated on her cheeks in the meagre sunlight.

Matthew too looked strained as he greeted them, before both couples headed into the funeral parlour.

A government-issue sedan pulled into the parlour's driveway and Grant Phillips exited from the driver's side. He walked around to the passenger side and opened the door for his wife, who waited for him to offer an arm. Then a pinch-faced Harriet let him pull her into a standing position.

How's it possible to be so physically and mentally frail? I wonder what her diagnosis actually is.

Jillian had long observed that, as a general rule, most couples made a certain physical and social sense. Attractive people were almost invariably aware that they were attractive and sought mates of a comparable physical level. The same could be said for the less attractive, the obnoxious, the stupid, the hateful. In Jillian's experience, like attracted like. When she'd met Aaron all those years ago, she had known that they were of a similar standing, physically and mentally, that his weathered face was matched with her square jaw, just as his bleeding-heart values complemented her stoic determination to apportion blame and find justice. But Grant and Harriet Phillips seemed an anomaly, some perverse trick of the universe. He was spry, witty, and tall enough that the individual elements of his looks didn't really matter. Harriet, on the other hand, was wholly unimpressive.

The judge's wife kept her eyes fixed firmly on some distant point as they negotiated what was becoming a crowd. It was clearly the judge who took responsibility for the social niceties the event required. Harriet merely stood by, ignoring her surrounds.

'Hello, Detectives,' he said as he approached the doorway. 'You remember Jillian, darling?' he asked his wife. 'And John?'

'Hello,' said Harriet, lifting her head but not looking directly at either detective. Jillian wondered if the clothing she'd chosen – figure-hiding, limb-concealing and plain – was part of whatever condition she had. She had been dressed similarly on the detectives' visit to her home.

Phillips gave an apologetic smile over his wife's head as the two of them walked in. Jillian remembered what Virginia Maiden had said about the dropped cash on the night of the party, how her retrieval of it had been greeted by Harriet with 'an episode'. Was it possible that this frail woman had killed her husband's friend in a mad rage? If so, had she perhaps not left the building with her husband? Or had she returned to the building alone?

There was a rustle of excitement deep amongst the mourners and a moment later Jillian found herself face to face with the chief judge. She realised she hadn't previously grasped the physical presence of Saul Meyers, the sheer breadth of him. Once upon a time, he might have been referred to as strapping, the type to play rugby or American football. Now he was merely big – a thick neck, hands the size of Christmas hams, tree-trunk legs. A woman with pale eyes and a tight bob stood next to him, lips pursed and eyebrows shaped in permanent surprise. Unlike the Phillipses, the Meyers made complete and immediate sense as a couple.

'Chief Judge,' Jillian said, and he gave the briefest of nods before looking pointedly away. Virginia Maiden arrived shortly afterwards, accompanied by a weak-chinned, slightly built man with sad eyes, just as the PA system inside launched abruptly into Van Morrison's 'Bright Side of the Road'.

McClintock raised an eyebrow at Jillian. 'You go on in,' she told him. 'I'll wait another minute, see who else pops up.'

Several late guests trickled in as Van Morrison's crooning came to an end. Jillian had just decided to go in herself when a taxi pulled into the drive. The driver got out, retrieved a pair of crutches from the back seat and then assisted a minuscule woman to disembark. Jillian waited for her to make her careful way, holding the heavy door to the funeral parlour open, and got an appreciative smile in return.

The reception room was filled to bursting point and it occurred to Jillian that the family had likely had the option of any manner of larger and more impressive venues. Had Bailey requested that her funeral one day be held here? Or was this a deliberate decision on the part of the family? A photograph of a younger Kaye Bailey in her barrister's robe and beaming with happiness sat on an easel beside a coffin covered with native flowers. On a small platform to the right of the photograph, a middle-aged woman with bright green hair and a broad Australian accent began describing the judge's life.

Jillian found herself quickly immersed in the story of Kaye Bailey. She learned that Kaye had started a regular charity bake sale in high school, that she had volunteered at a community legal service at university, and had once been arrested for defacing a statue of Robert Menzies, although, as the celebrant added, the charge was ultimately withdrawn. The crowd gave an appreciative chuckle at this before a classical pianist launched into a musical interlude. Then Ama got up to speak, of her mother's parenting, of her unfailing ability to comfort, to soothe, to care, even when she had spent all day caring. At this, Jillian experienced a familiar sense of uselessness.

Ollie will never get up and say anything like this about you. Or if he does it will just be a lie.

She glanced around the room, wondered if any of the other parents were feeling the same acute shame. She saw Tim Buxton sitting ashen-faced to one side, Grant and Harriet sitting just behind Bruce Singh, their faces tight with emotion. Matthew was sobbing into his partner's shoulder in the third row.

'Thank you so much, Ama,' the celebrant said when Ama had finished. 'That was so eloquently put and so moving.' She looked out into the crowd. 'And now, to share something of Kaye's professional impact, we've got Sigourney Harrison.'

The tiny woman with the crutches got to her feet with some effort and moved slowly down the aisle. Ama, who had just sat back down between her father and Hugo, got up again and went down the aisle to meet her. At the dais the two women held each other a moment, exchanging whispered words.

Sigourney Harrison climbed carefully onto the small platform and adjusted the microphone.

'My name's Sigourney, as you've just heard,' she told the room in a voice that ached with barely restrained pain. 'I'm sorry for the grand entrance, I've just had a knee reconstruction.' She smiled sadly. 'Ama has kindly offered to let me say a few words. For those of you who don't know, I began as a client of Kaye's almost twenty years ago. She was just starting out in law and she appeared for me pro bono because I didn't have any money.' She stopped and took a deep breath. 'As it later turned out, neither did she, because she didn't actually have permission to act pro bono and was paying her salary back to the firm to keep acting for me.'

There was an appreciative gasp from the mourners. 'I had been in a really nasty relationship with someone. He left me with lasting physical injuries. Kaye also arranged our escape from the house – me, my two kids and our dog. She picked me up herself, found me a refuge, at a time when they were almost impossible to get into, took in my dog herself, and then got my matter into court. She secured enough for me in the settlement to be independent and she ensured my kids were protected from this man, who had abused them as well as me. She literally saved our lives.'

Sigourney paused for another deep breath and repeated, 'She saved our lives. And when she started her own safe house, she invited me to be on the advisory committee, to explain to the board how women feel in such situations, what their needs are. She *listened* to me. She listened to all women and she cared, so very deeply. And that level of care, that dedication to her clients, wanting not just to win in court for them but to do every possible thing to help them, was indicative of her entire approach to life.' Sigourney wiped away a tear. 'So I am devastated,' she said after composing herself. 'But also so thankful to have known Kaye.'

The room was silent. Jillian, who had attended countless funerals during her time in Homicide, was always moved by them and always found motivation in the desire to bring justice to the mourning families. Now, though, for the first time, it occurred to her that justice, at least in this case, was a slippery premise. To the average man or woman on the street, justice was an arrest, a conviction, the knowledge that someone had been held accountable for a death. But many of the people in this room, those who were ostensibly servants to justice, understood intimately the cogs and wheels of the legal system, 'how the sausage is made', as Des would say. They would know better than anyone that murderers could plead to manslaughter, get a sentence reduction with an early guilty plea and that a murderer's actions could be weighed against their psychiatric history, their childhood, the rest of their lives, in search of some equilibrium.

Slow down. You can start by catching the guy.

A couple of other speakers followed and then, as Lou Reed's 'Perfect Day' began to play, Ama, Bruce, and two older women who Jillian didn't know carried the coffin slowly down the aisle. The mourners began to follow, and Jillian caught sight of Virginia Maiden and Saul Meyers, discrete amongst the tide of the crowd, move off to the side, deep in conversation and with their backs turned. She moved carefully around the perimeter of the room until she was only a few metres from them.

'I didn't say a thing,' the retired chief judge was saying. 'Just seemed easier. No need to make the cover-up worse than the crime . . .'

Did I hear that correctly?

'Well, me neither. And yes, I agree, and the other two don't know anything . . .'

'You good?' McClintock called from the door, and both judges looked around. Noticing Jillian, Saul Meyers had the grace to look slightly ashamed but Virginia Maiden merely sneered.

'Very rude to eavesdrop, Detective,' she said as she walked past.

Jillian shook her head in frustration as she went to join McClintock. 'What did you do that for?' she hissed. 'Couldn't you see I was doing something?'

'Sorry,' he responded. And then added with a laugh, 'Feels like I spend a lot of time apologising to you.'

CHAPTER 17

The wake was held at an Italian wine bar opposite the Northcote Town Hall, at the top of Ruckers Hill. It was a dark, cool space with jazz playing through the speakers and waiters in white shirts and black aprons. Jillian and McClintock positioned themselves in a corner close to the entrance, where they could watch who came and went without drawing attention to themselves. They had not spoken since leaving the funeral parlour, and Jillian was too irritated to tell him what she'd overheard.

Although really, what did I overhear? But they were definitely covering something up, right?

Grant Phillips arrived with Harriet and another much younger woman, with whom he was talking intently. She had bright red hair, wore a dress that billowed in an unflattering way at her ankles and spoke in an authoritative bellow that suggested self-importance. Harriet did not involve herself in the conversation but instead focused all her attention on her left hand, where a scar ran the distance from thumb to wrist bone.

Self-harming?

Two polished-looking men in their mid-thirties moved around Jillian to approach the bar. 'Jules tried to visit him the other day,' the taller of the two told his friend. 'She knows O'Neil well, he was her mentor when she started out. Anyway, his house had been busted open by the cops. I didn't even realise they were a couple. Can't see he's got anything to do with it, though. He's a softie.'

'You've gotta be kidding,' the other man said with a visible shudder. 'I wanted to cross-examine his client once, and outside court he got in my face and started tearing strips off me. Bloody awful. Obviously . . .'

There we go again with men and 'obvious'.

'Apparently Helen's freaking out about the Sharma trial,' the first man said, nodding a greeting to the woman talking with Grant Phillips. 'She's worried they might have to start again.' Then he added more lightly, 'Seriously, mate, just ask him out already.'

The other man looked over at them incredulously. 'You reckon she's keen on Phillips?'

Virginia Maiden walked past arm in arm with her husband, ignoring the detectives.

'Judge,' the first man said. 'Good to see you.'

'Martin, how are you?' Her face softened slightly. 'And Dean. It's almost like a little Brown's List Reunion, isn't it?'

Tim Buxton walked up and gave McClintock a familiar slap on the back, as though they were old friends. 'You good, mate?' he asked. 'Any updates for us?' He acknowledged Jillian with a nod, and not for the first time she wondered if her only means of gaining traction with the men in this world were extreme obsequiousness or explicit hostility.

What would you rather be, a doormat or a bitch?

Grant Phillips' smiling face was the tonic to this moment of bitterness. He had appeared from across the room, bringing the red-haired woman and Harriet with him. 'Lovely service, I thought,' he said, looking down at her.

'Helen McPherson,' said the woman, offering her hand. 'G'day Timmy,' she said to Buxton who had remained next to McClintock. 'Ya good? Any word from Screwy yet?'

Tim Buxton looked slightly awkward as he shook his head, as though he wanted to telepathically silence the woman.

'I keep thinking about the last time I saw him,' she continued, oblivious. 'Didn't mention he was going anywhere that night, but then that's not unusual, is it?'

Jillian realised with a start that this was likely the woman Michael O'Neil had been in conference with the night of Kaye's murder. In the last week she had spent some time harassing the barrister's clerk to obtain a name only to be told that O'Neil hadn't formally booked anything in and there was no 'backsheet' – whatever that meant.

'Could I have a word privately?' she asked Helen quickly, and led the way to the back of the room, off which she had briefly caught sight of a tiny courtyard.

'Detective Basset, Homicide,' said Jillian when they were out of earshot, and Helen McPherson looked perturbed.

'No wonder Timmy was giving me nothing – must have thought I was about to get Screwy in trouble for something. I must say, I feel a bit edgy talking to the police,' she added. 'Although I suppose people feel that way about lawyers too.'

'It's not uncommon,' Jillian said. 'So you had a conference with Michael O'Neil the night that Judge Bailey was killed? Is that correct?'

'That's right, I did. In his chambers. The longest bloody meeting I've ever had in my life. Awful stuff.' She shuddered dramatically.

'What time did you leave?'

'Close to eleven,' Helen said, 'I think. The client left at around ten and we agreed we'd go for another hour. By the end of it I could scarcely remember my own name, but Screwy wasn't going to be available for the rest of the week, or the one after, and the trial was meant to start the Monday after that – although obviously that got pushed back because of all of this.'

'So you left chambers around eleven, then what?'

'We left together. I'd parked at the Mint and it was fairly quiet, so Screwy walked me back to my car, which was nice of him.'

'Did he say where he was going?'

Helen McPherson frowned slightly. 'He mentioned he was hungry so I assumed he was going to go and get something to eat. We'd skipped dinner.'

'Do you remember him calling Judge Bailey at any point?'

'Yeah, I think he called her at one stage, I stepped out though while they were chatting.'

'How did Mr O'Neil seem to you, during your meeting?'

'He was good, his usual self.'

'And why was he going to be unavailable for the rest of the week, do you know?'

'He didn't say but I know he holidays a few times a year – I just assumed he was going somewhere for a break.'

'So he walked you to your car, then what direction did he walk in?'

'Back towards William Street. The Mint is in a dead end, it's the only way to get out.'

'And you haven't heard from him since that night?'

'No. I tried to call him when I heard about Kaye but he wasn't answering his phone. I assumed he'd turned it off, to just digest it all by himself. I popped by his house too, and saw you guys had already been. Look, Screwy can be hard as nails but he is also a real romantic. He wouldn't have hurt Kaye in a fit. She would have been the hard-arse in that dynamic. She said it herself at some function I saw her at – Women in Law or something – she said you can either be a good lawyer or a good wife, and that her choice had always been the law.'

This reminded Jillian of Bruce Singh's musing that morning. 'Can I ask,' she said, 'you're a solicitor, so you do the paperwork and work for a law firm, is that right?'

'It is. I do the grunt work, the barristers do the fancy court stuff.' She gave a masculine guffaw. 'And everyone else makes the money.'

'Right, so how much would you charge for a Binding Financial Agreement?'

Helen looked surprised. 'Well, that depends – on how much property there is, how complex the property is, whether there are trusts or businesses or self-managed superannuation funds. Also at what stage in the relationship the client is asking for it. I'm much happier drawing one up after people have broken up than doing the pre-nuptial ones. Those are an insurance claim waiting to happen.' She looked Jillian hard in the face. 'Is this for you?'

'No.' Jillian smiled. 'But can you give me a ballpark? Older couple, both previously married to other people, each with perhaps a house and some cash, some super, say. If they wanted to do a pre-nup, how much would it cost them?'

'Well, as I said, it would depend. I don't like doing them, they're the most complained about area of family law, so you charge a bit more to compensate for them one day going pear-shaped. But okay, for a relatively easy one, I'd probably charge between eight and ten thousand.'

'That's all?'

Helen McPherson laughed heartily again. 'Most of my clients would say, "That much?"'

'So you aren't aware of solicitors charging much more for one than that?'

Helen looked interested now. 'There are always ways of making something cost more,' she said. 'But I wouldn't. I'm sure some firms out there will milk a person for all they've got.'

'So, a prepayment of forty thousand dollars to a family lawyer would be considered a large amount?'

'For forty thousand dollars,' Helen said, 'I'd say you're looking at starting some pretty heavy litigation.'

CHAPTER 18

Through the lounge-room window Jillian could see the sky settling into a lazy dusk. She lay on the couch, replaying the events of the day in her head. 'Cover-up worse than the crime' came through in Saul Meyers' overripe accent, followed by Helen McPherson's bellow as she said, 'pretty heavy litigation'.

What on earth is going on?

She could hear Aaron trying to settle Ollie in the nursery. 'Shhh,' he would say, after which came rhythmic patting sounds, and then, Aaron having perhaps deduced that Ollie was finally asleep, a silence as he began the painstaking transition of their son from his arms to the cot. There would be a moment when the house exhaled in relief, only to be followed by Ollie's renewed screaming. Aaron had been at it now for over forty-five minutes.

You could go in there...

The thought terrified her, the very idea of being the receptacle of her child's emotions, of being responsible for whispering soothing words while he screamed in her face. She pushed the thought away by focusing again on the day. She had made a concerted effort to speak to Judge Maiden's husband alone, but the judge had firmly interrupted the attempts. 'This is a funeral,

Detective,' she hissed. 'Have some common decency. You can talk to Harold any other time.'

Both Meyers and his wife and the Maidens left as soon as they were politely able to. Jillian had watched with interest as the chief judge had paid his respects to Ama, who had stared him down before turning her back altogether. Saul Meyers' thick neck had turned crimson as he absorbed the snub.

'Did you hear me?' Aaron was standing directly above her, his face upside down as he leaned over the back of the couch. He looked irritated. His lips were pursed, his eyes narrowed. Her husband did not usually look like this.

'Sorry, what?'

'I said you could have got dinner on while I was doing that.'

'Oh.' It wasn't often that Aaron got grumpy with her. She was typically the irritable one, the one prone to bouts of snappiness at the end of a long day. 'Sorry, I'm just tired. I worked the whole day.'

'Well, so did I!' He stomped off to the kitchen, where she heard him angrily opening cupboard doors and slamming things down.

She got up, intending to help, but her phone, which had been sitting on her stomach, clattered to the floor with a resounding thump. The house inhaled. Then Ollie's crying began anew, more desperate, more furious than ever. Aaron stormed out of the kitchen, throwing her a filthy look as he returned to the nursery.

Jillian went into the kitchen and opened the fridge. There was a Tupperware container filled with day-old rice, some limp-looking vegetables and two eggs. She set to work heating sesame oil in the wok and cutting the vegetables into small chunks, adding soy and garlic until she had something that resembled fried rice.

She took two clean bowls from the dishwasher and unstacked the rest of the clean dishes as she listened to Aaron patting and talking to Ollie.

I don't know how he does it.

When at last he emerged she put the food on the table. He sat down and looked at his bowl. 'This is basmati rice,' he said.

'Yes.'

'So it's the wrong rice for fried rice.'

'Oh,' Jillian said. 'I guess I wasn't really paying attention. I did think it didn't look quite right.'

'Just forget it, I'll get a pizza.' Aaron got up and took his bowl back into the kitchen. She heard him scoop its contents into the bin and close the bin cupboard a little too loudly.

She began to feel the day's emotional toll in the back of her throat. Suddenly she was close to crying. 'I guess there's just nothing I'm good for in the house, is there?' she said aloud to herself, and then found that fat tears were streaming down her face.

She left the table and retreated to the bedroom, which was feeling more and more like it belonged only to her. She could hear Aaron on the phone ordering a pizza, one single pizza, and not the margarita that he knew she always preferred. She had never known Aaron to be spiteful before, or even this bad-tempered. If a car cut him off or a waiter was rude to him he would dismiss it as someone having a bad day. All throughout the period after Ollie was born, the really dark days when she and Ollie would take turns lying on a blanket on the ground and crying, he had remained calm and steadfast.

Maybe that baby has pushed him to breaking point too.

She felt sick as soon as she thought this.

What type of mother refers to her child as 'that baby'?

The front door closed and out on the street she heard the car starting. She was alone with Ollie again. He was silent for now, but what if he were to wake up?

She lay on the bed, scared to breathe. On Aaron's bedside table was a book on neuroplasticity with a thin layer of dust, a long-abandoned glass of water, and a photograph of their wedding day in a thick silver frame. For the first time it occurred to her that it was possible that they might not make it through this, that it might be too much for them to weather together, and that with this interloper in the nursery, their marriage might become unworkable.

What if I never love Ollie? What if Aaron and I end up hating each other? What if we end up in court?

What if Aaron loves Ollie more than he loves me?

Her thoughts came faster and faster, each one darker than the last. It seemed impossible that only a year ago they had been on holiday in Noosa, Aaron in a polo shirt and too much sunscreen, Jillian egg-shaped and overrun with the complaints of pregnancy.

Ten minutes later she heard the car pull up and tracked Aaron's movements from the squeaking gate to the reluctant front door. These sounds, so familiar and mundane on any other day, now filled her with trepidation. She wondered if she should go to him – apologise for not seeing to dinner earlier, for being a lazy spouse and a shit mother, for having dreadful, dark thoughts.

The bedroom door opened and Aaron came in with a pizza box, two plates and chilli oil balanced on top of it. 'Hello,' he said awkwardly, not quite looking at her.

'Hi.'

He pulled an old blanket from the armchair in the corner and put everything on top of it, before opening the box.

'I ordered the broccoli one because I was annoyed with you,' he confessed. 'I'm sorry, I just had a bad day with him today. He was so unsettled, we actually had to leave Scienceworks he was crying so much.'

'That's horrible. I'm sorry too.'

'Anyway, I've booked him in with Ed tomorrow, we'll see what he says but I'm sure it's just teething.'

'Ed?'

'Yeah, Ed. You know, Dr Ed. I told you about him. He's the one that used to work in Mildura. He's got a kid Ollie's age too, he called the kid River, remember?'

'Oh, right. River.'

She should have felt better, they had made up, Aaron was calmer, but her sense of inadequacy was filling her and she felt she might cry again at any moment. How was it she didn't know her own child's doctor?

'You should have told me,' she said, sounding more accusatory than she intended.

'Told you what?' he said through a mouthful of pizza.

'That he was going to the doctor.'

'It's when you're at work,' he said, eyebrows raised. 'And it's just for a check, it isn't like I've booked him in for surgery.'

'But I'm his mother.'

'Yes.' Aaron was measured. 'And I'm the one who stays home with him, so I book the appointments and stuff.'

'Because I'm so incompetent?' she responded. Now she was not just angry but furious.

'I've never said that,' Aaron said, putting his pizza down and looking hurt. 'What's brought this on?'

'Oh nothing, just being excluded from my own child's life.'

'I have never excluded you.' Aaron got to his feet and collected his plate. 'You know, I don't know if it's occurred to you or not, but the last eight months haven't exactly been a picnic for me either. I've had to hold everything together while you were in the hospital, while you were home, and then as soon as you go back to work you just disappear on us, not even trying to connect with Ollie. Do you think I haven't noticed that you're working insane hours to avoid us?'

She did not respond.

'See, you aren't even denying it. And when you do get home you don't even ask how he is.'

'That's not true.'

'It is. And don't think I don't know about the psychologist. I know you haven't gone back.'

Before she could respond to that, her mobile began vibrating on the bedside table.

'It's Des,' she said, picking it up.

'Of course it is.' Aaron walked out of the room and pulled the door closed behind him.

'Hi Des,' she said, trying not to sound wired, manic.

'You all good?'

'Yup.'

'Look, I've just heard. We got a call-out from Hawthorn.'

'Des, I've got my hands full with the Bailey case at the moment.'

'Yeah, I know. That's why I'm calling. It's that Judge Phillips, his wife has gone missing.'

PART TWO

CHAPTER 19

Grant Phillips was waiting at his front gate in a state of intense agitation as Jillian and McClintock pulled up. 'This is my fault,' he said by way of greeting. 'All my fault. I let her, I let her . . .' He trailed off, and his shoulders began to twitch. In the half-light provided by the porch lamp and the open garage door, he looked as haggard as his missing wife.

'Hang on, mate, let's get you inside and talk it through,' McClintock said. He sounded different to Jillian, not charming or smooth, just kind. She looked at him, surprised. Catching her eye, McClintock gestured for her to lead the way.

They went into the same sitting room they'd sat in days earlier. The darkness gave the impression that nothing existed beyond the windows except empty space. The house was silent save for the tick of a clock and the hum of the distant refrigerator. Jillian turned on an overhead light and the judge blinked absently.

'Sorry,' he said, 'I didn't realise how dark it had become.'

'Your dog is on his best behaviour,' Jillian said, recalling the shrill greeting they'd received on the previous visit.

The judge looked distressed. 'Oh Brasher, Brasher died. Day before yesterday. It was awful, just horrible. Poor thing. We don't know what happened, he just didn't wake up. I'm wondering if he had some heart issue we didn't know about or something. He wasn't even that old. Harriet was devastated.'

'So can you tell us what happened? When did you realise Harriet had gone?'

'After the funeral. I'd driven us there, and when we were about to leave she said she was going to go to the toilet. I waited at the bar, talking to Ama and Bruce. But she didn't come back. Initially I thought there might have been a queue, then I thought I should go check. Then some other woman came out. I asked if she'd seen her, but she said it was empty before she went in.'

'Did you look for her?'

'Yes, of course! Straightaway. I asked everyone. We asked people out in the street. But no one had seen her. As you know, she hasn't been herself lately and so then I thought maybe she'd just gone home, taken a cab, a tram – she's done that once or twice before, even though she gets nervous in public by herself. So I drove home and waited, and two hours later she still wasn't back. I called the wine bar to see if she'd showed up there again, then I called the hospitals – she's turned up there once before too – but nothing. I tried a few other places I thought of, then I drove out to look for her.' He paused for breath, looking stricken. 'She was already distraught about Kaye, and then there was the death of poor old Brasher – she just loved that dog. Last night she was in a complete state, saying all kinds of crazy things, but I thought she seemed better this morning, or I never would have taken her to the funeral.'

'What did she have on her, at the wake?'

'Nothing much, she doesn't have a mobile, has some strange ideas about radiation. Doesn't carry a wallet either. So if she did take the tram, maybe she was detained for not having a ticket?' He looked up at them hopefully.

'I'd like to think that an older woman in mental distress isn't going to be detained for not having a ticket,' said Jillian, thinking it was entirely possible that an overzealous ticket inspector could very well do just that. 'But I'll get someone to make those enquiries straightaway.'

'So, no wallet or phone – do you remember what she was wearing?' McClintock asked.

'A long dress, black I think,' the judge said, 'and a coat, something pale . . .'

'Any jewellery?'

'No, I don't think so. Maybe earrings, little ones, but I can't remember.'

'Grant,' said Jillian, 'what exactly is Harriet's diagnosis? Is it possible she was having delusions? Became psychotic?'

'We've been told a hundred different things over the years,' the judge sighed. 'Bipolar disorder, schizoaffective disorder, paranoid personality disorder. But as I said, yesterday morning she seemed okay, and at the wine bar she seemed okay – normal enough for Harriet, is what I mean.' He looked from one detective to the other. 'Is there anything I should be doing? What should I do?'

'You've called us, that's the best thing you could do,' Jillian said. 'May we see her room, please?'

Funny that I've assumed they have separate rooms. Projecting much?

The judge nodded and led them up the staircase. The house had an eerie quality in the night. Long shadows gave the heavy carpets a muddy look and in the hanging photos on the staircase wall only portions of faces and bodies were illuminated. It looked to Jillian as though the gilded frames bore ransom notes constructed of disjointed body parts.

'Harriet sleeps here,' Grant said, stopping at the door of a bedroom overlooking the back of the house. He flicked the light switch, revealing windows with thin bars across them. 'She made me put those in a few years ago,' he said, following Jillian's eyes. 'She was paranoid about intruders, and that was before all this.'

The room reminded Jillian of one you'd find in a decaying country manor. It might once have been grand but now looked merely run-down and dated. Pale cream wallpaper, floral carpet, an old Queen Anne bed, neatly made. Jillian walked its perimeter, trying to imagine the miserable creature she had met occupying this space, presumably obtaining comfort from it. On a nightstand, Jillian recognised a packet of tablets that were the same as those she was prescribed.

Just antidepressants then?

Am I as mad as Harriet? Will I become like her?

She peered under the bed. It was perfectly clean, not a stray hair-clip or speck of dust, nor any of the other things Jillian might have expected to reside in the gap between bed base and floor. The ensuite too was dated – a marble benchtop, a narrow medicine cabinet, a toothbrush sitting in an old glass tumbler. She took a moment to inspect the old-fashioned shower and bath behind a tulip-patterned shower curtain, just to be sure.

'Is anything missing? Anything she might have taken if she was planning not to come back?'

The judge opened the chest of drawers and the wardrobe. 'Don't think so. Harriet's fairly spartan, though.'

'It would be good to have the CCTV,' she said, 'see if anyone has been scoping you out. Can you email us the footage for the past few days?'

'Sure, I can do that right now.'

'I'm going to do a quick scout outside,' McClintock said, heading to the door.

Jillian and the judge returned to the sitting room and he opened his CCTV app.

'Maybe show me this morning's footage now, if you can?'

He dragged his finger along the bottom of the screen before handing the phone to Jillian. A clock in the bottom left corner of the image marked eight-fifty am. Jillian watched the Phillipses leaving the house together, Harriet trailing behind her husband as they walked into the garage. When the car emerged a moment later, the outline of both Phillipses could be discerned as the car backed out and the automatic gate swung open. Seeing this, Grant began to cry softly.

'May I email this to myself?' Jillian asked, gently. 'How many days does it store at once?'

'It deletes after seventy-two hours I think,' the judge said, slumping back in his chair.

On the wall behind him was a photo of the judge, Harriet and their son. They were standing on the Alexandra Bridge, the city in the background beyond the curl of the Yarra. Having emailed herself the footage, Jillian went over to examine it more closely. The Harriet in this picture was younger, prettier, but still recognisably her. 'Do you mind if I take this? Or is there a more recent shot?' she asked. 'We'll need to put something out publicly, so people know we're looking for her.'

Grant sighed. 'Whatever you need to do, of course.'

'That's your son?'

'Damien, yes. Did I mention he's in the UK at the moment? I haven't told him yet.'

'Perhaps do that now?'

She left him alone and went to see how McClintock was getting on. She found him carefully examining the front fence with his phone torch.

'Anything interesting?'

'A very nice vintage Jag that hasn't been driven in twenty-odd years and a Pinarello that's worth a hefty sum. But nothing useful for us. It's a real fortress, this place, isn't it?' he said.

'It is,' Jillian agreed. 'The first time I saw it, I was reminded of Sleeping Beauty in the castle.'

'What do you reckon?' he asked. 'She's topped herself, right?'

'I really don't know. Her state of mind is definitely a worry, but who's to say she isn't victim number two in some sicko's list? Warwick killed a wife, didn't he? Or maybe Harriet did Bailey and she's done a runner.'

'You reckon she could have done it?' McClintock was incredulous. 'Why wait till now to run in that case? And would she really be able to manage a strangulation?'

'Anything's possible,' Jillian said. 'You said you thought Phillips had the hots for Bailey. Maybe Harriet got jealous? If she knew chambers was a free-for-all that night, what was to stop her turning up after hubby was asleep? Maybe this weird anxiety thing is a bit of a smoke screen?'

'I still like O'Neil for Bailey,' McClintock said.

'Well, for the moment, they both look as guilty as each other. Which is to say, we don't have much on either of them. Open minds, Mick,' she added. 'I would have thought that was the obvious way to progress.'

CHAPTER 20

Jillian had not intended to return home but to go straight from the Phillipses' home to the office. However when she and McClintock arrived at the St Kilda Road station, Des, who was also just arriving and looking thoroughly irritated to be there so early, told them both to leave. 'You're useless to me at the moment,' he said. 'Go home and sleep, come back in a few hours. I'll get Mossman and Hastie cracking on the usual stuff and see if I can round up a few other troops too.'

When McClintock didn't argue with him, Jillian felt she also had no choice but to comply. It seemed opportune, too, to try and make up with Aaron, now that they had had some time to themselves. As she drove, she thought of him with increasing affection – he was so supportive, so good – he had carried her through the worst time in her life. By the time she had parked she was desperately conciliatory. However when she let herself into their old weatherboard, there was no sign of her husband or her son.

She went into the bedroom, drew the blinds and fell asleep fully clothed. When she woke at two pm, it was to an insistent vibrating next to her head. Uncharacteristically, she answered without checking.

'Jillian, hi, it's Ursula. You missed your appointment again the other day, so I just wanted to touch base and see how you were doing.'

It took her a moment to realise she was speaking to her psychologist. 'I'm okay,' she said, her voice hoarse, 'just had a big day yesterday.'

'Sure, of course.' There was a pause. 'Look, Jillian, I don't mean to seem rude, but my books are full at the moment. If you aren't ready to re-engage or you don't want to, I'd really like to offer your appointments to someone else.'

'That's fine,' she said, 'I'm fine. Okay, bye.'

She eased herself into a standing position and went out into the kitchen. The kettle was still warm and there were dirty dishes in the sink, but no sign of Aaron. She showered, changed her clothes and drove back to work.

St Kilda Road was more crowded than it had been in the very early morning and there was an air of unified purpose evident amongst the Homicide team. Someone had moved a television onto a table outside Des's office. On the screen was Harriet Phillips' face interspersed with shots of a serious-looking reporter whose words were muted. A text ribbon across the base of the screen ran the message: 'Police urgently seeking information about the whereabouts of Harriet Phillips, wife of family law judge, extreme concerns held for her welfare.' In addition to dealing with the media, which he typically detested, Des had also spent much of the day moving crews around to accommodate the enlarged scope of the investigation. As Jillian approached her desk she noted that all of them seemed to be gathered around McClintock.

'Nothing missing from the house, and she does have a history of mental illness,' he was telling his enraptured audience. 'They've got a pretty comprehensive CCTV system but it deletes after a few days. One of you can go through it, see if anyone was poking around.'

'Hey,' she said, feeling irrationally excluded, as though she had discovered all of her friends catching up without her.

'Hey,' he smiled at her, oblivious. 'I was just figuring out what to do with our new and expanded crew.'

'What's been done so far?'

'I spoke to the manager from the wine bar where they had the wake – they don't have CCTV but a few of the other places in the vicinity do, so I'm going to go out and see what we can get,' said Frank Donoghue, an older, sturdier presence within the squad.

'Great.'

'These two,' McClintock gestured towards two detectives who Des kindly referred to as 'legacy cops' and who seemed to float from team to team, 'are going to doorknock along the tram routes she'd have needed to take. See if anyone saw her, spoke to her, that type of thing.'

'Good, yes.'

'And we were just chatting about what Hastie and Mossman here could get to. The husband says she's previously talked about drowning herself. I thought one of them could liaise with the divers, check the Yarra, other water bodies near her.'

'Alright,' Jillian said, her mind moving quickly. 'Good idea. Liaise with them but let Donoghue be the main contact. I need you to focus on the commonalities between Bailey and Phillips, in two different ways. Hastie, we know that both judges heard cases about Brian Shanahan and we still haven't had any luck locating him. Track him down. Paula, can you go through all Bailey's records and tee them up against Grant Phillips' – I want to know every other litigant that they've both dealt with. Once you've done every litigant at the court, find out who Judge Bailey's clerk was when she was at the bar, plus the names of every client she had back then and when she was a solicitor. Do the same for Phillips and then compare those as well.'

'Are they really going to have records going back that far?' Mossman asked. 'Wasn't Bailey at the bar more than seven years ago? And Phillips must have been there even longer.'

'They should have something, and even if the clerks don't, Bailey and Phillips might have kept their own records.'

McClintock looked at her incredulously. 'That's a lot,' he began, 'given Harriet's mental . . .'

She glared at him and he stopped talking.

'What about the husband?' Hastie asked. 'He ties the two of them together. He might have topped them both.'

'CCTV from a few places around the court shows him leaving the night Bailey was killed,' Jillian said. 'And not coming back as far as we can tell. Sure, he could be a suspect for his wife, but the quickest way to figure that out is going to be chatting to anyone who saw him and her in the later stages of the wake. He's already told us a few people he spoke to and who helped him look. We'll need to start verifying that too. We'll regroup before we knock off tonight. Alright?'

She returned to her desk and to thirty-five unopened emails. 'I've got data from Citylink,' she called out to McClintock half an hour later, 'that puts a car registered to Virginia Maiden and apparently driven by her husband en route from the city to Armadale at half past twelve the evening Bailey was killed and a shot of the two of them in the car.' She sighed. 'But that conversation with Meyers at the funeral was seriously suss. Even if she didn't do it, she's hiding something.'

McClintock grunted an acknowledgement.

'And they're still trying to rebuild all the data in Bailey's phone. Not that I'm expecting much to be there.'

Her desk phone rang and she answered absently, still consumed by her inbox. 'Hello?'

'Yes hi,' said a female voice, 'this is Lisa Nettle, I left a message?'

'Ms Nettle. Yes. How can I assist?'

'I know what happened to the judge,' the caller said, her voice rising into a hysterical giggle. 'And the other one, the new missing one. And I've got proof.'

Lisa Nettle confirmed to Jillian that she and her children had vacated the property at which McClintock had tried to visit her. 'It wasn't safe,' she whispered into the phone, 'so we're in an Airbnb nearby until everything cools down.' This house was only three blocks away from her registered address which Jillian thought a curious choice. If she were that afraid of being located, why had she not changed suburb at the very least?

The new home was a freshly renovated Californian bungalow off Glen Huntly Road in Carnegie. 'I lived in a share house in this street,' McClintock said wistfully as he parked out the front. 'Can't remember what number. They've all been done up since then. God, it was a dump.'

That was a surprise. Jillian hadn't picked him as the type to have lived in a share house, ever. She'd taken her colleague for the sort who remained within the protective arms of their parents until such time as they'd saved the deposit to purchase their own home.

'When was this?' she asked as they pushed open the gate.

'Straight outta school, I did a few years at Monash.' He gestured towards the monolith of the Caulfield campus, discernible in the distance.

The garden path was covered in chalk drawings of butterflies, and several layers of children's shoes were piled untidily on either side of the front door, along with two scooters, three bicycle helmets and a skateboard. Jillian rang the doorbell and Lisa Nettle's approaching shape was immediately visible through the stained glass. When she opened the door she was exactly what Jillian had expected from a brief examination of social media sites – a small blonde woman, thin but with muscular arms that suggested routine strength training. Her cheeks and lips were lightly plumped, but the underside of her eyes were a purple-grey and her nails had been bitten to the quick.

'Come through,' she said, ushering them down a hallway of miscellaneous mess to a large open-plan kitchen and living area. The unmistakable tang of wine followed in her wake. 'Welcome to hell. He doesn't know you're coming, does he? I didn't think you'd call him but I just want to check because –'

'We don't make a habit of advising members of the public who we might be meeting,' Jillian said, assuming that the 'he' referred to was Lisa's ex-husband.

In the living area every surface had items pertaining to the interests of children: dolls, Lego, puzzles, iPads, schoolwork, running shoes, all piled comically high wherever there was room for them. There were other signs of the children too, on the smudged walls, the windowpanes.

Something to look forward to. If Aaron doesn't leave you.

McClintock assessed the mess with barely disguised distaste. 'Lovely house,' he said, nodding at the yard, where a swimming pool bobbled with children's floaties and a cat lay sunning itself on the deck.

'I hate it. The yard is the only good thing about it. None of us like it. The kids can't sleep properly, I can't sleep properly, but we can't go back to the rental because he knows about it. He's been trying to give me a nervous breakdown for ages. Another one, I mean.' She gave a bitter little snort. 'Sorry about the mess, but the cleaner doesn't come until tomorrow. I used to have one every week but Rahul couldn't cough up for that, could he? No, and he says he's too depressed to work more . . .'

As she spoke she directed the detectives to a couch. McClintock sat down and shifted a school blazer to make room for Jillian, who instead moved to an adjacent chair.

'No, I'm going to sit there,' Lisa said, and added, 'I'm deaf in my left ear, if I sit here I'll be able to hear you both.'

She positioned herself in the chair and said, 'I've been trying to get to talk to you since Judge Bailey was killed.' She sounded petulant. 'And now this other lady's gone too.'

'Why do you think your ex-husband might be involved?' Jillian asked.

'Because he's a psychopath and he hated her,' Lisa said, as though this were completely obvious. 'We got told the judgement was coming down, my lawyer got a call saying we had to be there in the morning. Rahul would have got the same call. A few hours later someone's killed her – not rocket science, is it?'

'But is there something specific that he said or did that makes you think it was him?'

Lisa Nettle clicked her tongue impatiently. 'Well, it isn't just a coincidence, is it? There are no real coincidences in the world and especially not with Rahul. I learned that the hard way.' She gave another bitter laugh.

McClintock asked, 'Is there a reason you think he might have been near the court that day?' Jillian, whose patience with the woman was already wearing thin, was struck by how gentle he sounded and felt immediately guilty. Lisa Nettle was clearly under significant stress, albeit psychological rather than material. She deserved compassion.

You've been there too, remember.

'All I know is the Wednesday night, he said he wanted to have dinner with the kids. I told him that was okay, not that I have a choice with the court orders, got them ready, and he never showed up.'

'So he made an arrangement and then cancelled it?' Jillian clarified.

'Arrangement, that's not what I'd call it. It's not really an arrangement when you don't give the other person any choice.'

'Was it unusual for him to . . . make a plan with the children and then not follow through?' asked McClintock.

'Oh, he'd cancel on the kids all the time.' Lisa Nettle sounded exasperated, as though the detectives were not understanding her. 'One of his ways of getting to me, his little mind games. And then next time he saw them he'd tell them that I'd told his lawyer he wasn't allowed to see them, or some rubbish like that.'

McClintock frowned. 'Does he have a history of being violent towards people?'

'Of course he does! Why do you think I'm half deaf? If you get on the wrong side of him he won't stop until he's destroyed you. He really hated that judge, she was just the type to get under his skin – talked over him, didn't give a shit that he was famous. Here!' She got to her feet and disappeared briefly, returning with a thick document secured with a bulldog clip. 'Here! Read it. Read it!'

Jillian took the bundle of papers. She recognised the front page: it was the report she had looked at in Judge Bailey's chambers, the psychological assessment of the two parties.

'It's on the last page,' Lisa said, immediately taking the report back and turning the pages with her raw fingertips. 'Here, this one.'

Noting that the parties have completely differing accounts of their relationship, and further noting that the evidence has not been tested, I am unable to make formal psychiatric diagnoses of either party. In the event that Ms Nettle's account is accepted by the court then it may be that the husband's behaviour, including presumably lying during this consultation, is indicative of a narcissistic personality disorder. In the event that it is the wife who has misrepresented events to me, I am inclined to think this likely relates to her previous diagnoses of borderline personality disorder and difficulty in regulating her emotions. It is also entirely possible that each party holds the diagnosis I have previously indicated. In any case, it is clear that the prognosis for both Dr Sharma and Ms Nettle is likely to be grim.

Jillian handed it to McClintock when she'd finished reading.

'Did you read it all?' Lisa demanded. 'It says he's a narcissistic psychopath.'

Well, not exactly.

'Did the court accept your version of events?' McClintock asked.

'They haven't given us the judgement. But the new judge the other day, he said maybe in the next few weeks. My lawyer reckons we're gonna win. The independent children's lawyer, she was a bitch too, but my lawyer says she liked me better.'

'Who's the new judge?' Jillian asked.

'That's what I've been trying to tell you! Last week we had a hearing about what was to be done with the judge dead and the final judgement missing, and my lawyer sent me a copy of the orders the other day and it's him – the one whose wife's gone. So the first judge gets killed the day before we're meant to hear her decision, then another judge has a hearing with us and then his wife disappears. Come on, it isn't a coincidence, is it?'

Jillian and McClintock looked at each other.

'Sorry,' Jillian said when Lisa looked as though she was about to begin again. 'You said the judgement had gone missing?'

Lisa nodded vigorously. 'That will have been Rahul. When he went and killed her he would have found it and taken it, just to mess things up for me.'

'But there's an electronic copy,' McClintock said. 'We've seen it on her laptop.'

'Yes,' said Lisa, 'but they don't know whether or not she made any more changes to it on the hard copy. That was what the new judge told us the other day. Unless it turns up or we reach some agreement he said he might have to listen to the court transcripts and rewrite the judgement. He sounded almost as angry as I felt, actually.'

How did we miss this?

'But Rahul will appeal anyway,' Lisa continued. 'So really, it doesn't even matter what the new judge decides. Rahul will just appeal and appeal. Go to the Supreme Court or the High Court, whatever.' She narrowed her eyes. 'You know, the court hasn't returned any of my jewellery. Rahul made a big fuss about a few of the rings he'd given me – an engagement ring, anniversary ring – demanded I hand them over as exhibits, said they were evidence of something or other, but he knows as well as I do he was talking shit. I'm never going to see them again and that's deliberate. They're worth a heap. It's basically theft, isn't it? Apparently it happens all the time. I read about this guy online, his whole file, with these really personal photos, just got stolen in the middle of a trial. Maybe you can investigate that?' she added hopefully. 'Or ask the court? I really need that jewellery.'

'We can't intervene in the court's process,' McClintock said, still so patiently.

How is he doing that?

Jillian was keen to end the interview. She needed to consider what they had just been told, do some checking. 'Alright,' she said, 'perhaps you could give us your husband's contact details, tell us where he's likely to be?'

They obtained a rough understanding of Rahul Sharma's schedule, including slights and criticisms with every salient detail. 'First thing he goes to the gym, that's where he met the new girlfriend, she was his PT of course. Twenty-two if you can believe it. Poor thing. Part of me wants to warn her. Another part thinks it'll be better for her to find out for herself. Then Monday to Wednesday he shoots *Please Fix Me*, from five until five. Thursdays he says he's in his rooms but I had a private investigator on him at one stage and he didn't see him go in there at all. And Fridays he's at home, I think. Again, that's what he says, but who knows really. He told the court he would need to see extra patients on that day, to be able to cover the cost of spousal maintenance and child support, but he was too depressed – bullshit – yet somehow I'm hiding in this place and the kids have to take a bus home from school if I'm at the gym, or if I have to go pee in a cup whenever some Legal Aid lawyer who's meant to be representing the kids tells me to.'

The detectives managed to extract themselves at last and bid goodbye to Lisa Nettle at the front door.

'Well,' Jillian said once they were in the car. 'Seems like we fucked up!'

CHAPTER 21

'What, you think Rahul Sharma went up to chambers, stole the judgement and killed the judge?' Des boomed into the phone, sounding incredulous. 'And then pinched the wife of the next judge at a wake? A celebrity whose mug is known to all and sundry. How would he have even got near her?'

'I agree it's pretty out there but we do have a missing judgement, Des. Presumably the only people who would benefit from that would be Lisa Nettle or Dr Sharma. She had her mother staying with her on the night Bailey was killed and the mother's confirmed it already. That leaves Sharma. He could have been staking Bailey out for a while, waiting for his opportunity. This might have been in the works for ages.'

'It's due diligence,' McClintock said too loudly in the direction of Jillian's phone as he turned onto North Road, towards Brighton where Rahul Sharma lived in the former matrimonial home, a reno-vated Georgian mansion mere metres from the foreshore. 'Unlikely as it is, we need to check. Famous people do insane things too.'

So you don't think Harriet Phillips is a suicide now?

'Yeah yeah,' Des said. 'I'm not saying don't check, I'm just saying don't waste too much time.'

'Okay,' Jillian said, 'we're all in agreement then.'

'What do you make of it all?' McClintock asked when Des had signed off.

'I really don't know. It does seem pretty far-fetched, but doctors have murdered before now.'

'Do you ever watch his show?'

'Nah, you?'

'Sometimes. My mum's into it, but it's not the type of thing I'd go out of my way to look at alone. He comes across as a nice enough bloke, but then people can have different sides. Don't think I'll be able to watch it again after meeting her, though. I reckon she's a classic battered wife.'

'Really?' Jillian was surprised by his generous assessment. 'I had her pegged as a spoiled drunk.'

'Maybe she's both?'

He stopped the car outside yet another extremely high brick wall. It was nearing six already and the street was taking on the long shadows of its many multi-storeyed homes. A sharp ocean breeze slapped at their faces as McClintock searched for and located an intercom.

There was no answer.

McClintock tried again, and again they were met with resounding silence.

'How long do you reckon it takes him to get home from shooting?' McClintock asked thoughtfully.

'The city to Brighton, driving like a doctor, in peak hour, maybe forty minutes? We might need to try him at work. There any cosmetic surgery you're in the market for?'

'The only doctor I need is a good shrink.' He laughed as he said it but Jillian felt immediately paranoid. Was he hinting that something was wrong with her? Did he somehow know about her discussion with Ursula?

You sound really crazy.

They returned to the car. 'I'm hungry,' Jillian said aloud to herself as McClintock negotiated the peak-hour traffic.

'You need to prioritise eating more, you just snack. Don't you think in the morning about what you're going to eat for the day?'

'Mick, I have a small child, I can hardly think about anything,' she snapped. 'And having you criticise my eating habits isn't helpful.'

'Jesus,' McClintock said, momentarily lifting both hands off the steering wheel. 'I can't do anything right, can I?'

He drove on in silence and did not directly address her again until the team were congregated in the meeting room to report on their progress. 'You taking the lead?'

'Yup.'

She informed the rest of the team about their meeting with Lisa Nettle. 'Obviously we have reason to be sceptical but we also have reason to pursue it. We'll see where the next few days take us. Now, how did everyone else go?'

The disappearance of Harriet Phillips, with all its ambiguities and peculiarities, was a source of vigorous debate amongst the members of the team. The older detectives who had doorknocked the tram routes had come up empty-handed. They had also contacted every crisis service they could think of. She had not appeared at any hospital, halfway home or other outreach program. The wine bar that had hosted the wake had three possible entrances through which Harriet, or someone taking her, could have left.

'The CCTV I've managed to get so far doesn't seem to show her walking anywhere along High Street, which suggests she left or was taken from the back entrance which is closer to the toilets, but which backs onto a mostly residential street,' Donoghue said. 'I've done a doorknock but not many people were home and it doesn't look like a security camera–heavy area. No joy from the divers yet either.'

Hastie's update was slightly more optimistic. 'The threats to Judge Bailey from the burner email addresses – we're almost one hundred per cent sure a bunch of them are from Shanahan. The most recent one was sent about a month ago. We're waiting for confirmation but should have it soon.'

'That's good.'

'The dick pics, though,' he continued with a slight smile, 'aren't from the same ISP, which is weird. I mean, it's probably still him. I've been reading through one of Kaye Bailey's old judgements and the bloke's pretty bloody shameless, and a freak to boot. He sent a frozen rat to one of the barristers who represented his wife at a hearing, and he got caught pinching documents from the court file and sticking them to the underside of the bar table. The lawyer acting for the wife saw him under the seat with Blu-Tack when he thought he had the room to himself. Still no sign of him either in New South Wales or at his place, though. I've traumatised two of his exes by calling to see if they know where he is. Neither of them wanted a bar of him.'

'I'm working through what the court was able to give me straight-away,' Mossman said, 'but it's slow progress. It will take a few days.'

'That's fine. Des, anything you want to say?'

Her boss touched his stomach lightly. 'Spoke to Legal about this business with the law firm – whether or not we can subpoena like you suggested and whether or not we're likely to be successful. They aren't optimistic but they're working on other options as quickly as they can.'

Jillian left the office an hour later, feeling groggy and with her sense of time askew. The streets were dark and quiet as she drove and she called Aaron, aching for his voice. 'I'm on the way back,' she told him. 'Big day. How are you?'

'Have you stopped taking your meds?'

'Aaron . . .'

'I found them in the bin. We agreed you'd try them for the full year and see. You promised you'd try.'

'I don't like taking them – they make me sweat and yawn and they screw with my sleep. And they remind me . . .'

'You promised,' he said again.

Something inside her snapped. 'We aren't children, you know! Just because I promised something when I was depressed doesn't mean I'm bound to it for the rest of my life. We agreed I'd go back to work and that's helped more than anything else.'

'It isn't just about you, it's about the whole family. I feel like you're withdrawing.'

'Withdrawing?'

'We'll talk about it when you get home,' he said with an air of finality before hanging up.

Withdrawing from the family!

She found that comment particularly irksome. Did he not realise how large an adjustment it had been for her to make the family, to become a mother? How dehumanising it had felt to just be referred to as 'mum' by midwives in the hospital? How intrusive it had been to have strangers reach out and touch her, or warn her or comfort her or worst of all, ignore her and focus all their attention on Ollie? Aaron had not had to contend with the judgemental looks of the psychologists and psychiatrists when she told them what she was really thinking. His identity had not been subsumed by a minute bundle of flesh. Was it not understandable that she would want time away from that? Want time to just be her?

Am I a bad person? Am I selfish? Why can't things be how they used to be?

She and Aaron hugged and apologised when she arrived home but she sensed that this was not a fight that had quite blown over. He spent the night dealing with Ollie and when she woke in the morning, he was still fast asleep. As she was walking out the door her phone rang and a put-upon administrator from the Royal Melbourne Hospital introduced himself.

'We've got a Michael O'Neil here,' he explained. 'We got told to call you if he turned up.'

CHAPTER 22

The Royal Melbourne Hospital precinct was an area busy with conflicting purposes. Grattan Street, which ran from the old slums of North Melbourne past the hospital in Parkville, the brutalist School of Veterinary Sciences at the university and on to the genteel restaurants of Carlton, was at present closed to the public and inhabited by a series of large construction vehicles. These vehicles, part of the crew for the Metro Tunnel, moaned and roared at each other while pedestrians negotiated footpaths diminished to accommodate the mighty machines.

The lobby of the hospital itself was a microcosm of the broader Australian population. Every race, every profession, every age and gender was represented within its walls. There were scrubs and turbans, hijabs and miniskirts, a plethora of languages. Jillian found it soothing after the sterile whiteness of the Melbourne she had spent the past weeks immersed in. This was more like her city. The heterogeneous entity she proudly called home.

At the reception, McClintock applied his usual charm to obtain direction to the ward onto which Michael O'Neil, barrister, had been admitted. He had had a fall at the train station, the administrator had told her on the phone. 'He'd just got off a Sydney train according to the people at Southern Cross. Possible concussion, but also dehydrated and malnourished.'

What on earth has he been up to?

The uniformed police officer sitting next to O'Neil's bed got up eagerly as the detectives approached.

'There you go,' O'Neil said to the young constable, 'you're relieved from being further lectured about the relationship between the police force and systemic racism.'

The constable gave a nervous smile before leaving the detectives with his charge.

The Michael O'Neil lying in the hospital bed was a vastly changed creature from the one Jillian had researched online. His face was sunken, his arms were thin and he was looking contemptuously at the detectives. Jillian could not get an immediate read on him. He didn't appear to be a man who would require the massaging of ego, but nor did he have the easy friendliness of Grant Phillips. Before she could talk, McClintock began. Too aggressively, Jillian thought.

'We've been looking for you for over two weeks. You don't answer your phone, your clerk doesn't know where you've got to. Bit suss, wouldn't you say?'

Not sure this is going to warm him up . . .

'I've been up near the Blue Mountains,' the barrister said calmly, 'doing a silent retreat. You don't take your phone and you're uncontactable. That's the point.'

Jillian recalled Aaron going on such a retreat when he had developed an interest in transcendental meditation some years earlier. Typically a man of few words, he had returned from his two-week course filled to the brim with pent-up conversation.

'You got any evidence that you were away by yourself, being quiet?' McClintock demanded, still unnecessarily aggressive.

''Course I bloody do,' O'Neil snapped, frowning at him. 'You ask the organisers – they picked me up from Town Hall Station Thursday morning and dropped me back there last night. I only found out what happened on the train,' he said, his face becoming pained. 'Someone had left a newspaper, I saw Kaye's picture. Look,' he addressed Jillian in a way that suggested he found her the more sensible of the two detectives, 'I didn't kill her, so how's this for a plan – tell me what you need and I'll tell you what I know.'

Jillian ran through the preliminaries with him, verifying his movements on the night Kaye Bailey was killed.

'I had a conference for a trial – mess of a matter – thought that I'd be done by nine but things just kept popping up. My instructor was there until quite late so I walked her to her car, went back to chambers and then went straight to the station.'

'We understood you were expected at Saul Meyers' retirement party?'

'I ran into Grant earlier in the day, said I might make an appearance, but I got bogged down and Kaye was busy anyway so I skipped it.'

'And the afternoon and evening of 1 May?'

'Still at the retreat. Why do you want to know about that?' he asked.

'That's the day Grant Phillips' wife went missing.'

'Ah. And you reckon the two things are definitely related? Suppose it would be too much of a coincidence. Some bloody anti–family law nutter then? I blame Hanson for this shit. And the Liberal Party, stirring it up when it suits them. Unconscionable.' The barrister paused, then added, 'I have heard Harriet is quite unstable – mentally, I mean. You sure she didn't disappear by design?'

'We aren't sure about anything at this stage,' Jillian said. 'Can you think of any reason why Kaye might have engaged a law firm that specialises in family law and employment law?'

'She did what?' Michael O'Neil looked genuinely surprised. 'First I've heard of it.'

'Well, was it possible that she had instructed someone to prepare a Binding Financial Agreement for the two of you?'

O'Neil gave a weak laugh. 'I can guarantee that whatever she was doing had nothing to do with a Binding Financial Agreement,' he said. 'For two reasons. The first is that Kaye and I had no intention of ever moving in together, let alone getting married. The second is that Kaye didn't believe in them. It was her view that people should go into relationships with their wallets and hearts open. She'd never do one.'

'She did one with her ex-husband.'

'Yes, but that was at the end of their marriage, that's different.'

'Then do you have any idea why she might have transferred funds to FarrugiaPerriam? They're a Sydney firm.'

'FarrugiaPerriam?' O'Neil's eyes widened slightly. 'Well now, that's curious.' He leaned back into the pillows as he considered. 'She asked me, perhaps a few months ago, what the best law firm in Sydney was. I told her FarrugiaPerriam – I do a bit of Sydney work every so often and they've briefed me a bit. They do good stuff.'

'She didn't say why she wanted to know?'

'No. She didn't. And I didn't ask.'

'And she never mentioned needing legal advice about anything that was happening at work?'

'You mean Saul telling her to bugger off whenever she tried to raise matters of security with him? No, she never said anything to me about taking that to a lawyer. But Kaye wasn't expansive, you know. She was very mindful of confidentiality, of her ethical obligations, and she never wanted to create any conflict of interest for me. She also didn't tend to burden others with her thoughts. Although Saul would say differently, of course. You know she requested multiple meetings with him last year about her safety? And he ignored them. God, I would have liked to see his face when he found out she was going to replace him. I'm sure he was hoping it would be Virginia Maiden. I'm sure Virginia was too.'

'You don't sound very keen on Judge Maiden?' Jillian said, thinking back to that still unexplained conversation she had overheard between Maiden and Meyers.

'Virginia is very...' The barrister searched for the word. 'Puritanical. Someone like that shouldn't be in family law, she doesn't have any natural empathy, any understanding of how the other half lives. Plus, she's a real groomer. I've never liked that.'

'Groomer?' McClintock said, sounding alarmed. 'What do you mean, exactly?'

'Oh, not like a child sex offender, that's not what I mean. Although I suppose there's a commonality. I did a big defence, years ago, when I was in criminal law – a member of the clergy, a number of historical abuse allegations, scant evidence. The kids he'd allegedly molested all had poor mental health, were druggies, that type of thing. We were fairly confident we'd get him off but he was found guilty, which was a good thing as he almost certainly was guilty. But the character witnesses he produced for sentencing – politicians, senior barristers, bureaucrats, just extraordinary. I realised he'd groomed these people for years, they were all utterly convinced he was this incredible man, could do no wrong. And it's the same with Virginia – she's a complete dragon to the litigants, the solicitors, a lot of barristers, but if you saw her working the room at some function, you'd think it inconceivable that she'd ever behave the way I've personally seen her behave.'

Jillian asked, 'Is it possible that Virginia might have wanted to harm Judge Bailey?'

'I'm sure it is. But I'd be very surprised if she actually had. Virginia's not one to get her hands dirty. At least I don't think so. I suppose you never know.'

'How did Judge Bailey sound on the night she died? We understand you spoke to her?'

'Stressed, I'd say. She'd been working on a really nasty judgement.' O'Neil considered for a moment. 'Although I suspect part of her was also enjoying the drama. Everyone had an opinion on that case, you know, and on what she was planning to do with it. She'd basically said a thousand times where she stood.'

'Where she stood with what?' Jillian asked.

'Sorry, I sometimes forget not everyone inhabits the same sad world as us. Family law property settlements – the law as it stands says that a number of things are to be taken into account when deciding how to divide property at the end of a relationship. You start by looking at whether it would even be just and equitable to do a property settlement. If it is, then you look at what each of the parties brought into the relationship, what they did during the relationship, what their future needs and earning capacity are, and then you consider whether the outcome of those things is just and equitable too. Kaye had a publicly expressed view that there were situations where one party might have come into the relationship with no assets of significance, and not earned much during the relationship, but due to family violence might be entitled to damages for pain inflicted on them. Now, while she didn't say as much, to me anyway, I'd bet she was going to make an order for one of them, probably the wife, to receive damages. Have they released the judgement yet, by the way?'

'Actually,' Jillian said, 'no one knows where it's got to. The final hard copy, that is.'

O'Neil looked incredulous. 'Well, there'd be an electronic copy of course, but that's really odd . . .'

'Did Kaye say whether she was expecting anyone to visit her at chambers that night?' McClintock asked.

'No, she didn't.' Michael O'Neil looked suddenly tired. His eyes started to close, apparently involuntarily. 'No, she just said she'd see me when I got back.' He made an effort to rouse himself. 'Come to think of it, she said hopefully all the blood would be cleaned off the walls by then.'

The detectives returned to the lift, each quiet and contemplative. When the doors opened onto the lobby Jillian was inundated by the smell of hospital-grade disinfectant and lavender oil, the latter spilling out of a diffuser in the gift shop. She felt as if someone had pulled her lungs from her body and she staggered forward.

'You okay?' McClintock asked.

'Fine,' she tried to say, but instead made a gasping noise.

'Here,' he said, directing her towards a seat next to the public phone. 'Sit.'

'I just need the bathroom,' she managed to say, and propelled herself in the opposite direction. Everything felt far away, blurry and unclear. She took herself into an alcove, sank to her knees and breathed deeply, again and again.

What the fuck was that about?

CHAPTER 23

They arrived at the station to find Mossman in a state of excited agitation. 'I was just about to call,' she said, 'I think I might have something.'

She led the detectives to her desk and showed them an elaborate spreadsheet she'd created. 'This was so I could keep track of everything,' she said, pointing at the screen. 'I asked the former clerks to send through the booking information for every client Bailey and Phillips had. I'm still working through it all – there's a lot – but I've got a hit. A woman called Kim Surle.'

'Kim,' Jillian repeated. 'As in, "Kim, 1 pm, DJ" – the post-it note in Bailey's chambers.'

'That's right, and guess where she works?'

'You're joking. That obvious?'

'What am I missing?' said McClintock.

'David Jones,' Jillian told him. 'One o'clock at David Jones.' She looked at Mossman. 'But how do you know she works at David Jones?'

'The same way I know she liked a bunch of Brian Shanahan's Facebook pages,' Mossman said, again struggling to contain her excitement. She minimised the spreadsheet and returned to her internet browser. There on the screen was Kim Surle's Facebook page.

Kim Surle. Single. David Jones. Women's fashion – Australian designers. Melbourne.
Likes:
Everything you wanted to know about family law.
Which property valuer should I use?
Family Court Survivors association.
Survivors Victoria.

'She's an open book,' Jillian said. 'I'm surprised she doesn't have her mobile number and address there too.'

'I know, right? Luckily I have those for you anyway.' Mossman pushed a post-it note towards Jillian. 'I rang and she has her lunch break at twelve-thirty. She's expecting you.'

'Well done,' McClintock said and Mossman beamed with pride. 'That's really good work.'

'It is,' Jillian agreed, wishing she'd got in first. 'Really good work!'

Jillian had once worked in David Jones herself, as a Christmas casual when she was at university. As she and McClintock negotiated the crowded men's cologne section with its shining metallic surfaces and glistening display bottles she felt a pang of nostalgia. Not for the job as such, although she'd enjoyed the people-watching and the staff discounts, but for the ease of that time in her life, the person she had been then.

They found Kim Surle in the downstairs coffee shop, sitting in the farthermost seat against an internal wall. She was in her early forties with grey-blonde hair and dejected eyes. Despite being neatly made up and attired, there was a coarseness to her, in the sag of her mouth, the way she slumped over her coffee cup. She had taken her shoes off under the table and stretched her stockinged feet onto the seat opposite.

'It's not bad work,' she told Jillian as McClintock ordered drinks for the three of them from a bow-tied barista. 'We get celebrities sometimes, and the girls I work with are lovely. But your legs are killing you by the end of the day. I've told my own girls, if you end up in retail, get a job at ALDI, they get to sit down. I do get a thirty per cent discount, but.'

When McClintock returned to the table Kim put her feet down and her shoes back on. She seemed suddenly nervous.

'As my colleague explained on the phone,' Jillian began, 'we're investigating the murder of Judge Kaye Bailey, which you may have seen in the news recently. Could you tell us the last time you saw Judge Bailey?'

Kim Surle answered without hesitation. 'It was the eighteenth, I remember because it was my mum's birthday.'

'And did you catch up often? We understand she represented you in a family law matter some years ago.'

'She was my lawyer in my property settlement with Ted, my ex. I never caught up with her after that, until last month,' Kim said. 'I was in the fitting rooms a few weeks ago, working away. Kaye was in there trying something on, can't remember what, but she needed a bigger size and pressed the assist button. I went to help her and she recognised me straightaway, remembered my name. It took me a minute and when I put it together, I wasn't that happy to see her, I'll admit.'

'We understand Kaye worked primarily with family violence victims at that time...' McClintock had adopted the same gentle tone he'd had with Lisa Nettle.

'Oh, Ted wasn't violent,' Kim said, surprised. 'No, he was just in denial about the end of the marriage. He just couldn't cope with it.

He stayed in the house and didn't want to give me anything. I had three kids and no money. I only took him to court as a last resort.'

'Why were you not happy to see her then?' Jillian asked.

Kim looked confused for a moment. 'I'd just put all that behind me, you know,' she said after a pause. 'The court stuff, it was so stressful. Worst time in my life.'

'But you agreed to catch up for a coffee?'

'Yes. I didn't really want to but she said she'd pay, just wanted to see how I was going and all that . . .'

'You're saying it was Kaye who wanted to catch up?' Jillian clarified. This struck her as strange. Why would the judge seek out an old client in this way?

'That's right,' said Kim. 'She just wanted to see how I was, she said. She remembered the girls too, knew their names.'

'And when you caught up,' McClintock said, 'what did you talk about? Anything in particular?'

'She asked after the girls again, what they were interested in, where they were up to in school, and about me – where I was living, how work was – small talk, you know?' Kim looked down at her hands. 'To think she was killed that same night, I can't believe it. We were sitting right here.'

'And how did she seem that day?' Jillian said.

'She was nice, just like I remembered. She told me she was a judge now and that . . .'

Kim trailed off and Jillian had the impression there was something she wasn't telling them.

'Yes?' she prompted.

'She just, like, she was a good person,' Kim said. 'I feel awful for her family.'

'Were you aware that since Judge Bailey was murdered, a woman she knew has gone missing?' McClintock asked. 'Harriet Phillips. She's married to the man who represented you in court back then – Grant Phillips.'

'Yes, I remember,' Kim said thoughtfully. 'So they're connected? You reckon the other lady is dead too?'

'We aren't sure. But until we know more we're proceeding on the basis that her disappearance is related to Judge Bailey's murder.'

'Fair enough.' Kim shrugged.

'Tell me,' Jillian said, 'how did you find Grant Phillips when he was your barrister?'

Kim looked closely at Jillian, as though trying to deduce something. 'He was fine,' she said eventually. 'Got me what I wanted and didn't charge me.'

'He acted for you pro bono, you're saying?' Jillian said.

'Yes. Like I said, I didn't have much back then. Don't have much more these days, actually.' Kim looked at her mobile and said, 'I need to get back now.'

'Just for our records, Kim, can you tell us where you were in the early morning of the nineteenth of April?'

Kim sighed. 'The girls and I went to netball, picked up some Macca's on the way home, and then watched something, can't remember what. We would all have been asleep by ten, though.'

'And you didn't leave the house again at all?'

'No.'

'And on the first of May, after midday?'

'Was that when the woman went missing?' Kim pulled up her calendar on her phone. 'I was here, working.'

'Do you know a Brian Shanahan?' McClintock asked.

'Brian Shanahan,' Kim Surle repeated blankly. 'I don't think so. Who is he?'

'He runs a bunch of Facebook sites for people he calls family law victims. We can see you were involved in a few of his pages.'

'Was I? When? I haven't used Facebook in years, I don't think . . .'

McClintock took out his phone and showed her screen captures of her membership of various groups. 'See? There.'

Kim squinted at the phone. 'God, they're from five or six years ago, whenever everyone was getting on Facebook. The girls set it up for me. I don't even know what my password is anymore. I'm guessing this was just when I was joining anything that got suggested to me.' She stood up and put her bag over her shoulder. 'I'm sorry, I've really got to go now. I hope you catch whoever did it.' She pushed her chair back in and turned towards the escalators.

'That was weird, right?' Jillian said when Kim had gone.

'Yeah, I don't think she was telling us everything.'

'And she was a bit dark on Phillips even though he acted for her pro bono.'

'She's a strange unit,' McClintock said. 'That's for sure. Doesn't exactly have criminal mastermind vibes, though.'

'No,' Jillian agreed, 'she doesn't.'

CHAPTER 24

Permission for Jillian and McClintock to attend the Brighton residence of Rahul Sharma was finally provided the following Monday after several days of protracted negotiations. The doctor's lawyer, John Hammond, had demanded the detectives sign non-disclosure agreements and provide a list of interview questions in advance. When it was explained to him that this was not something Victoria Police could do, there had been several hours of silence before Des received an email inviting the detectives to Dr Sharma's home. The implication was that the interview would be an act of goodwill on his part, unrelated to any moral or legal imperative to assist the police.

'The lawyer's a fucking dickhead,' Des warned them. 'Total weasel. He's adamant nothing is happening without him present.'

Jillian was subdued on the drive there. The last few days had been painfully slow as she was forced to wait for other people in order to progress the investigations. Bailey's work emails had finally been disseminated and read through in their entirety, and had provided nothing beyond the threats that they were already aware of, and, as O'Neil had promised, several emails from Bailey to the chief judge requesting a meeting to discuss 'serious matters'. There was no email from Saul Meyers regarding the suspension of the proximity cards, which meant, Jillian reflected, that Bailey and her associates were likely the only people in the building unaware that the building was unsecured on the night of her death. The judge's phone, too, had finally revealed small and unsatisfying pieces of information – a screen capture of a ticket to an exhibition and a photograph of a dress hanging on a rack.

To maintain her sense of purpose Jillian had spent the entire weekend reading every publicly available piece of information on Rahul Sharma, including several academic studies he'd been involved in at Oxford and an article he had had published in *The Lancet*. She had fallen asleep some time after three that morning listening to the doctor being interviewed for a health and wellness podcast.

Rahul Sharma was forty-one years old, had trained at the University of Melbourne and interned at the Royal Melbourne Hospital. After his intern year he attended Oxford University as a Rhodes Scholar, and on his return to Australia he became the youngest doctor in the country to be admitted to the Royal Australasian College of Surgeons. He had ignited a social media firestorm after stating that he was not opposed to performing breast augmentations on teenagers if it could 'materially improve their self-esteem'. He had first come to the attention of television executives after performing reconstructive surgery on the Australian victim of a terrorist attack in Indonesia and had been offered his own program shortly thereafter.

Pictures of his and Lisa Nettle's wedding had made it into *Who* magazine – Sharma in a navy suit, Lisa in a pink and cream wedding dress that Jillian guessed was meant to replicate the one Gwen Stefani wore when she married Gavin Rossdale.

Weird choice. That marriage did not end well.

According to LEAP, both Sharma and Nettle had mutual Intervention Orders in place. Both orders had been made 'by consent and without admission of any wrongdoing'. Lisa Nettle also had a drink driving offence. Rahul Sharma had been investigated for but not charged with an assault on his estranged wife. There were various reports of police attendances in which one or both parties had requested assistance, but no evidence that anything had progressed further.

Jillian found it hard to reconcile the LEAP record with the smiling faces in the *Who* spread. How had two people who presumably once loved each other allowed their feelings to not just weaken but actually curdle? Was it possible that this would happen to her and Aaron? Would they end up as wretched creatures of the court, each following a barrister out of a trial and asking, punch drunk, what on earth had happened?

Don't be silly! You're just going through a rough patch. Everyone says the first year after having a kid is a huge adjustment.

'You alright?' McClintock asked.

'Yup. Why?'

'You look tired.'

'Mick, do me a favour and promise you will never, for the rest of your life, tell another woman that she looks tired.'

There was silence in the car. Once again, Jillian's outburst had thrown her.

This just keeps happening. Maybe this isn't normal?

She glanced across at McClintock, who was looking abashed. He opened his mouth to speak.

'Don't!' she said. 'No apologies. Just don't ever say it again.'

'Alright. I was actually going to tell you there are some brownies in the glove box.'

Without saying anything, Jillian opened the glove box and removed a brownie. She had not eaten that day and she devoured two, spraying crumbs all over the car and, noting McClintock's winces, hastily cleaning them up.

'Thanks,' she offered. 'Sorry about the crumbs.'

McClintock pulled into Sharma's driveway and pressed the intercom.

'I read online that he got a twenty-five-metre swimming pool installed here,' he said, 'as well as a tennis court. Place must be worth twenty million at least.'

The automated gate opened and they drove through, to be waved to a stop by a short man with a generous stomach whose dark hair was combed into a thick wave on the top of his head.

'Lovely to meet you both,' he said, through the car window. 'John Hammond's my name, the good doctor's solicitor. Would you park just over there, please.' He waved a hand to indicate. 'I'm glad you haven't come in a marked car. Dr Sharma would not have liked that.'

'Nice to meet you too,' Jillian said with as much politeness as she could muster. The lawyer's voice was as slick as his manner. 'Just so you know –'

'Dr Sharma's quite adamant that he wants me here,' Hammond interrupted smoothly. 'Not to worry, I'll be like a fly on the wall.'

'Do you represent him in the family law matter as well?' McClintock asked as they followed the solicitor towards the house. The garden, the grounds and the mansion were all in a state of opulent display, done strictly to impress, Jillian thought. There was no evidence of children.

'Goodness no.' Hammond made a theatrical grimace. 'I wouldn't touch family law with a ten-foot pole. No, I deal with the corporate stuff – the expansion of the business, some of the criminal stuff too, if I have to. Rahul's had a number of spurious allegations made against him by his ex-wife and I've been managing those as they crop up. It's rather like playing whack-a-mole. You knock one down and up pops another. She's quite prolific.'

Jillian found herself repulsed by this little man. It was all very well for him to distance himself from the nastiness of the world in which he made his living, but she thought it in bad taste to treat it like a bit of a joke.

Dr Sharma was waiting for them at his ornate front door wearing a linen shirt, dark shorts and boat shoes without socks. He had a light etching of stubble on his cheeks, and a too-white smile as he invited them in.

He led them through a modernist interior that clashed with the antiquity of the building. A broad, open area at the end of a hallway was dominated by a huge Roy Lichtenstein print and two large triangular-shaped couches in cobalt blue.

'The decorating was all my ex-wife's doing,' Dr Sharma said, sitting down on one triangle sofa and gesturing for the detectives to take the other. 'She was very into pop art, thus,' he indicated the cushions which all bore Andy Warhol prints of Marilyn Monroe's face.

John Hammond inserted himself into an egg-shaped seat suspended from the ceiling by a thick chain. He positioned himself with some difficulty and, after adjusting his weight, balanced a note-book on his lap. The chair rocked back and forth as he made his face attentive, trying to ignore the oscillations. Jillian sensed McClintock trying to suppress a laugh.

'So,' Sharma said, fixing his automatic smile on each of the detectives. 'How can I help you?' He leaned forward as he said this and Jillian was reminded fleetingly of an interview she had seen with Tom Cruise many years before. Like Tom Cruise there was a strange magnetism to this too-smooth man. It was as though all the energy in the room were concentrated in his body.

'We're here to talk to you about the murder of Judge Bailey,' McClintock said. 'And the disappearance of Harriet Phillips. We're following up some information we've received.'

'I see,' Rahul Sharma said, his brow crinkling in concern, with some effort. 'Anything I can do to help. What would you like to know?'

His phone rang loudly and after looking at it he apologised, got to his feet and moved into the corridor to take the call.

As the doctor closed the door behind him, Jillian took in the sparkling kitchen at the far end of the room, all stainless steel and gleaming surfaces. The upper walls were covered in a monochrome wallpaper print of Campbell's Soup cans. She could see two coffee cups on the bench and a fruit platter that, although already half eaten, looked as though it could have been served at a royal banquet.

Who has time to make that for breakfast?

'Sorry,' the doctor said when he was back, 'not a good time. The ex has been creating chaos as usual, someone anonymously reported me to AHPRA for god knows what, and my business partner just told me he wants out. Where were we?'

McClintock cut to the chase. 'Could you confirm for us where you were on the morning of 19 April between midnight and two am?'

Hammond immediately moved to interject but Rahul Sharma waved him quiet. 'It's fine, John. I've got nothing to hide.' He looked at McClintock and then at Jillian in a way that showed his media experience. 'I'll need to check my calendar, one moment ... Yes, I thought so,' the doctor said, frowning into his phone. 'I was off that night. I had an op in the day that we were filming, that was at the Epworth, and then I came straight home. I was meant to be in court the next day for the judgement, you see. Usually I would go out and have dinner with the kids but I was just too nervous so I stayed here all night.'

'Was anyone with you?'

'No. Just me.'

His phone rang again and he answered it with an apologetic grimace. 'Hi Rob, no, no, I have no idea either. He's completely pulled the plug. Personal problems maybe. Yes, that's the plan. Can I call you in an hour? Great.'

'And did you leave the house at all?' Jillian asked.

'Not that I can recall.' He smiled.

'And what about during the day on 1 May?'

Sharma swiped his mobile screen with a neatly groomed index finger. 'I had the day off, actually. I dropped in to see a patient at the hospital around four, I would have left around five. I had a production meeting by video at nine pm and that was it.' He looked up at them. 'I think I would have watched *MasterChef* on catch-up, if that's any help.' He gave a little chuckle. 'You know who loved *MasterChef* actually, and this is true – Judge Bailey. She mentioned it in court one day, had everyone laughing. Very warm, approachable woman. I often thought if we'd met in different circumstances we might have been friends.'

As Jillian tried to envisage that unlikely friendship, Sharma launched into a diatribe.

'She saw right through Lisa, too. Lisa was always trying to have things adjourned, saying she needed more time for this, that or the other. There was one point, I remember, when Lisa was crying poor – that was one of her specialties, you know – she was claiming I hadn't paid her spousal maintenance, which was a lie, I'd paid the kids' school fees directly because that was what she wanted it for – thirty thousand a term for the three of them. I told the judge what had happened and Judge Bailey read her the riot act, told her lawyer that she should be more pragmatic about the applications she was bringing. The next time we're at court the judge announces that she received correspondence from Lisa that was abusive, asks Lisa if she wished to pursue the allegations she made. Lisa denies she ever sent any correspondence, said I'd probably made my own account up and done it, but the judge knew. She looked at her differently after that which was good, because I don't think she realised until then how crazy my ex could be.'

Christ.

'Lisa has told us that you were responsible for her losing hearing in one ear,' McClintock said, his tone light, unnaturally so. Jillian realised that her colleague detested this man.

'She tells everyone that,' Rahul Sharma said. 'It's not true. She lost her hearing when she hurt her head while she was drunk. She fell down the stairs you walked past on your way in here. Told everyone I'd pushed her, too.'

'So,' Jillian said, 'to be clear, no one is able to alibi you for the times stipulated on either of those days?'

'Oh.' Dr Sharma sounded surprised. 'Yes, I suppose that's right. Well, I was on the phone for the production meeting, so my team would be able to confirm that, and I suppose my computer would show what programs I was watching.'

'Are those your kids?' McClintock asked abruptly, pointing to a picture on the wall of three small children, all with dark eyes and pale hair.

'Yes. My most precious things. I can't wait for them to move back here. The things she said about me.' He shook his head. 'All I've ever wanted is to be with them, to love them, care for them. You know, the judge that's taken over wanted to know whether we wanted to write submissions about why he should or shouldn't release the version of the judgement he has. I said, just tell us what's going to happen. This system, it's bizarre.'

'That would be Judge Phillips?' Jillian clarified.

'Judge Phillips, yes, I think that's right.'

'Our understanding,' John Hammond interjected, looking up from the notes he'd been taking, 'is that getting someone else to deliver the judgement is slightly complicated. I think the new judge is just trying to confirm whether he's actually able to deliver it or not, given that the reasons in it aren't his, and no one knows whether it's Judge Bailey's final version of her reasons. Although, as I said earlier, I'm not actually across that area of the law.'

'So you knew that your judgement had gone missing, Dr Sharma?' Jillian asked.

'Only when the new judge told us. My first thought was that maybe Lisa did it, you know, because she didn't like Judge Bailey, but honestly, if it happened between midnight and two am she would have been well into her third bottle of wine. She wouldn't have been able to get herself to the city.'

'So you had no concerns about the judgement? You didn't want to see it in advance?'

'Me?' The doctor shook his head. 'No concerns at all! If someone stole it and it wasn't my ex, I can only assume it's because they recognised my name, got interested. Maybe they thought they'd sell it.'

'It would be a bit of an incriminating thing to sell, wouldn't it?' McClintock said.

'Probably,' the doctor agreed, 'although criminals aren't always the smartest.'

John Hammond leaned forward in his egg-shaped chair, giving the impression he was about to hatch from it. 'Is there anything else Dr Sharma can assist you with?' he asked.

Jillian looked at McClintock, who shook his head. 'I don't think so,' she said, and they allowed themselves to be ushered out.

'What was that about?' she asked as they were waiting for the automatic gate to release them. 'You looked like you wanted to throttle him.'

'He was slimy,' McClintock said. 'Prick.'

'Sure, but –'

'But nothing. You know what, I reckon he did it!' McClintock's face was set in brutal determination.

What the hell has got into him?

CHAPTER 25

Driving home that night, Jillian turned over everything they'd learned thus far, trying to fit the details into some cohesive whole, to bring everything into perfect clarity. The investigation felt like a tiny fruit tree sprouting branches in a hundred directions, expending energy that would ultimately go unrewarded. Most of the branches would be nothing but dead ends, clipped back and refined as other, stronger lines of investigation took hold. The difficulty was that at the moment she had no idea what case theory, what scenario, fit.

It was still possible that one of the party attendees was responsible for Bailey's murder, but the most likely candidates among them, Saul Meyers and Virginia Maiden, were verified to have left the city prior to her death. Dr Sharma had motive, and the disappearance of the judgement would almost certainly be of benefit to him. But had he also kidnapped and possibly murdered Harriet Phillips?

Surely not.

A request had been put in for his phone data and access to his computers, which should show his movements that night.

Brian Shanahan also remained a possibility, but the man had not been seen locally in weeks. Was he staying elsewhere, waiting to pick off the judges or their spouses one at a time in a sadistic attempt to punish the courts for what they had stripped him of? Or had Harriet Phillips killed Judge Bailey and either suicided or gone to ground afterwards?

We need to find Harriet!

Mossman had emailed her and McClintock further information about a multitude of matters that Bailey and Phillips had worked on together as solicitor and counsel. The junior detective had marked names she thought might have particular relevance, cross-referencing them with social media pages, other online presences and any other information to hand. It seemed that most parties, having gone through the family court system, tried to forget it as soon as they could. They remarried, moved country, changed jobs and names.

Her mind turned to Grant Phillips. She wondered what it was that had held him and Harriet together for so long. Was it an old-fashioned sense of duty on his part, perhaps? Or loyalty? Surely there was no romantic or sexual attraction anymore? Like McClintock, she had noticed the almost ethereal way the judge described Kaye Bailey. She had gone so far as to ask Grant Phillips whether he and Bailey had ever been in a relationship, but the judge denied it with genuine surprise.

Her street was silent save for the murmur of distant traffic. At the front door she carefully jiggled the handle into the right position so she could open it without too much squeaking resistance. It was quiet inside the house, too quiet. She looked at her watch – nine o'clock. 'Aaron, you here?'

'Yup,' he called from the couch, where he was sitting in the darkness.

She kissed his forehead and put her workbag on the table.

'Why are you here in the dark? Ollie gone down already?'

'He's at Mum's place.'

'How come?' Had they planned something she'd forgotten about?

'He's at Mum's,' Aaron repeated, 'because I went over there earlier and put him down. I'm going to head back soon. I just wanted to talk to you without having an ear out for him at the same time.'

A dreadful sensation, something darker than fear, began in the pit of her stomach and crawled towards her chest. 'What's the matter?' she said, coming around the couch to face him.

He stood up. 'What do you think is the matter, Jillian?'

'I don't know.'

Liar.

'What's the matter is I feel like a single parent. What's the matter is you spending every waking hour at work and, when you do finally come home, not showing one iota of interest in anything that's happened in my day, let alone Ollie's. We've been over this before.' He sounded as exasperated as she'd ever heard him. 'You've gone back to work so you can forget you ever had a kid.'

'Aaron! How can you –'

'No.' He held up a hand to silence her. 'It's true, don't argue, don't try to tell me I'm interpreting it wrong. I hoped going back would be good for you, I hoped it would be helpful, that you'd remember who you were. I didn't expect it to mean you'd forget about us. And I didn't think you'd use it as an excuse to avoid working on yourself.'

How she hated that expression, 'working on herself' – there was something so embarrassingly earnest about it.

'I know you're still not taking the medication. I know that you cancelled your psychologist's appointments. You clearly have no desire to get better, you just want to stick your head in the sand.'

Jillian was surprised yet again by the strength of her sudden anger. 'Okay, fine, what do you want me to say? Oh, how interesting that Ollie did some crawl or clap or whatever. What do I care?'

'That's my point! You should care!'

'Well, I don't.'

He looked physically wounded and said nothing further, just turned and left the room.

She got into the shower and took a long time, much longer than was necessary to wash her hair and body and shave her legs. She tried to breathe deeply. Part of her wanted to cry. She had never been able to tell Aaron just how bad it was in those months alone with Ollie. Her husband was so in love with their new son, so enamoured of their new family unit, that she could not bring herself to describe to him the dark thoughts she had, the images that would bombard her when she closed her eyes. Part of her also worried about how he might react, that she might look into his eyes and see disgust, or worse, fear.

She blow-dried her hair, pulled on a dress, and emerged to see Aaron in the kitchen taking pouches of homemade baby food from the freezer and putting them into a shopping bag. Ollie's baby bag was open on the kitchen table and had been filled with nappies and clothes.

'What's up?' she asked, trying to sound light-hearted even as she knew she wasn't going to like what he said next.

'I need to get away from this,' he said. 'I need you to figure out whether you actually want to get better or not.'

'I am getting better,' she insisted, 'I am better, I'm just doing it my way.' Her throat began to constrict as she uttered the words so that she felt as though she were choking on them. She knew that she was lying but she was also afraid of telling the truth.

He'd never be able to look at me the same way again.

'Are you?' he said. 'Really?' Then he picked up his phone and keys and walked out the front door.

CHAPTER 26

She left for work the next morning while it was still dark, not entirely sure why. It was no longer necessary to avoid Ollie. The office was quiet and still and in the half-light, surrounded by unoccupied desks and silent phones, she ate every piece of food she could find at McClintock's desk and tried to think only of work.

The rest of the team slowly filtered in, Mossman with tales of her appallingly behaved children, Hastie with complaints about the traffic. Des, never one for mornings, offered only a passing nod. Only the bravest or most foolhardy detective would bother trying to engage him in conversation before his second instant coffee of the day.

At eight-thirty there was still no sign of McClintock.

'Anyone heard from Mick?' she asked and was greeted with silence or shaking heads.

She refreshed her email again and again, hoping that Rahul Sharma's phone records might miraculously have been expedited, that Shanahan might have been sighted somewhere, that something, anything, might have happened.

At nine forty-five, her desk phone rang.

'Detective Basset, it's Angela Hui. Do you think you could come to the law courts? As soon as you can. We've had a threatening letter arrive, and something else. Judge Phillips, Christianne, everyone is in a real state.'

Jillian got to her feet. 'I'll be there in fifteen,' she told the registry manager.

Angela met Jillian in the now too familiar lobby, her cheeks red and her eyes wide.

'This way,' she said, setting off at once towards the public entrance to the large courtroom they had previously met the judges in, talking all the while. 'To give you the background, Glenda – she's the woman who does the mail for all the courts – is training a new employee at the moment. Typically the process is, if things are addressed to the registrar or directly to the court we open them down here, and if they're addressed to an individual judge or associate, or to chambers, they're taken upstairs unopened. Glenda told the trainee to take a letter to Christianne in court. She's sitting with Grant at the moment in 2A. Christianne opened the mail while court was in session, and . . . Anyway, Grant's adjourned till the afternoon so that this can all be dealt with. He shouldn't even be here given the stress he's under at present.'

Angela knocked on the door to 2A and was met with the brief clicking of the lock, followed by Christianne D'Santo's skeletal face trapped in the same agonised expression as the morning Jillian first met her. 'Hello, Detective,' she said dully. 'It's on the table, near the computer.'

The associate pointed to a single piece of paper lying next to a standard-sized Australia Post envelope and two small, glinting objects. The paper contained only one sentence, written in black texta in a bold hand: *Don't think this ends before I want it to.*

Jillian looked at the envelope. Unlike the note, the address had been typed. The stamp indicated a postbox on Elizabeth Street that Jillian suspected was one of the busiest in the city. It was marked to the attention of 'Judge Philip'.

'Spelled his name wrong,' she said absently as she moved to look at the objects that had accompanied the letter – two diamond stud earrings.

'I noticed that too.' Grant Phillips had materialised from behind his bench. He was still wearing his judicial robes and had a troubled expression on his face. He unclipped the hidden gate that separated his platform from the greater courtroom and came to survey the items with Jillian.

'They're Harriet's earrings,' he said with an attempt at calmness. 'I'm ninety-nine per cent sure. I know they're common enough, but I gave them to her; think I helped her put them in before the funeral too.'

He made to pick them up. 'Don't,' Jillian said. 'There might be DNA or prints.' She pulled on a pair of latex gloves and transferred the earrings, note and envelope to an evidence bag.

'Well, DNA would be something,' the judge said, with the smallest hint of optimism.

'Is there anything we should be doing?' Angela asked Jillian. 'Do we need to close the building again? Most of the judges are doing everything remotely but obviously I can't put the non-judicial staff at risk either.'

'I don't think so,' Jillian said. 'We've already got increased security, we'll liaise with uniform about a further increased presence and we'll take prints from all of you but that will be about all, I'd think. I'm sorry, this must have been an awful letter to receive.'

Christianne gave a sniff and Angela looked towards her compassionately. Grant Phillips left Jillian's side and came to stand by the young associate. He held her shoulder with one hand. 'You head home whenever you need, and take a taxi. Alright? Angela, can you organise for one of the other associates to relieve Christianne for the afternoon?'

Angela nodded. 'If you're sure you want to stay too, Judge? I can get Matthew down here with you. Christianne, I'm going to get security to drive you home.'

'That might be good,' the associate conceded. She was looking up at the judge, her eyes dull. 'Is there anything else you need me to do? Before I go?'

'You're a good girl,' Grant Phillips said. 'If Detective Basset says it's alright I'm happy for you to leave right now.' He looked expectantly towards Jillian who, after confirming that she would contact Christianne later, agreed that she should go home. The young woman got to her feet shakily and left the courtroom through the public entrance.

Both the judge and the registry manager looked after her as the heavy door swung shut. Angela locked it immediately. 'I've suggested counselling,' Grant Phillips said, apparently to no one in particular. 'She says she's not ready yet. She's lost whatever weight she had after Kaye died and cries at her desk half the day but what else can I do? It's not good, Ange.'

'I'll talk to her again,' Angela assured him. 'Tell her she needs to take some proper leave.'

Jillian followed the judge and Angela out of the courtroom. 'I didn't think you'd be back in court so soon,' she said to him as they waited for the lift.

'I'd be going stir-crazy at home,' he said, 'just waiting to hear something. I'd almost convinced myself last night that she's going to turn up dead somewhere. I was sure of it. And then we get this. It doesn't read like she's dead, does it? I mean, if she's dead, why not just leave her somewhere, or tell me outright?'

'That's the question. Obviously we hope she's indeed alive, but there's no ransom note we'd typically expect in a kidnapping. I think we all need to remember that we're not dealing with a normal person here.' They boarded the lift and Angela pushed the button for level twelve. 'Someone who's willing to kill in cold blood isn't going to behave the way everyone else might.'

'I suppose,' Phillips said, 'this means the two things are connected. Why else would someone take Hari if not because of me? My work? Poor Damien. He desperately wants to come home to see me, but I've told him not to. I don't want him anywhere near me until we know what's going on. If something were to happen to him too . . .' He looked at Jillian. 'Do you have children? I can't remember if I've asked you.'

'I don't,' Jillian said.

Why did I say that?

Angela excused herself at her office and Jillian followed the judge to his chambers. He directed her to the rooms next to Virginia Maiden's. 'I swapped,' he said by way of explanation. 'Used to be next to Kaye but I couldn't cope with walking that way every day, thinking about what happened. These are Saul's old chambers. He's almost wrapped up now.' He opened the internal door. 'So I've got Saul's old chambers and Kaye's old associates. Mine both finished up earlier in the year, went to the bar,' he added as an aside.

'I was wondering,' she said when they were seated, 'whether you recalled a woman called Kim Surle?'

He thought for a moment. 'I don't think so. Should I?'

'She's an old client of yours and Kaye's, before you became judges. Her name's just come up in our enquiries.'

'Really?' He looked interested. 'Do you know anything about the case? About her?'

'She's employed in retail now. I suppose you would have seen her about fifteen years ago; she's around forty-five now, blonde. Said the husband wasn't violent, just a property settlement.'

'Doesn't ring a bell at all. The ones I remember from those days tend to be the difficult ones. The real prick clients. Engineers – they're always awful, too smart for their own good, and can't get their head around the idea that parenting is considered to be an equal contribution to whatever money they were bringing in. Doctors are usually nasty too – god complexes, not used to being told no.'

'You did this case pro bono, she remembers that,' Jillian said.

This time there was the merest twitch of the judge's eye. 'Did I? I did do that a bit, back in the day. Mainly for women without much money, obviously – they were Kaye's bread and butter for a while. Back then I was charging about three thousand a day and working five days a week. If I made twelve grand rather than fifteen every so often it didn't really materially change my life. I used to do it a bit. I suppose I felt it renewed those women's faith in the male species and helped them out that tiny bit. I suspect that was one of the reasons Kaye used to brief me so much, she knew I was a softie.'

'The hearing you had with Rahul Sharma the other day – did anything of significance happen in that, anything that might have upset him?'

'No, not at all.' The judge leaned back in his chair. 'It was very quick, all by agreement in the end, we were just determining how to proceed. This issue with the missing judgement has created a few problems – primarily that we can't be certain that the version on our server is identical to Kaye's final version; that the reasons in the two versions are the same. But as I explained to them both, the doctor and Lisa Nettle, the actual orders are clear. Sharma represented himself, that was the only surprise – he's previously been legally represented but he indicated he wanted to seek some different legal advice. So we've adjourned for a few weeks to allow him to do so. We'll see what he says once he's had that. The version I've read is very much what I would have expected, I'd be surprised if the final version was at all different. Personally, I think she got it wrong, but that's neither here nor there.'

He looked out his window for a moment and then back at Jillian. 'Do you really think DNA might be retrievable from those earrings?' he asked.

'Or the envelope or note,' Jillian said. 'We'll ask the lab to look at them as a matter of urgency.' Her eye caught the judge's wallet and keys, sitting on the corner of his desk. She could see the very edge of a five-dollar note and thought of Virginia Maiden's story about Harriet. 'Did you happen to see the interaction between Judge Maiden and your wife at the retirement party?' she asked. 'Something about some dropped cash.'

Grant Phillips shook his head. 'Only the aftermath. That was all over before I realised what was happening. Think I might have been chatting to Saul. Harriet was standing near me but I wasn't paying attention. Do you really think there might be DNA?' he asked again. 'Wouldn't that be something?'

Jillian looked again at the items she had tucked into her bag. The earrings, if they had been freshly removed from Harriet with the intention of terrorising her husband might surely have some speck of her on them, although that was not terribly useful in itself. She was not optimistic about there being anything on the note. The envelope was a new one and had been secured with tape rather than licked, but tape could trap the smallest of fibres. She examined what she could see of the adhesive through the evidence bag and realised with a jolt that there was something trapped under the tape. When she saw what it was, hope flared in her that this time, obtaining DNA was in fact a real possibility.

This could be it! This might break it open.

But why did you tell him you didn't have a kid?

PART THREE

CHAPTER 27

As she drove back to St Kilda Road, Jillian experienced a strong dissonance between the emotions she thought she should have and the way she actually felt. The revelation that Harriet Phillips had most likely been taken gave the investigation renewed purpose and clarified the best avenues of enquiry; it was also probable that they would be able to obtain a DNA sample. And yet her mind churned instead with guilt.

Did I really do that? Deny having a kid?

Yes, but only because I'm private.

Liar! That wasn't why.

What kind of a mother lies about that?

The type whose husband leaves her?

By the time she'd parked the car, she was so overwhelmed she felt dizzy. She wanted to confess to her husband and child, and have them forgive her – not just for denying Ollie's existence that morning, but for every negative thought she'd had about him. She wanted absolution.

Kind of sounds like you're having a bit of a panic spike.

Aaron doesn't want to talk to you anyway.

She breathed deeply, trying to calm herself by counting to eight with each exhalation.

'Oi!' The yell was matched by a sharp rapping on the car window. It was McClintock, his face urgent. He rapped again. 'Where have you been? I've called you about seven times.'

'What's up?' she asked, getting unsteadily out of the car.

'Shanahan's back. Come on, I'll drive.'

They did not talk much on the drive to Lara. The outbound city traffic was languid – a succession of roadworks had reduced the major arterials to single lanes. Prior to Ollie, Jillian and Aaron had taken this road a few times a year to a favourite Airbnb in Torquay, where they would spend a week drinking wine, cooking for friends and attempting to surf.

She had messaged Aaron and hoped for a response by now, something soothing telling her he would see her in a few days, that he just needed some space – but there'd been nothing. In the entirety of their relationship, this was the first time they had argued to the extent that she felt genuinely concerned for their future.

You might have done it this time.

'Let's talk about Shanahan,' she said, not wanting to dwell on Aaron or the awful things that had been said. 'What's our theory? He somehow finds his way up to chambers last year and messes with Bailey by taking her wallet. After that he does nothing for a while. Then he sneaks up again, kills her, then bides his time before kidnapping Harriet Phillips?'

'I agree,' McClintock said. 'It's a long shot, but the guy is definitely deranged so anything is possible. That initial security breach might have been a test run, a chance to orient himself.'

'What about Harriet? How does he get to her at a wake?'

'Well, the funeral details were publicly available, and there was a

huge crowd,' McClintock said. 'All he really needed was an opportunity and the balls to go through with it. He might not even have been
after her in particular, could have just been opportunity.'

'But where's he been staying while all this is going on? Why
haven't we been able to find him? And why come back to his block if
he's lying low?'

'Doesn't need to be anything particularly methodical about what
he does, does there? He could have dumped Phillips in the Yarra for
all we know.'

'We've already looked there.'

'You know what I mean.'

'I guess.'

She filled him in on the morning's events and when they were
idling as traffic merged, showed him the evidence bags containing the
envelope and the earrings. 'Jesus Christ,' he said. 'An eyelash. Please
God, don't let it be Christianne's or Harriet's or Phillips'. If we can get
a sample from Shanahan today and match it –'

'You've ruled out Sharma then, have you?' she asked.

'Not totally, but your note makes it clear Harriet isn't a suicide.
And I don't reckon Sharma's necessarily hiding her in his wine cellar.'
He sighed. 'I'm keeping an open mind. Shanahan's a good option.'
McClintock handed her his phone. 'Open my email and have a look
at the most recent judgement Angela Hui sent through. I think its
subject line is Argyle and Wang.'

'Who's Argyle Wang?'

'Argyle and Wang,' McClintock explained. 'They're the pseudo-
nyms the court used for Shanahan and one of his partners when they
published the judgement. Angela couldn't find an unsanitised version
which is what she was sending us all beforehand.'

'Sanitised?'

'Anonymised.'

'Ah. I thought we'd read them all? Can't believe there's another one.' Indeed, within the team everyone knew at least one instalment of Brian Shanahan's love life off by heart.

'Nope, this is the Grant Phillips one – Shanahan appealed the judgement Saul Meyers did and it got sent back to be heard again by a different judge. Lucky Phillips. There's some sections in there from a report – psychologist or psychiatrist, I can't remember – about him. Have a read.'

'What's your passcode?' Jillian said.

'2404 – my birthday.'

'Who makes their code their own birthday?'

'I'm single and I don't have a kid,' he said. 'I have limited options.'

She opened his phone and was unsurprised to find that he had way fewer unread emails than she did. Of course, he was the type to read every email upon receipt and immediately file or delete it, whereas she restricted herself to the pressing ones and never deleted anything. She found the judgement and skimmed the initial pages, which involved a long series of orders regarding a child referred to as 'B' who was only one year old. This child was to live with his mother and spend two separate nights with his father each week, on the condition that 'the father obtained suitable accommodation for himself'. Orders had also been made giving the parties 'equal shared responsibility' and for both to begin a parenting course. Jillian suppressed a snort.

Well, that's bloody pointless.

'Which bit are you reading?' McClintock asked.

'Just the orders. They seem ridiculous to me. If these people needed a judge to help them decide where the kid is going to live and when to see the other parent I don't think a parenting course is going to be much help.' She continued to skim the minutiae of the early stages of the relationship – the parties had met on an internet dating site designed to match Asian women with Western men, they had only ever dated online before marrying, and within two weeks of the parties moving in together in Australia there had been an 'incident of family violence'.

There followed details of the circumstances of the breakdown of the relationship, the claims and counter-claims made by each party. Several experts had been consulted, one of whom was a 'Family Report' writer who had noted 'a great deal of immaturity on both sides but more concerningly on the part of the father, who is almost twenty-five years older than the mother'. They later noted:

> It seems to the writer that the father has a number of personality traits that make interpersonal relationships difficult for him. He is a man who is heavily focused on his perceived persecution within the family law system, which he feels has been solely responsible for his separation from three children from previous relationships. The father spoke at length about his treatment by another judge of the court who he felt had previously been biased towards him. He continued on this trajectory even after I explained that it was not relevant to my recommendations. He then told me 'the whole system needs to be blown up and something done about undemocratic judges'.

Jillian whistled softly.

'You just read the bit about blowing up the courts?' McClintock asked.

'The report writer does clarify that he meant it metaphorically,' Jillian said. 'Nevertheless, it's something alright.'

'And further evidence that he was still hating on a judge, which can only have been Bailey, last year.'

Jillian read the rest of the judgement. It was a sombre affair, and there was a clear expectation, at least on the part of the judicial officer, that the parties would be back in court again.

They took the Lara exit and followed ambling roads to the dirt track that marked Brian Shanahan's property. This time, signs of life were immediately evident on the block. The gate was open and as they drove past the letterbox, three Jack Russells and a kelpie surrounded the car, nipping at the wheels and leaping in excitement. McClintock drove slowly and Jillian leaned her head out the window, paranoid about accidentally running over one of the dogs. When they got out of the car the animals swarmed around their legs, searching for scent.

A shade cloth had been erected over the front of the caravan, and underneath, two camp chairs and a worn picnic table sat on the weedy dirt. The table was laden with several tins of dog food, a new-looking laptop, and bulk grocery items – rice, cashew nuts, dried pasta. As the detectives approached the caravan door the dogs followed, their barking becoming more frenzied.

There was movement at the window and Jillian saw a woman's face, broad and serious. She looked out fleetingly before pulling the curtains abruptly shut. A moment later, Brian Shanahan appeared at the door wearing a T-shirt advertising Beer Laos. He was a strange-looking man, much older and more physically diminished than his online presence suggested. He seemed to Jillian a wiry, stooped personification of middle-aged grievance. His hair was greying, his flesh slightly raw.

Shanahan eyed the detectives suspiciously as he placed a thin metal whistle to his lips and silenced the dogs, who retreated behind the van.

'What do you want?' he demanded. 'Who are you?'

Jillian saw the woman reappear at the window, in the thin gap between the old-fashioned lace curtains. She caught Jillian's eye before quickly moving out of sight once more.

'We're detectives,' Jillian said, 'here to talk about some family law judges with you, Brian. Can we come in and have a chat?' There was something about this man in his pitiable kingdom with his courtier dogs that she found so pathetic she wanted to avert her eyes. This was despite knowing that he was likely abusive towards his intimate partners, dangerous and definitely deranged.

You can be pathetic and a killer.

'Nope.' Brian Shanahan puffed his compact chest out. 'Not having you snooping around and bothering my wife.'

'We heard about the wedding,' McClintock said. 'Congratulations. Who's the lucky lady?'

Shanahan looked at McClintock with undisguised but impersonal hate. 'None of your business. Now say what you came to say and then bugger off.'

'Shall we sit here?' Jillian gestured at the picnic table. Instinct told her that this was a man who needed women to coddle him, that the price of a conversation was allowing him to return to a childlike state where he could do no wrong. In this way, she reflected, he was not dissimilar to Saul Meyers.

Shanahan looked intently at her, his head cocked slightly to one side, and she knew that her assessment was correct. He sat down and she followed, while McClintock remained standing.

'Well, Brian,' she said gently, 'you may or may not be aware that Judge Kaye Bailey has been killed. We understand that you've previously had some issues with her?'

The effect of hearing the judge's name was immediate. 'That woman.' Shanahan's eyes darkened and his lean little body inflated with ill feeling. 'That woman, that piece of shit ruined my life.' He drew a ragged breath. 'I went to her and told her my ex was gonna run away and take my kid, I was never going to see him again. I told her that. I said the ex is telling the cops all this bullshit about me and she's got her mates in on it and all I want is for my boy to stay here, he can see his mum whenever he likes. And do you know what Kaye Bailey did? She bloody smiled at me!' Shanahan's eyes narrowed further. 'Smiled and said to me, "Mr Shanahan, I'm not convinced that you're demonstrating much insight into the needs of a young child."' He licked his lips. 'Then she goes, and this is word for word what she said, "I don't see any evidence of risk being immediate in the material." I was representing myself, for fuck's sake!' He clenched his jaw. 'Ruined my life, ruined my kid's.'

'I see,' Jillian said, wondering which parts of the story he had omitted or amended. 'When was the last time you saw Judge Bailey?'

'When I was last in court,' he said without any hesitation. 'Went into the wrong room by mistake, she wasn't my judge this time. But there she fucking was, looking down on me like I was fucking nothing. Her and that little bitch minion who follows her around looking all smug. Walked right bloody out again.'

'And do you remember when this was?'

'Dunno. Last year sometime. Maybe when I was getting me trial done before the fat bloke, or one of the others.'

'And you're quite sure you haven't seen her at all since then?'

'Yep.' Shanahan was shifting around in his seat, as though his inner turmoil required a physical outlet.

'You don't like the courts much, do you?' McClintock observed.

'No,' Shanahan snarled. 'I don't like the courts at all. I don't like systems that punish children, reward false claims against hardworking people, separate families and ruin people's lives. The number of people I've spoken to who've attempted suicide . . .' He shook his head. 'You probably don't realise this with your little cop mind, but the whole fucking system has been designed to oppress people, and it's corrupt from the top down. You ask that chief judge how he got his swish gig at the top of the tower. It was the same with Kaye fucking Bailey. It's who you know and what you do for them, and fuck it if you don't know anything about how real people think or live.'

At the end of this tirade Shanahan sat back in his seat and crossed his arms.

'That day you saw Judge Bailey in the wrong courtroom,' Jillian said, 'you didn't happen to let yourself into her chambers, did you?' She asked this lightly, as though it were a bit of a joke between the two of them, and caught the merest flicker in his left eye.

'Nope. Why would I want to do that?'

'Did you ever write any emails to Judge Bailey or her associates?'

'I send lots of emails,' he said, and again there was the slightest twitch of his eye.

'Then can you tell us how some particularly nasty emails have been traced back to you?'

He stared at her. 'If you're gonna arrest me, just do it,' he said. He was, Jillian knew, trying for bravado.

McClintock moved forward as though to take immediate advantage of this offer but Jillian held a hand up.

'What about Grant Phillips?' she asked. 'Have you come across him in your dealings with the court?'

'What's he look like?'

'Tall, thin, greying hair.'

'Oh yeah, that show pony. Too busy bloody making eyes at the lawyer on the other side to pay me the slightest. Thought he was god's gift. Glad I only had him once, he was almost worse than the fat one. Human bagpipe, I called that chief judge to his face. He was pretty pissed off at that.'

Jillian swallowed a laugh. Shanahan's description was unfortunately apt.

'So when you were before Grant Phillips, you didn't like his decision?'

'I don't like any of their bloody decisions! They don't listen.'

'Brian, can you tell us where you were on 19 April between midnight and two?'

'I've been on me honeymoon for the last month.'

'But on that day specifically, where were you?'

'We woulda been on the road. We drove to Albury to see me brother.'

'Did you stay anywhere on the way?'

'Nope, drove straight through. Got married in the morning at the registry, then came back here, packed and got moving that night. Wanted to avoid traffic.'

'What's your brother's name?'

'Nathan Shanahan.'

'Right, and Nathan will confirm that you were there, will he?' asked McClintock.

'I'd say so,' Shanahan snarled. 'Given that I was.'

'Could we speak to your wife?' McClintock cocked his head towards the caravan window.

Brian Shanahan gave him a scathing look and said nothing.

'It would help us,' Jillian urged, 'and then we could get going, leave you in peace.'

He thought for a moment and then yelled something in what Jillian took to be Thai. A moment later his wife emerged. She was much younger than Shanahan, perhaps thirty or so. She eyed Jillian with wary curiosity before looking to her husband, her eyes asking a silent question. He said something else to her.

'What was that?' McClintock demanded.

'I just told her who you were,' he said. 'Her English isn't great.' He turned back to her and spoke again. His wife looked at Jillian and announced in a monotone, 'I've been here with him every day in Australia.'

'There we go,' Brian Shanahan said decisively. He gave Jillian a slight nod. 'Now, I think it must be time for you to get going, unless you're going to charge me?'

'Brian, would you consent to us taking a DNA sample?' Jillian asked. 'At the station? It just means we can rule you out of our enquiries.'

He looked at her suspiciously. 'Yeah right, you want me to help you stitch me up. I don't think so. I don't have to consent and I won't. Come back here with a court order or whatever you need, or better still, stop wasting my time.'

CHAPTER 28

'Well, if the human bagpipe is killed next we'll know for sure,' McClintock said as they pulled into the station carpark. 'Shanahan's a miserable prick but he knows a good insult.'

Jillian chuckled. 'We should find out what time he got married, whether it was at the registry office in the city – that puts him nearby. Albeit several hours earlier.'

'I still reckon we should have brought him in. If Harriet's alive and he's holding her somewhere . . .'

'That's why we're getting the surveillance happening. If he's got her, he'll be panicking about the DNA. We wait and see where he goes and we follow . . .'

In the lift Jillian caught sight of her reflection. McClintock had somehow restrained himself from mentioning it, but she looked dreadful – not just tired but stressed. The skin under her eyes had become a dark purple, like Lisa Nettle's; there were fine lines on her face that she was sure had appeared overnight, and her lips were dry. She had a good centimetre or two of regrowth at her hairline.

I need to dye my hair back to normal. What was I thinking?

'If Shanahan was in the city and did wander down to the court, do you think it's possible someone tipped him off?' she mused.

'About the security being down, you mean?'

'Yeah. Unless he's been staking the place out permanently, why that day – it's too much of a coincidence, isn't it?'

'What are you thinking?' McClintock asked.

'Not sure. Only that we're missing something. Some connection. My best guess would be Christianne, only because it seems like she was around for the last security breach he was involved in. Although I really don't see it.'

'What, you think Christianne might have colluded with Shanahan to allow him entry to the building?' McClintock looked incredulous.

'Probably not, but as I said, there's something or someone that we're missing.'

Upstairs Mossman waved from Des's office, where Jillian knew they were already putting together the necessary information to apply for a warrant to monitor Brian Shanahan's phone conversations, to take an involuntary DNA sample and to search his home.

Hastie looked up as they passed, his desk phone to his ear. 'Sharma alibi check,' he mouthed. So far they had only been able to verify Rahul Sharma's movements up until eleven pm on the night Bailey was killed, after which he claimed to have been asleep. His solicitor had provided two months' worth of CCTV video files, none of them labelled or in order, that he said proved his client had not left the house after finishing work that night. Concurrently, the doctor had phoned them three times to ask if there was anything they could do to prevent Lisa Nettle from contacting the hospitals he admitted at to try and confirm his hours herself.

'We need those DNA results from the envelope ASAP,' Jillian said to McClintock once seated at their own desks. 'How's this for a plan: you take them over yourself and work your charm with the lab, then check how Hastie's going with Sharma's phone records and the CCTV. I'll do the paperwork to organise the DNA sample for Shanahan. Then I'll have another chat to Christianne, just to be sure she isn't a closet psychopath, and we'll regroup in a few hours.'

McClintock nodded. 'I'm on it.'

Jillian completed the Shanahan paperwork quickly then called Christianne, who didn't pick up. After leaving a voicemail she searched for her social media pages. Like most people in her age range, the associate seemed to have given up on Facebook but maintained Instagram enthusiastically. A photo of her university graduation showed her with the young man who had accompanied her to Kaye Bailey's funeral, standing hand in hand in front of the University of Melbourne's Wilson Hall. The Christianne of old had fuller cheeks and vibrant skin, a pretty face. In other photos, too, taken at weddings, birthday parties, a baby's christening, she looked much healthier. She had not posted anything new since a week before Judge Bailey died. Jillian looked at her list of followers. Most of Christianne's friends seemed to be people of her own age, although she also recognised a few colleagues from the courts including Angela, Tomir and Matthew. Finding nothing interesting or surprising, Jillian sighed and closed the search window.

She then phoned Angela Hui, who sounded flustered when she answered.

'I was wondering whether Christianne was in? I'm keen to have a quick chat to her.'

'She's back tomorrow but Grant's put her on light duties,' Angela said. 'Honestly, I don't think she should come back, she's a nervous wreck. But at the moment he's lent her out to Saul Meyers. She'll be over at his house tomorrow to pack up an awful lot of files he'd taken home. She'll bring them back to the court. I think this is Grant's way of keeping her distracted without the stress.'

Jillian took down Meyers' address and rang off.

The following morning, Jillian pulled up outside Saul Meyers' home.

The recently retired chief judge lived in a single-storey, double-fronted Victorian red brick in Kew, exactly the type of house Jillian expected. Unlike Kaye Bailey and Grant Phillips, Saul Meyers apparently did not hold concerns for his personal safety: his front fence was low and there was no security gate with intercom. The house was proudly visible from the footpath and Jillian could see a baby grand piano through a window unencumbered by blinds.

She wondered whether Saul Meyers might come to regret his casual approach in the event that Brian Shanahan was the culprit, as surely Meyers, 'the human bagpipe', was next on the list.

It was his wife, Pamela Meyers, who answered the door, her blank face notable for a total lack of curiosity. 'Saul and the girl are just in the garage,' she said, unperturbed by the presence of a detective. 'They should be back any minute. You're welcome to wait if you want to.'

'That would be wonderful,' Jillian said. 'Thank you.'

'I'm just sitting in here,' Pamela said, ushering Jillian through to the room with the baby grand piano. They sat together at a round table on which a number of brochures for cruises and a notebook and pen were placed.

'Sorry about the clutter,' said Pamela, but making no effort to move it. 'Just sorting out Saul's retirement present while he's busy.' Jillian looked at the brochures. The cruise packages had titles like

'Caribbean Dreams' and 'Island Paradise'. 'Starting at $30,000 pp' boasted a brochure for something called 'Tropicana Sunset'.

How could a man like this possibly make judgements about ordinary people?

'Where are you thinking of going?' Jillian asked, to make small talk.

'This one comes recommended,' Pamela said, taking up a brochure. 'Fiji, Vanuatu, New Caledonia. We've never really done an island holiday before. Saul always wants to go to Europe.' She tenderly replaced the brochure on the table.

'Ah,' Jillian said lamely.

Where are *those two?*

'Do you play?' she asked, looking at the piano.

'I did, years ago,' Pamela said, not particularly interested in Jillian's presence. 'But not for a long time. Our granddaughter has just started, which is why we bought this.'

Best to be prepared, in case she becomes a concert pianist.

Jillian noted that Pamela Meyers had the strange practice of completing a sentence and falling silent. In Jillian's experience, most people, regardless of whether they were suspects, victims, witnesses or altogether unrelated to an investigation, assumed a certain jitteriness in the presence of police. They became nervous or shifty or overly accommodating or even hysterical, depending on the circumstances, but they rarely remained wholly unmoved.

Is she really that disinterested? Is that why Saul Meyers married her?

'Did you know Judge Bailey at all?' she asked. And to her surprise, Pamela Meyers' face immediately darkened.

'That woman,' she said, leaning forward slightly, 'was a bully.'

'In what way a bully?'

'She was always on at Saul about something or other, trying to get him to change this or that, make this a policy, fire that person. At one stage she actually threatened to report him to the attorney-general, can you believe that? She was one of those nasty fighting women, you know the type? Always busy interfering, and whenever something doesn't work out they say it's because of gender, that men don't take women seriously. She said that about Saul.' Pamela straightened in her chair. 'Saul doesn't have a sexist bone in his body.'

'Do you know why Judge Bailey told your husband she was going to report him to the attorney-general?'

'I can't remember exactly, but it was to do with some policy she wanted to see adopted that Saul didn't agree with. She was just a killjoy. She didn't like any of them relaxing, having a drink, making a joke. It was so silly, she pretended she wanted to make things at the court better for the staff, but really she just wanted him gone, that was what it was about.'

'Do you know if the attorney-general ever got involved?'

'I don't know for sure. You'd have to ask Saul. All I know is he was very upset, said she was trying to make things awkward for him.'

'So you're not –' Jillian began, but Pamela Meyers was on a roll.

'She did it to Ginny too, you know?' Her voice had become higher and more urgent. 'Had a go at her, accused her of having a conflict of interest. I remember we had dinner with her and her husband that weekend, the one before Saul's party, and Saul and Ginny were both beside themselves about the trouble she was causing. Saul said it was all ridiculous.'

'What was the conflict of interest, do you know?'

'I just can't remember. But Ginny was very upset.'

'And you don't remember what Judge Bailey might have been trying to get your husband to agree to?'

'No, I can't, it wasn't very interesting. But she was nasty. She started rumours about people, wanted to bring down those who might have wanted to be chief judge, didn't care about anyone else's reputation or family.'

'You weren't at the retirement party, were you?'

'No, our youngest is pregnant and sick so I was helping her. Lucky too. If I'd been there I'd have had a thing or two to say . . .'

Jillian heard the front door opening and Saul Meyers' rich baritone.

'Someone's parked right out the front!' he boomed to his wife from the hallway. 'Don't recognise the car, it's no one on the street. I'm going to write to the council, it should be permits only.'

Meyers poked his head around the door to seek his wife's agreement, and saw Jillian.

'What are you doing here?' He looked from Jillian to his wife, whose face had regained its blank composure.

'I needed to have a quick chat to Christianne,' Jillian said lightly. 'Thought it might be easier to grab her here.' She smiled at the associate. 'Can we have a word out the front?'

'Has something else happened?' Christianne asked anxiously once they were away from the house.

'No, I just wanted to check a few things with you. To do with the security breaches last year. Can you tell me how the theft of Kaye's wallet happened?'

Christianne blushed deeply. 'It was so embarrassing. We had an interim defended hearing in court, but the parties had gone away to see if they could settle it between themselves. I usually wait in court and work from the courtroom computer when that's happening. Kaye asked me to go and see how things were going while she went to the bathroom and I knew that the barristers had gone down to the registry to look at the subpoenas so I went there. I was only gone for a few minutes, but I'd taken my lanyard off and that must be when he came in. Once we discovered that Kaye's wallet had been stolen I offered to resign, but she wouldn't let me.'

She looked as distressed as if it had happened that very morning. *No duplicity here, I'd say.*

'What about the other security breach?'

'Mastromonica – she was scary. We were in the duty list. There were lots of people in court. I got out of my seat for a minute because a barrister wanted to hand me something and they're not allowed to approach the bench. She just threw herself forwards. We adjourned, called Tomir. It was over quickly at least. Kaye was furious afterwards. Not with me,' she added quickly, 'with him.' Christianne nodded towards the house. 'And Tomir. She told me she'd asked for security to sit in for that list because Mastromonica had made trouble before and the CJ and Tomir told her just to use the panic button.'

As if on cue, Saul Meyers came out of the house. He placed a large cardboard box in the back of the silver SUV parked in the driveway. 'When you're ready, Christianne,' he called pointedly.

'I'd actually like a quick word with you too,' Jillian said, turning to him.

'That's fine,' he said, 'just not right now. You can see I'm busy.'

'I'd like to talk to you about the conflict of interest involving Virginia Maiden,' Jillian said loudly.

Christianne looked from the detective to the judge, clearly surprised. 'Conflict of interest?' she repeated quietly.

Saul Meyers had turned deep red and looked as though he wanted to hit Jillian. She was aware that she was about to land Pamela Meyers in trouble.

'Really?' said the former judge, drawing himself up. 'Well, I'd like you to fuck off.'

When Jillian arrived at St Kilda Road, Des immediately beckoned her into his office with a single raised finger. 'Take a seat,' he said, 'and tell me what the fuck happened between you and the chief judge.'

'Nothing happened, he just got stroppy when I challenged him. He and Judge Maiden are hiding something that I think is significant. I don't know what it is, but I asked him about it.'

'Well unluckily for you, he and the Chief Commissioner went to school together. Guess who just rang me up spitting chips.'

'Oh. Sorry.'

'Why didn't you take McClintock with you?'

This caught her off guard. She would have thought that of anyone, Des would understand why she might have chosen to go alone. 'I was just chasing something up. I didn't think it would be a big deal. I wasn't even intending to talk to Meyers, the associate just happened to be with him so that's where I went.'

Des frowned. 'Are you alright?' he asked. 'You seem a bit more wired than usual. This isn't the Jilly I know. You're the people whisperer. McClintock's the one who pisses people off.'

'I think he only pisses you and me off.'

'Back to my question though, are you okay? Do you need to take a step back for a bit longer, spend some more time at home?'

'No!' Her reaction was too loud.

'You sure?'

'Absolutely.'

'And how's Aaron?'

'Fine.'

'The little one?'

'Also fine.'

'Well good,' he said, although she could tell he didn't believe her. 'Look, can you take the rest of the day, just so I can tell the big boss I've done something about the situation. I've told him you're a bloody good officer but I need to make a token gesture.'

'Fine.'

'That's the way.'

CHAPTER 29

Jillian was halfway through a very old and particularly expensive bottle of grenache that she and Aaron had received as a wedding present when her phone rang. She leapt from the couch and tipsily ransacked various surfaces. She had sent Aaron five messages during the course of the day, none of which he'd responded to.

But when she located the phone it was not Aaron, but her mother. *Ugh.*

'You good, honey?' Marion Basset asked in her familiar, slightly high-pitched warbling voice.

Immediately, Jillian's mind turned to excuses for ending the call. She would say she was tired, she'd call back tomorrow. But even as she thought this, she found herself saying, 'Fine. How are you?'

'I'm good, darl. Although my hip's playing up again and I've been a bit flat. Alice reckons I might have seasonal affective disorder.'

Alice was her mother's best friend and enabler-in-chief. The two of them would sit together on Marion's front porch day-drinking, smoking joints and encouraging each other in elaborate conspiracy theories, far-fetched health diagnoses and fits of hysteria. Every time Jillian visited her mother, she wondered how the neighbours coped with the sound of two drunk, dope-smoking old hippies bitching and whining from midday to long after midnight. As far as Jillian could make out, they did this at least four times a week.

'That's no good.' She returned to the couch and her bottle of wine, and began flicking between television stations for something to distract her from her mother's voice, which had a Pavlovian effect on Jillian's central nervous system. Her mother had always had that skill. No matter what might have been happening in Jillian's life, a telephone call with Marion was guaranteed to push all other sources of stress to the periphery. It wasn't the conversations in themselves that pained her so much as the way they reminded Jillian of the things she liked least about herself.

It's her fault you're a bad mum. You didn't have anyone to learn from.

On the one hand, the thought was comforting. It absolved her of any responsibility, placed the blame squarely at the feet of a woman who had often waxed lyrical about her hatred of parenthood. But the thought also depressed her. Was it really the case that Jillian's experience of being mothered destined her for failure as a mother? The optimist in her wanted to believe that this was not so, that with each generation there was an opportunity to right the wrongs of the previous. The pessimist in her thought that while generational change might be possible, she herself was probably not the right woman to prove the theory.

After all, you've already blown it, haven't you?

Marion had just begun an anecdote about volunteering for a local community organisation, and the 'unreasonable' and 'stuck-up' manager she'd clashed with there, when Jillian's phone beeped with a message from Aaron.

'Mum, I've got to go, sorry. Something urgent has just come through from work.'

'It's always urgent with your work,' Marion said reproachfully, but she did not protest as Jillian ended the conversation.

I'm basically just free therapy for her anyway.

She opened the text message.

Sorry, not ignoring you, phone buggered. Will sort it out first thing. Talk tomorrow.

A second later there was another beep.

Ollie's fine, by the way.

Jillian sighed. She felt exhausted and confused. She emailed her psychologist, not with the intention of actually booking a new appointment, but so that she could tell Aaron she had made some effort.

Have emailed psych, she texted.

And when he did not immediately respond she wrote, *I'm glad Ollie is okay.*

To force away thoughts of Aaron and Ollie and their imminent family breakdown, she flicked onto a reality TV show and turned the volume up. A young man with a substantial facial injury was talking earnestly into the camera while his mother sat next to him, her arm wrapped protectively around his shoulders. 'It would just be nice to be able to go out and not have the first thing people ask me be "What happened?"' the boy was saying, tears welling. 'It would be nice to have a girlfriend one day.'

His mother began to cry too. 'That's why we're so grateful,' she said to whoever was interviewing her off screen, 'to get this type of treatment done. The waiting list was astronomical and we don't have private health insurance or any savings, so we feel so thankful to Dr Sharma.'

Sharma!

Jillian sat up, all her attention on the program. Rahul Sharma was now freshly shaven and had a thick layer of stage make-up on.

He spoke in a calming voice to the young patient and his mother about the risks of the surgery and the exact process the operation would follow. His bedside manner was indeed remarkable, a gentle soothing that instilled absolute confidence.

The scene changed to the young man being wheeled into an operating theatre, and an anaesthetic being administered. Then Dr Sharma began the surgery.

Jillian watched intently. The procedure was being done not, as she had assumed, at one of the large Melbourne hospitals, but at the Australasian Centre for Cosmetic and Restorative Medicine, whose branding featured prominently in several shots. Googling the centre, Jillian learned that it was Rahul's own business, and that it had thirteen hospitals in Australia and South-East Asia. The company had recently made an initial public offering.

No wonder he can afford the fancy house.

The show wrapped up fifteen minutes later, after confirmation that the operation had been an unqualified success and a reveal of the boy's newly recovered face. The boy and his mother tearfully hugged Sharma. The credits began to roll, a long list of crew and medical experts followed by several acknowledgments. 'Dr Rahul Sharma and Dr Andrew Maiden would like to thank everyone at . . .'

Andrew Maiden?

Jillian immediately googled the name. An egg-headed man appeared in several pictures and articles about Dr Sharma. She scanned the links. On the third one she found a photo with the caption: 'Dr Andrew Maiden and his mother, Her Honour Judge Virginia Maiden, at the Royal Children's Hospital annual gala.'

I think I've found our missing link, she texted McClintock. *And our conflict of interest. I might even know where the judgement is.*

CHAPTER 30

The detectives met in the station carpark early the next morning. Donoghue and Hastie had been dispatched to confirm Jillian's suspicions and she felt possessed of manic energy as she and McClintock waited for the phone call to come. 'Was I right?'

'You know it.'

She gave McClintock a thumbs up.

'You see Hastie's email?' McClintock asked when she got into his car. 'A bit more CCTV from the day of the wake showed up.'

'I'll look at it now,' Jillian said, opening her email and clicking on the file. 'Anything jump out at you?'

'Nah, but maybe you'll pick something up.'

The footage was black and white, low quality, and the camera angle wasn't the best. It looked out onto the residential street adjacent to the wine bar. There were several minutes of nothing, and then the smallest wedge of a light-coloured head appeared on the bottom of the screen, followed a moment later by the hint of something which Jillian thought was a car roof, driving away.

'Is that Harriet?' She rewound, squinting. 'Looks like it could be. So perhaps someone forced her into a car?'

'Or she got into it voluntarily,' McClintock said, leaning over at a red light to see for himself. 'God, it's quick. I didn't even see it.'

She emailed the footage on with a request that everything be done to enhance and clarify the vision. Her hands shook slightly as she typed – the consequence of finishing an entire bottle of wine by herself.

McClintock yawned. Glancing across at her colleague, Jillian thought he looked as rough as she felt. McClintock was typically cleanly shaven, well rested, and in either a neatly pressed shirt or some type of athletic wear. Today he had not shaved and his eyes were slightly bloodshot. Beneath whatever aftershave he had applied there was a lingering, stale scent.

'Big night?' she asked. 'Hungover?'

'Something like that. Andrew Maiden was a good find,' he said, changing the subject. 'I should have ... Anyway, I thought *Please Fix Me* wasn't your cup of tea?'

'It isn't. I was just talking to my mother, needed something to distract me from her insanity.'

'That's no way to talk about a mother,' McClintock said in mock outrage as he turned onto High Street from St Kilda Road. 'Who was on phones last night?'

Jillian suppressed a yawn. 'Mossman. She's already texted. Very boring conversation between Brian Shanahan and his brother that seems to verify he arrived there when he said he did. And he hasn't left his house at all.'

'Hey listen,' said McClintock, 'there's something I need to tell you about Andrew –'

Whatever he was about to say was interrupted by the abrupt braking of the car in front of him. A boy and a girl, both in bright purple blazers, appeared to have walked directly into traffic without looking and were now being abused by the driver of a yellow BMW M3.

'Jesus, mate, they're just kids,' McClintock said incredulously.

'Rich kids, though,' Jillian added. Her heart was pounding and the sudden braking motion had made her stomach bounce around her chest cavity. 'Who think traffic should stop for them. What were you saying?'

'Oh,' McClintock said, 'nothing important.'

The Maiden residence was located in Armadale, in a quiet street that ran off Kooyong Road. The home displayed a different type of opulence to those of Grant Phillips or Saul Meyers or even Rahul Sharma. Once a Victorian terrace, it had been gutted and reimagined as a modernist monolith. They were shown inside by the weak-chinned and diminutive Harold Maiden who led them along a corridor enclosed on one side by the view of a lap pool that gave the home an oppressive, subterranean feel.

Virginia Maiden was sitting at the kitchen island with several documents in front of her divided into neatly organised piles. Harold presented the detectives before retreating up the corridor. Virginia Maiden was demurely dressed and wore her usual impervious expression. She carefully placed the documents in a single file and pushed them to the side before giving her complete attention to McClintock.

'John, lovely to see you again,' she said brightly, ignoring Jillian entirely. 'To what do I owe this early-morning visit?'

'Judge Maiden,' he nodded in greeting, 'we just need to ask you some questions about Rahul Sharma.'

Before he could continue, a voice said, 'Good heavens, is that you, Johnny?' and Jillian turned to see a man she recognised from her internet search as Andrew Maiden standing in the corridor. 'It is, isn't it. Wow, small world.'

Jillian looked at McClintock in surprise. The detective's neck had coloured slightly.

'Hey Andrew,' he said, 'how are you?'

Andrew Maiden was now upon them, extending a hand. 'Mate, it must have been twenty years,' he said.

'You two know each other?' Virginia Maiden said, evidently delighted. 'Tell me how?'

'Well, school,' McClintock conceded.

'Johnny here was on the rowing team with us, footy too,' said the doctor, sounding genuinely thrilled. From the expression on McClintock's face Jillian suspected the delight was not mutual.

'Just crazy,' he continued, 'and you're a cop now, weren't you going to do –'

'It wasn't for me,' McClintock interrupted.

'Wasn't your old man a cop?' Andrew said. 'I think I remember him coming in to do a talk one time. Showed us his gun and all that.'

'That sounds about right.'

'Well, there you go,' Virginia Maiden said. 'Didn't I ask how I knew you when we first met?' she said to McClintock. 'I thought you looked familiar.'

'And you're looking into the judge's murder, are you?' Andrew Maiden said. 'God, what a relief. We've been worried sick about Mum, taking it in turns to stay over, although she insists she doesn't need guarding. But Dad isn't well, you know. I'm so glad they've got you on it.'

'Judge Maiden, perhaps while Andrew and John catch up, I could have a word with you?' Jillian suggested.

'I suppose,' the judge said reluctantly. 'What about?'

What is her problem?

'Rahul Sharma.'

Both Maidens paled slightly and the doctor threw a fleeting look at his mother.

'If it's about Rahul, I might be able to help,' Andrew Maiden stammered. 'You know he's my business partner? Was my business partner,' he corrected himself.

'We do,' Jillian said. 'And we'd like to talk to you too, but separately, in a moment.'

'Of course,' he said, trying and failing to sound casual. 'In that case I'll leave you to it. Got some calls to make anyway.' He took himself out into the courtyard visible beyond glass sliding doors and pulled his phone from his pocket.

Without asking, Jillian took a seat at the kitchen island and pulled another stool out for McClintock.

'Judge Maiden, could you tell us what your relationship is with Rahul Sharma?'

'Relationship?' Virginia Maiden raised her eyebrows slightly. 'He's Andrew's friend from university, Oxford. Why do you ask?'

'As you're aware, the matter Kaye Bailey was working on when she was killed was about Rahul Sharma and his former partner. We're trying to get a sense of what connections he might have had in the building.'

'Well, I didn't let him into the building to kill Kaye, if that's what you're asking.' From the fear in the judge's eyes, Jillian could tell that the power dynamic between them had finally shifted in her favour.

You're toying with her a bit, aren't you?

'Were you and he close?'

'Not really. He and Andrew are, of course, but I wouldn't say Rahul and I had any particular involvement with each other.'

'When was the last time you spoke to Dr Sharma?' Jillian asked.

'I don't know, I can't remember off the top of my head! We weren't in regular communication. As I've told you, he's Andrew's friend, not mine.'

Jillian knew that this was likely the case. They had found no evidence of contact between the judge and Rahul Sharma but the older woman looked gloriously unnerved, which Jillian could not help taking malicious pleasure in.

'Two of our colleagues went by your chambers first thing this morning,' Jillian said.

'Well, that was silly. I told my associates I wasn't going to risk going in for the time being unless I absolutely have to be in court. If you'd bothered calling them they would have told you that.'

'They were there to search your chambers,' Jillian explained, and for once she had Virginia Maiden's full attention.

McClintock said, 'They found Kaye Bailey's missing judgement there. In the shredding pile.'

There was a silence that seemed to stretch on for minutes. 'Oh for goodness' sake, it was just a harmless joke,' the judge said finally, trying to muster condescension. 'We'd all been drinking, we were just being stupid. I happened to see it on her associate's desk as I went to the bathroom and Saul and I knew it would irritate her a bit. I mean, she was the new CJ, it was just a bit of teasing. But,' she added firmly, 'she was still alive and well when we left.'

'We don't quite buy that,' Jillian said. 'That it was a harmless joke, I mean. We don't think you killed Kaye Bailey, but your theft of the judgement wasn't a spur-of-the-moment prank.'

Virginia Maiden audibly gulped.

Emboldened, Jillian went on, 'We know that Kaye Bailey had raised the issue of a conflict of interest, regarding you and the Sharma case. Saul Meyers ignored it, as he ignored everything Kaye told him, inconvenient truths that made his life difficult and his friendships more awkward. She wanted Saul to move your chambers to a different floor and for there to be an information barrier until she'd handed down the judgement. She was worried that she or you would be compromised, that there was a risk of you seeing or hearing something in advance. Your son and Rahul Sharma were in business together, and the allegations going around in the Sharma case had the potential to create problems for them. Judge Bailey was referring their entire business to Consumer Affairs, and Rahul to AHPRA. Going by some of the practices she outlined in the judgement, it's just a matter of time before Andrew ends up with the health regulator breathing down his neck too.'

Jillian took a moment to look hard at the judge.

Can't ignore me now, can you?

'The night of the murder, you and Saul went into her chambers, ostensibly to say goodnight, apologise, congratulate her one more time, all that. Except that really you just wanted to get your hands on the judgement and Saul was happy to go along for the ride. Her office door was shut or almost shut, you saw the judgement on Christianne's desk and you took it. When you read it you realised that your son might be in serious shit when it was published. On the way home that night you called him. You told him he needed to make a report to AHPRA himself, as soon as possible, and extricate himself from dealings with Rahul. Your precious boy would be saved the indignity of having his professional reputation tarnished and the family name would be protected.

'We assume you took it back into work intending to replace it the next day, then once you heard about Kaye, you realised how bad that would look. That's how it happened, isn't it? You thought you'd just ensure everything was okay for your son, and toy with a woman whom you didn't like as a bonus, and instead, you implicated yourself in a murder. If only you'd deigned to do the shredding yourself, you'd have destroyed the evidence. Instead you left if up to your poor associate. Useless.'

CHAPTER 31

Jillian watched the sushi plates move hypnotically along the track, edamame beans and slivers of tuna glistening under the bright restaurant lights. Japanese had been McClintock's idea – motivated, Jillian suspected, by the opportunity to ensure she ate 'real food' rather than the chocolate bars in the kitchen.

It had not been a productive morning. A full twenty-four hours had passed since Virginia Maiden had been brought in for questioning. Noting the extremely unusual circumstances of the matter, Des had insisted that they seek the advice of the lawyers within the police force before formally charging her with anything. While they waited for this advice, Jillian felt as though they were treading water. The momentum that had been building had also been stymied by other hold-ups beyond the detectives' control. DNA analysis of the letter sent to Judge Phillips had not yet been processed. Nor had there been any sightings of Harriet Phillips beyond the scrap of hair that just may have been her in the CCTV footage. Brian Shanahan had been reluctantly swabbed but as yet they had nothing to match his sample to.

'I can't stand that guy,' McClintock said, having extracted the DNA sample, 'and his place is like something from fucking *True*

278

Detective.' He had delivered the swab to the lab himself, assuring Jillian that he would convey the urgency of the situation, and had come back an hour later with his tail between his legs. 'They reckon at least three days.'

'I thought you were charming the lab into processing everything ASAP?' Jillian said, trying not to sound accusatory.

'There's only so much charming I can do. They're going as hard as they can but everyone thinks what they're working on is urgent, as they all told me again and again.'

Jillian unlocked her phone and checked her emails while McClintock helped himself to his sixth plate. 'I don't understand why everything's taking so long.'

'They'll come when they come,' McClintock said.

That sounds like something Aaron would say.

Her heart lurched a little. Aaron was still waiting for her to 'meaningfully engage with treatment', as he'd put it in his most recent text. He sounded like a social worker, not her husband. She had restrained herself from writing something snarky back.

The phone tap of Shanahan had provided nothing of interest. The man spoke to his brother with extraordinary regularity. Their conversations were tedious affairs that traversed whatever sport they had both watched, the many ways in which Nathan's boss was trying to 'screw him over', and Brian's efforts to seek a judicial review of a decision by the education regulator to prevent him from teaching. Aside from briefly mentioning that 'some cops tried to pin that judge on me', their suspect had been entirely silent on the looming threat of an arrest.

Surveillance of his home had revealed the most mundane of existences. Shanahan ran his family law websites from his caravan while his wife worked, Jillian suspected off the books, in a cafe at Werribee Plaza. They left the house only when he drove her to work, and when they went grocery shopping together.

'Poor woman,' McClintock said after one such report had come back to them. 'What a horrible life, stuck with him.'

'She might actually like it,' Jillian said. 'We don't know. Maybe this was a better option than whatever life she had before.'

'Then poor her for having had that life.'

Jillian scrutinised the revolving dishes and took another plate of vegetable maki just before it slipped out of reach.

Food is so much more enticing when there are only finite seconds in which to reach for it.

'I keep thinking about Harriet Phillips and those earrings,' she said. 'Why would he send them to us?'

'Not to us, to Phillips.'

'You know what I mean. I just don't really understand the point of it. What was he trying to tell us?'

Jillian ate the rolls, sucked the remaining soy sauce off her chopsticks and rotated her shoulders. There was an agonised cracking objection from her bones that caused McClintock to recoil.

'That's not normal, you need to get that looked at.'

She ignored him. 'Come on, let's head back – watch the paint dry with everyone else.'

Hastie, who had been responsible for annotating many of the Shanahan tapes, was slumped over his desk when they returned. He looked up when he saw them and said, 'If I have to listen to him talking about fishing for one more minute . . .'

'Don't,' Donoghue said from his desk. 'I've spent the last day and a half looking through CCTV from every shop on High Street Northcote that might contain a light-coloured car. Do you know how many light cars were in the area on the afternoon of that wake?'

'Take a break, both of you,' Jillian said. 'Get some fresh air, eat, come back.'

In her absence, Grant Phillips had phoned her, something he'd taken to doing daily. She called him back. 'I don't have any updates on Harriet at this stage, I'm afraid,' she said.

'Is it true that Ginny was hiding the judgement? That's the hot gossip around court, that she was raided first thing yesterday.'

'I can't talk about that,' she said firmly, even as she was tempted to describe the particular satisfaction that interviewing Judge Maiden had given her. 'But we have found the judgement, and at this stage we don't think it's related to Kaye or Harriet.'

Grant Phillips signed off and she opened her email. 'Judge's data – a bit more' was the only unopened message. Any excitement she felt was immediately extinguished by the message from the analyst who had tried to resurrect Kaye's phone. *I'm sorry, I've tried everything I can think of. Almost everything is corrupted. There are a few more random bits and pieces we've been able to access which I've attached. Just pictures, no text. Give me a call if you have any questions.*

The first attachment was a photograph of a beautiful Burmese cat, its eyes illuminated by the sun, whiskers alert. The second was of Ama and looked to have been taken several years ago; it showed her arm in arm with Hugo at some formal function. The third was a shot of a woman's upper arm and back, covered in a thick round of purple bruising.

Weird. What's this doing on her phone?

Jillian scanned the photo. There was no trace of hair, no tattoo or other distinguishing marks. All that could be deduced was that the woman was white, relatively thin, and presumably still in some pain – the bruises looked fresh. The photo had been taken at eleven-fifteen pm on 16 December 2017.

'What's that?' McClintock said, leaning back from his desk to look at Jillian's screen.

'Bailey's phone. Do you reckon that's her? Mirror selfie might be possible?'

'Suppose so. Why else would she have it? Yikes, looks like she got manhandled something shocking.'

Jillian phoned Ama, who she knew was intending to remain in Australia for another few weeks. 'Did your mum have some type of accident around December last year? A fall maybe, or a fight with someone?'

'Not that I'm aware, why?'

'We've found a photo on her phone of someone with substantial bruising on their shoulders, arms, back. Can't tell who it is, though.'

'Doesn't ring any bells. But Mum was pretty stoic, and she didn't like telling me things she thought would upset me. So it's possible she had a fall and didn't say. Hey, have you heard from that law firm yet? My dad wrote to them explaining the situation and saying that he or I could be appointed to give instructions if we knew what Mum engaged them for, but they're just ignoring us.'

'Sorry, we don't have an update there, unfortunately,' Jillian said. 'We were advised not to subpoena them by our lawyers. Last I heard they were going to get their own advice to see if they could be more specific without breaching any of their duties but they're making slow work of it.'

Jillian then phoned Michael O'Neil, who was similarly perplexed by the idea of Kaye Bailey having an injury.

'What date did you say again? Let me check the calendar.'

She could hear him getting to his feet and the rustling of several pieces of paper before he returned to the call. 'Ah, here we go, 2017. December. On the sixteenth I have myself attending something called the Melbourne Law Foundation Gala Function. God, that sounds tedious. Why did we go to that? Oh, I remember, actually, Kaye was a speaker. Something about a new women's refuge in the city. She spoke very well, that's right.'

'And you don't recall her having a fall, for example?'

'I don't.'

'Do you remember if she drank much?'

'I don't, no. In fact the only thing I remember about that night is – but no, that won't be important.'

'What's that?' Jillian asked.

'Well, I hate to speak ill of a colleague, and I do genuinely respect her, she's a really good solicitor, but that was the night we realised Helen McPherson and Grant might have been more than just friends.'

CHAPTER 32

It was late and Des, who had spent much of the day reading through all the evidence that Jillian and McClintock had obtained to date, looked exhausted. He removed his hands from the back of his head to clap them together, before returning them to their perch. 'Alright, shoot. What're you thinking?'

'We're ninety per cent sure it isn't Sharma,' Jillian said. 'He seems to have been home all night, judging from his CCTV. He finally let us have a poke around on his devices, too. We can see he spent a fair bit of time both on the night of Bailey's death and the day of Harriet's disappearance online – mainly just watching himself on YouTube.'

'I still like Shanahan,' McClintock said. 'He's got motive for Bailey, and we know he's got into her chambers before. He's got motive for hurting Phillips too. Plus he's a nutter.'

'But,' said Jillian, 'his brother has unequivocally alibied him, as has his wife. Neither of them is particularly reliable – Nathan Shanahan gives me the impression he'd agree to anything on Brian's behalf, and the wife is totally at his mercy – but they are alibis. We're still waiting on the DNA from the eyelash. We could arrest him now for the threatening emails – we know those were him. Well, a lot of them have been confirmed as his.'

'Alright,' Des said, jotting down 'alibi? DNA?' next to Shanahan's name. 'Are we satisfied it wasn't anyone who was at the party? Because if we're going to accuse another judge I'd like to know sooner rather than later.'

'We're satisfied,' McClintock said immediately.

'Jilly?' Des asked, as though McClintock hadn't spoken.

McClintock's phone beeped with an incoming text. He ignored it but the sound stirred Jillian's memory.

'I'm not quite sure,' she said, chewing her bottom lip. 'Kim Surle – I keep thinking about her. It's just so weird that she saw Bailey that day, after all those years without any contact. And Kim knew Phillips, too. I just can't figure out how it all fits.'

'Well, we know she went over and above for clients from that eulogy at the funeral,' said McClintock. 'If anyone was going to catch up with an old client for lunch it would be her.'

'I suppose so. Then there's this business with Helen McPherson. We know that something has been going on between her and Phillips. What if Helen came to chambers that night? We know Michael O'Neil walked her to her car which was parked at the Mint but he didn't see her drive away. Perhaps she was hoping to rendezvous with Phillips? Perhaps she had her own beef with Bailey? We don't know what their relationship was like. You said you thought Phillips fancied Bailey. Maybe Helen was jealous?'

'What is she thinking? He's so old,' McClintock said.

'Old but charming.'

Even though I don't normally trust charming men.

'Plus, Helen has a motive for getting rid of Harriet. It's possible she wanted the wife out of the way, and she was at the wake with her.' But even as she said this, Jillian knew it didn't quite add up. Helen had assisted in looking for Harriet in the immediate aftermath of her disappearance and had been spoken to by the team.

What aren't I seeing?

'YEAH!' McClintock yelled, getting to his feet with his phone in hand. 'Woo hoo!'

'What on earth?' Jillian demanded.

'We just got the DNA results,' he said. 'It's a match with Brian Shanahan.'

Brian Shanahan's peaceful evening cup of tea was interrupted by the attendance of the detectives. 'What the fuck is this bullshit?' he demanded as it was explained to him that he was being arrested. 'You can't do this!' He looked at his wife, who was cowering by the caravan door. 'Don't say anything about anything,' he yelled at her as officers directed him to stand. 'They're just looking for an excuse to put us both away.'

McClintock escorted the confused woman to a waiting police car with gentle assurances that she was not under arrest and that a Thai interpreter would be available at the station.

Brian Shanahan, watching her go, reminded Jillian of a toddler whose favourite toy had been confiscated.

He himself did not go quickly or quietly. Jillian and McClintock were subjected to sustained expletives as he was moved outside and his caravan was searched.

Jillian had been involved in any number of searches during her time in the police, and for an endless variety of homes. She had spent time in the houses of hoarders, of millionaire gangsters, internet paedophiles and white-collar criminals, but she had never seen so many things crammed into such a compact space as in Brian Shanahan's caravan.

The bedroom area, which only had room for the double bed and a wardrobe the size of a broom cupboard, somehow hosted the memorabilia of his entire childhood, from primary-school awards to high-school art projects. Photos tracked Brian Shanahan from a tiny prep student to an athletic high schooler. There was a house captain certificate and even a final-year history assignment. It startled Jillian to think of this man as once being young and full of hope, unburdened by grievance and not set on vindication. What had gone so wrong? How had he become the husk of a creature he now was?

'That's bloody personal,' he yelled, looking through the window from outside the caravan, where he was being detained by uniformed officers. 'Get out of my bedroom.'

In the kitchen area she bagged his laptop and five portable hard drives. From cupboards she retrieved several boxes of family-law documentation, relating not just to his own cases, but also to those of people who'd written to him seeking advice. One box was labelled 'Wives', and looked to contain every interaction Shanahan had enjoyed in each of his doomed marriages, from first meetings to Intervention Orders and divorce certificates. There were envelopes filled with strands of thick black hair mixed in with his own, pictures of babies, plus several photos of the women in various stages of undress.

A photo fluttered to the floor and as she bent to pick it up, Jillian's eye caught the underside of the kitchen table. She recalled the account of Shanahan hiding court documents under the bar table and squatted down to investigate. Sure enough, a large envelope was lodged into one corner, held in place with duct tape. She leaned in and pulled it out.

The envelope contained print-outs from Shanahan's various Facebook pages. She flicked through and came to one that caught her interest. Someone writing under the name 'Jekyll and Hyde' had posted names and addresses for several of the family law judges.

Bailey – 49 Merriton Street, Northcote
Perriam – 9 Vance Avenue, Williamstown
Meyers – Kew
Davies – 6 Fyfe Street, Camberwell
Maiden – Potnet Street, Armadale (no. unknown)
Phillips – Hawthorn (don't know where)

As Jillian had not previously seen these on his Facebook pages she deduced that Shanahan had deleted the posts but retained copies for himself. The information was out of date – Kaye Bailey had moved in the months prior to her murder – and ultimately irrelevant, as Bailey had been killed in chambers and Harriet taken from Bailey's wake. But why had Shanahan kept it? And why conceal it in this way?

Driving back to St Kilda Road, McClintock was jubilant, tapping his fingers on the steering wheel in excited beats as he navigated the traffic. But Jillian was subdued. Shanahan was a man whose entire identity had been subsumed by hatred, of the courts, of its officers. He was pathetic to her.

When they arrived at the station he was processed and put in an interview room, where he sat small and sad with his legs spread far apart as though trying for a gesture of control.

'Why the fuck am I here?' he demanded. 'And where's my wife? What are you doing with her?'

Pear Chen, as the new Mrs Shanahan was in fact called, was awaiting the presence of a Thai interpreter in another interview room.

McClintock took a seat and placed the various pieces of evidence in a pile, allowing for the enormity of the case to dawn on their subject. Shanahan looked at it with contempt. McClintock began with a photo of the earrings and the note.

'Never seen either of them before in my life,' Shanahan insisted with a sniff, although Jillian saw that his eyes lingered on the note.

'Is this your handwriting?' McClintock asked.

'Given I didn't write it, how could it be?'

'What's this about, Brian?' McClintock asked, showing him the print-out of the judges' names and addresses.

Shanahan shrugged. 'That's just some bullshit someone posted on one of my Facebook sites. It's months old. I printed it off so I'd have a record of it but I had to delete it from the site because we can't publish stuff like that. It's against the rules.'

'Brian,' Jillian said, pushing another piece of paper across the table, 'here are a number of email addresses and passwords. These were found at your home with the list of judges' addresses. Are these your email addresses?'

'Nope,' he said, although now he looked slightly troubled.

McClintock took up a sheet of ISP reports and pushed them towards Shanahan. 'Do you know what these are?'

'Nope.'

'These reports tell us the ISP addresses for particular pieces of information on the internet – social media posts, emails, web pages. What these reports reveal is that someone using your ISP, and using the email accounts we previously showed to you, was sending Judge Bailey abusive and threatening emails.'

'Oh,' Shanahan said. 'Fancy that.'

'Can you provide an explanation for this?'

'Nope.'

McClintock produced print-outs of several of the emails. 'Have a read through these, Brian, let us know when you're done.'

The former teacher scanned each page efficiently, looking put out. 'So?' he said when he had finished.

'Do you remember sending those, Brian?'

'No. Because I didn't send them.'

Jillian showed him a selection of the photos of penises that Kaye Bailey had received. 'Do these ring a bell, Brian?'

This time he recoiled slightly. 'That's not me!' he said. 'What would I want to send pictures of a bunch of dicks for?'

'For the same reason that you might want to send a bunch of nasty emails?'

'No,' he said, crossing his arms. 'Wouldn't bother. That judge wasn't worth the effort. And I wouldn't send those, they're filthy.' Jillian thought he might be telling the truth this time.

'Do you know Christianne D'Santo?' she asked.

'Nope, who's that?'

'She was Judge Bailey's associate. A security pass went missing from her desk in court last year. Coincidentally on the same day that someone entered Judge Bailey's chambers and stole her wallet, and, also coincidentally, the same day that you were at court for a hearing. Judge Bailey noticed you in her courtroom that day.'

'Never happened,' Shanahan said.

McClintock produced another page, this time a laboratory report comparing the eyelash that had been caught under the tape on the envelope containing the earrings with Brian Shanahan's DNA profile.

'You left a trace, Brian,' McClintock said. 'You left an eyelash and it matches the DNA sample you so reluctantly provided to us.'

Brian Shanahan took a moment to process this information. Jillian could see his mind working through the possibilities. Finally he said, 'That's impossible, that's bullshit. You're stitching me up and you know it.'

'Tell us where Harriet is, Brian,' McClintock said. 'If you help us now it'll be a lot better for you than waiting for us to find her on our own. And we will find her.'

'I want a lawyer,' Brian Shanahan said. 'I'm not saying another word until they arrive.'

CHAPTER 33

'L awyer can't get here until first thing tomorrow,' Des said. It was eleven-thirty and the older detective looked exhausted. 'We'll hold him overnight, chat again in the morning. Let him stew for a bit.'

'Sounds good,' Jillian said.

'Is it too early to have a celebratory drink?' Mossman asked.

Des looked interested. 'Maybe a quick one. Need to go somewhere shit, it's a Friday night, I'm too old to deal with crowds.'

'Shall we say the Duke's Arms in half an hour?'

McClintock slapped his hands together. 'I'm gonna ride there,' he said. 'I'll get changed and head over, try and get a table.'

'Okay, see you there,' Jillian said. The day had been so frantic she had barely looked at her mobile. She checked her messages. Aaron had sent through a picture of Ollie sleeping in the cot at his grandmother's house.

Jillian thought back over the past few tumultuous weeks and was surprised that she didn't feel a greater sense of achievement at being so near the end of the case. She could not work out what was bothering her, professionally at least. On the personal level, well, that was another matter.

*

Des mopped at his brow with a serviette and got to his feet. 'That's me out,' he said, looking at his watch. 'We've got Adam coming over for breakfast in the morning with the girls, and Deb will bite my head off if I'm too seedy to help out.'

It was not unusual for Des to speak this way about his wife. Jillian had met Debbie multiple times over the course of working with Des, and the impression he gave of her – as being a tiny shrew with a huge mouth and the capacity to scream the house down – was completely at odds with the sweet, quietly spoken woman who attended the Christmas parties with gifts for everyone.

We can all be someone else behind closed doors.

'That's me off too,' Mossman said, getting giddily to her feet and banging into the next table. 'There's a train in ten.' Jillian imagined her arriving home to her children slightly the worse for wear. Mossman's husband was a police officer too and Jillian wondered how they managed that – not just the hours, but the inevitable trauma, the need to blow off steam.

Her mind returned to Harriet Phillips, who was around the same age as Debbie. How different those two women were, as different as Jillian was from either of them. All of them mothers, though. Each had gone through the wretched process of giving their bodies over to a child. Each had presumably done the best they could within the limitations they faced.

She pulled herself out of her thoughts and saw it was just her and McClintock still in the pub. 'Come on, my round,' she told him. Her voice sounded blurry and far away and her cheeks felt numb. 'What will you have?'

'A soda water with lime, please. But only if you're getting yourself something.'

Jillian was startled. 'Soda water? You got something on tomorrow?'

'No,' he said briskly. 'I don't drink.'

'Yes you do,' she insisted.

'No. I don't.'

'You were hungover the other day,' she said. 'You looked dreadful.'

McClintock laughed. 'Did I just? Thanks for that. You realise you told me off for saying the same thing to you in the car outside Sharma's house? You made me promise never to say anything like it again.'

Jillian had to laugh too. 'You're right. I really did.'

He smiled at her, a relaxed, more genuine smile than the one he used to charm reluctant witnesses.

'I can't believe you don't drink,' she said when she returned from the bar with his soda water and her own gin and tonic. 'I feel so betrayed. Why were you all seedy the other morning then?'

McClintock looked at her as though deciding whether or not to tell her. 'Actually,' he said finally, 'I was studying all night.'

'You were? What are you studying?'

For someone usually so sure of himself, he looked bashful.

'Law,' he said. 'Well, I'm studying to get into a law degree.'

'Wow. So you want to go to the dark side?' Jillian took a chip from the bowl Des had left half eaten on the table.

'Yeah, I do. I actually got accepted after high school but I dropped out. Then I became a cop and realised I'd made a mistake. So now I'm trying to sit the LSAT, get in as a postgrad.'

'Well, that's cool,' Jillian said. 'Why'd you drop out?'

McClintock looked down at his glass and poked the slice of lime listlessly. 'I wasn't very well.'

'As in . . .?'

'I had some issues. My dad passed away at the end of my second year. He was a nasty piece of work, a big drinker – actually, a total alcoholic is more like it. We had a difficult relationship and then, yeah, he died. I got fairly depressed after that. I couldn't study. I couldn't do anything, really. I had to sort myself out. So I travelled, focused on fitness, did criminology and eventually went into policing instead.' He sighed. 'Anyway, I'm ready now.'

'So that's why you don't drink? Because of your dad?'

'Partly, yeah.'

McClintock's revelation shocked her. She had not seen it coming, that this man who presented as so confident, so calm and self-assured, who she'd assumed had had a privileged life, had struggled so much. Aspects of his personality that she'd found at best perplexing and at worst irritating came into new focus. Were his fanatically clean car and desk a means of ensuring order in a mind that could become disturbed? Was his enthusiasm for sport a way of connecting with people that did not require him to drink? Was this why he had an obsession with healthy eating?

Jesus. I got him so wrong.

They were each silent. Jillian wanted to offer some sort of apology, for misjudging him, for not being more welcoming, but she wasn't sure how to say it.

Perhaps she looked troubled, because he asked, 'Are you okay?'

Two days ago she would have slapped him down for asking. Now she only sighed. 'No, actually,' she said. 'I don't think I am.'

Did I just admit that?

'What's happening?'

'Not sure where to start, really. I was miserable at home with Ollie so I came back to work. Then I got totally involved in the case and

I guess I used it as an excuse to avoid dealing with stuff.' She stopped, unsure how much to reveal. She took a risk and continued, 'Stuff that happened around Ollie's birth and afterwards. So now Aaron, my husband, has left, he's gone to his mum's place. With Ollie. I guess to give me an opportunity to decide whether I'm ready to deal with everything I went through.'

How strange it felt to have said all of that, to have released her most private worries into the universe where other people could acknowledge and respond to them, could judge her.

'What happened at Ollie's birth?' he asked.

'Well, nothing, but also everything.' She sighed. 'The birth was alright, fine really. A lot of women would kill for the type of birth I had. But a few hours after he was born, I started feeling really . . .' She searched for the right word. 'Wrong, maybe? I started having these weird thoughts, things I'd never have thought about previously. I'd be looking at him and my mind would be saying, "You know, you're going to ruin his life". The thoughts just went around and around in my head until they weren't just thoughts, they were gospel. And everything just escalated from there. I started thinking about him dying. Started thinking about me dying. Started thinking about whether or not I might hurt him. I didn't want to be alone with him – I worried that I'd do something terrible. Part of me knew I wouldn't, but another part would see me, like, putting a pillow over his face or something. It was awful. Then I decided I wouldn't get too attached to him, because it made me feel like a fraud, enjoying his company and thinking all these terrible things at the same time. I got to the point where I was really afraid to be around him. I didn't trust myself and I suppose I thought if he knew my face too well then it would be worse whenever the bad thing happened, whatever that might be.' Jillian stopped. 'Sorry, none of it makes much sense, I know.'

'Fuck,' McClintock said with genuine compassion.

'Yeah, it was really scary. I was okay for a little while after I got home from hospital; I could hold it together in front of Aaron at least. But one day, after he'd gone back to work, he must have been worried about me because he came home, and I'd gone out and left Ollie on his own. I just couldn't be around him. I was admitted to the mother and baby unit at the hospital for a bit, with Ollie, and because I'm good at talking the talk we didn't have to stay too long. But I wasn't better when we left, just pretending. Aaron was already onto me, of course, so he took leave and stayed home with Ollie. And in some ways that made it worse, because he was so bloody good at being a dad. There was no point me being home when I had nothing to contribute, so I went back to work. Aaron thinks I haven't really dealt with it all properly.'

'Well, have you?'

'No,' she said quietly. 'But the psychiatrist at the hospital, he asked me these horrible questions and then wrote down my answers. And then I had to see this psychologist but I just found her so judgemental and talking about it made it feel so much worse than keeping it inside and I don't want to do that again.'

'Talking to someone helps,' McClintock said with absolute certainty. 'Not straightaway maybe, but after a while. Trust me. I've done it.'

'Have you really?' She shouldn't have been surprised, not with what she'd heard tonight.

'Yup. I still go now, when I'm feeling a bit down. Just to get myself back on track. The other day, the day Harriet's earrings turned up at the court, I was late in because I'd gone to see my psychologist.'

Jillian had completely forgotten he'd even been late.

'The Rahul Sharma stuff,' McClintock went on, 'and Brian Shanahan too, they dragged up things I hadn't thought about for a while. My dad used to act the way Lisa Nettle describes Sharma acting. He was such a nice, smooth guy in front of a crowd, but the second no one else was around, he was the worst. He beat the shit out of Mum almost every day.'

'Jesus, that's dreadful, I'm sorry.'

'Thanks.'

'How are you feeling now?'

'Fine. Once I talked it out.'

Jillian looked at him. 'When you go to the psychologist, what do they ask you? When I've been, I just feel like I end up reliving the worst moments of my life. There's no catharsis or anything. It doesn't make me feel better at all.'

He smiled slightly. 'It does suck, I agree. But if you can find the right person to talk to, and the right type of treatment, it will be okay. You don't even realise how much it helps at the very start. You know, I thought you might have been going through something. You just don't talk about your kid, you get weird whenever other people mention babies, and I remember you being lively in training. You were funny! These days you seem kind of flat. Plus there was that panic attack at the hospital.'

'Oh. I thought I got away with that. The smells triggered me.'

'Also, everyone always said how collaborative you were, how good you were to work with, how generous. I was really excited when I found out I was going to be on the same team as you. But you always seem like you just want to get on with it by yourself.'

Jillian found it hard hearing this. She knew it was true.

'Talk to someone,' he said again. 'You won't regret it.'

He got to his feet. 'I'm going to head off. We've got a lot on tomorrow. You right to get home? Need me to dink you to Yarraville?'

She laughed. 'I'll grab a cab, but thanks for the offer.'

Outside the pub, he unlocked his bike and bid her goodnight. Jillian walked towards the city, looking for a taxi. She passed a saxophonist playing 'Moon Dance', and as the music bounced along the street she felt almost festive. She had told McClintock her deepest fears and the sky hadn't fallen in. She hunted in her bag for a coin, turned back and placed it in the busker's sax case.

Ahead of her a cab was idling in a loading zone. She knocked on the window but the driver shook his head. 'Sorry, I'm waiting for someone,' he said through the glass.

Waiting for someone.

The second no one was around.

In that moment, the events of the last few weeks fell into place.

Oh my god. I know exactly what happened.

She woke in the morning to the edges of a headache and a text message from McClintock.

There's a postnatal anxiety disorder program run out of the Women's. Strictly outpatient. You can get referred by your GP. If you aren't meshing with your current psych, this might be another option. – Mick

She replayed their conversation from the night before, not feeling mortified as she might have expected, but almost proud. She had opened up and she had survived. She googled the program he had suggested and left an urgent message with her GP requesting a referral be written for her first thing on Monday morning.

I can do this.

She showered and when she next looked at her phone there was a text from Des sent to both her and McClintock. *Just spoken to higher-ups re Shanahan. Lawyer not coming until Shanahan's brother puts funds in trust. Apparently Shanahan burnt him a few years ago and he's refusing to risk it. Will hold until first thing Monday. Only come in if you need to.*

Jillian tapped out a response. *That's fine. I put a few things together last night. I think I know how everything went down.*

Within seconds both Des and McClintock had tried to call her.

I'll explain soon. Just got some family stuff to do first.

Jillian showered, changed and checked the time. She wanted to call Aaron, but it was still early and if he had had a bad night with Ollie she might wake him up. Feeling nervous, she left the house. As she walked a meandering route from Yarraville to her mother-in-law's home in Seddon she thought about how simple it all now seemed – of course she needed treatment, of course it would be hard, but of course it would be worth it.

At nine-thirty she knocked on the door of Margot's house feeling anxious, hoping she had not misjudged the situation and that her presence would be welcome. She needed to look Aaron in the eye and promise to do better, because that was what he and Ollie deserved.

Jillian dreaded the sight of Margot, her concerned face as she made herself scarce or offered to take Ollie while 'Mummy and Daddy talk'. At the same time she felt the beginnings of guilt for the way she had treated her mother-in-law, who unfailingly provided the guidance and affection that Jillian's own mother did not.

Aaron opened the door, Ollie in his arms. 'Hi,' he said, his eyes widening.

Surprised but not unhappy. That's good.

'Hello,' she said, already feeling tears welling. 'Can I come in? You were right. You were right about everything. I know I need to do something about it. I'm just really bloody scared. What if I end up in hospital again? What if I end up institutionalised? What if we end up divorced? What if I'm just a really awful mum like mine and I ruin Ollie's life?'

Aaron opened the door wider to let her through and she impulsively threw herself into his arms. 'I'm so sorry,' she said, 'so sorry. I'm going to do better. I've asked for a referral to a postnatal anxiety program and I'm going to go to every session and do whatever they tell me to do.'

Aaron held her, rocking her back and forth with Ollie nestled between them, gripping her hair in his little hands. 'It's alright,' Aaron said, 'it's alright. You've got this and I'm going to help you.'

'I've been such an awful mother. I guess I just felt like there was no chance for him with me,' she sobbed.

Aaron laughed. 'Well, there's no chance for me without you, so I say we both just sort ourselves out.'

CHAPTER 34

'I still don't understand why we're here,' McClintock said by way of greeting when they met outside the Commonwealth Law Courts the following Monday morning. The building had almost returned to its pre-tragedy state – the only evidence of anything amiss was the uniformed officer stationed next to the door, and a sign warning practitioners and litigants that they could only be admitted fifteen minutes before a scheduled court list. 'Can't you put me out of my misery now?'

'I told you my theory,' she said. 'We know Kaye didn't do anything by halves. If I'm right, the other things she was doing to help weren't enough. She'll have wanted to do this too. But we won't know for sure until we hear the judgement, and I've confirmed with Grant Phillips that that will be this morning.'

'Hmmm,' said McClintock. 'I reckon we're going to have more than enough anyway, assuming you're right about Harriet.'

Jillian looked at her watch. 'We should find out about that pretty soon, I reckon. And if I'm wrong, we'll be back in time to chat to Shanahan and his lawyer.'

They were too early to be admitted, and rather than stand in line they ordered coffees and sat in the cafe, watching as the lost souls of the court system began to arrive.

'I'll be glad to see the last of this place,' McClintock said, taking a sip of his latte. 'Bloody miserable.'

'Me too. My parents went through it when I was young. Not over me, but the property. I can still remember my mother crying into the phone whenever she talked to her lawyer.'

'Yeah, my cousin's –' He stopped. 'Hello,' he said, 'look who's here.'

Jillian turned to follow his gaze and saw Rahul Sharma in a dark suit and neatly pressed white shirt. He had the spring in his step of a man expecting good things to come. He was with a young woman, very blonde, wearing a pair of red Christian Louboutin heels. As she neared the building she stopped to take a selfie on her phone, before joining Sharma in the line.

So that must be the personal trainer?

Helen McPherson arrived shortly afterwards wearing thick-heeled shoes and an unflattering suit. She looked towards the detectives and then away.

'Doesn't want to say hello then?' McClintock said with interest.

A few moments later Lisa Nettle walked past, her hair freshly blown out.

'Surely Phillips shouldn't be dealing with the matter if he's having a thing with the solicitor,' McClintock said. 'That doesn't seem ethical.'

'I suppose it wasn't his matter to start with, and now he's only reading out someone else's judgement.' She had not yet had an opportunity to ask the older judge about his relationship with Helen McPherson. McClintock had thought it unnecessary anyway – 'marriages are complex' he had said wisely – but Jillian viewed the confident solicitor as a loose end.

'Shall we?' she said when they'd finished their coffees, and they took their places in the line.

As they waited for their bags to be checked at the security counter, Jillian eavesdropped on the lawyers surrounding them. Virginia Maiden's abrupt resignation was a topic of much speculation and an apparent relief to many of those who had appeared before her. Others wondered aloud about Saul Meyers' new replacement. 'It's a damn shame about Kaye,' one barrister sighed to his instructor, 'she would have worked wonders in this place.'

Inside, the vast majority of people were congregated at the still locked door to courtroom 2A. Rahul Sharma had positioned himself in the middle of a long bench, the young woman next to him. They both eyeballed Lisa Nettle who stood with her besuited lawyer outside the interview room in which Jillian had interviewed the judges in the immediate aftermath of Kaye Bailey's murder. Sharma immediately averted his gaze from the detectives, while Lisa gave a nod of recognition. Presently, the courtroom door was opened from the inside and Christianne D'Santo emerged. She stuck a piece of paper to the outside of the door. There was only one matter listed before Grant Phillips, 'Sharma & Nettle & Independent Children's Lawyer'.

Christianne gave the detectives a smile before allowing the crowd entry. Jillian and McClintock stood at the back of the room as she greeted the parties and marked their appearances then moved the judge's chair into its position. She disappeared and a moment later three knocks reverberated from the other side of the far wall. 'Silence, all stand and remain standing,' Christianne called. 'The Federal Circuit Court of Australia is now in session.'

Grant Phillips appeared at the bench, where he nodded to those below.

'Please be seated,' Christianne directed. 'Calling the matter of Sharma and Nettle.'

Lisa Nettle, who was sitting in the front row of the gallery, turned to watch as her ex-husband made his appearance and confirmed he was self-representing. Her lawyer followed suit, as did Helen McPherson.

Embarrassed, maybe? I would be.

'Well now,' Grant Phillips said, looking around the crowded courtroom, 'I must say I did anticipate something of an audience, although perhaps not this extensive. Before I pronounce the orders, I would like to make some comments. The first is this – the court orders contained herein and the reasons for judgement are not for outside publication. While I understand that there is public interest in this matter, the interest here is not sufficient for me to consider denying the parties, and more importantly their children, privacy. Any mention of this matter in the news media including social media will be a violation of section 121 of the *Family Law Act*. I have no doubt everyone will do the right thing.'

He looked around the room again, his eyes finding Jillian's and widening ever so slightly. 'I also want to note explicitly that the reasons herein are the reasons as determined by my sister, Her Honour Judge Bailey, who is sadly no longer with us. I would also like to thank the parties and the other people involved in this matter for their patience. I know you have been waiting for this judgement for some time, and that it can be tempting in circumstances such as these to lose faith in the justice system. I hope that today can provide some resolution.' He gave each party a brief smile before clearing his throat.

'I confirm the orders made are as follows. First, with regard to parenting, I order that the mother, Ms Lisa Nettle, have sole parental responsibility for the children. Second, that the children live with the mother . . .'

There had not been sufficient time between the first and second orders being pronounced for those watching to react immediately, but by the end of the second order there was a low murmur throughout the gallery, and from Lisa Nettle's end of the bar table.

Jillian could not see Rahul Sharma's face but she noticed an abrupt stiffening in his shoulders. The woman accompanying him let out a loud theatrical wail. The doctor paid her no notice. Grant Phillips also ignored the woman's outburst as he continued to pronounce the orders.

'Third, that the mother be restrained from consuming alcohol to excess while the children are in her care. Fourth, that the father spend time with the children for one weekend per month from nine am to five pm on either the Saturday or Sunday as nominated by the mother. Fifth, that both parties are restrained from discussing these proceedings with the children or within hearing of the children.'

Jillian's mind turned to the manner in which Michael O'Neil had described Kaye Bailey's agony over her recommendations, so troubled was she by having to choose which parent would harm the children less. What was it, Jillian wondered, that drew people to this world, where the administration of justice routinely meant the lesser of two evils?

Grant Phillips read on, through a long and prescriptive succession of parenting orders. Jillian was astounded by the breadth of them. Orders were made allowing the mother to travel with the children, to obtain passports for them without Rahul Sharma's involvement, and restraining both parties from discussing the proceedings with the children. Lisa Nettle began to weep, while her former husband's posture became more and more tense.

Grant Phillips took a deep breath. 'And now for the property,' he said. 'First, I order that the father retain for his sole use and possession:

a) the former matrimonial home at Summers Road, Brighton; b) the property situated at 12 Longhorne Street, Port Melbourne; c) the property situated at 9 Main Street, Portsea, this being the property referred to as 'The Portsea Property'; and any other real property in which he has an interest. Second, that the husband pay to the wife the sum of eight hundred and sixty-four thousand dollars.'

Lisa Nettle reached for her lawyer. 'How much is that?' she mouthed. 'I don't think it's enough.' The lawyer waved her client silent.

'Third,' said Grant Phillips, 'I order that the parties each retain the motor vehicles currently in their possession and do all necessary things and sign all necessary documents to transfer those motor vehicles into their respective names.'

'What about the Lexus?' Lisa Nettle whispered loudly to her lawyer. 'Didn't we ask for that?'

As the judge moved on to superannuation, Jillian overheard a robed barrister nearby whisper to another, 'How much do you reckon that is in percentages?'

'Not enough,' the other responded. 'It can't even be five per cent of the asset pool. I reckon Bailey actually did it.'

'Did what?' whispered McClintock to Jillian. 'Do you reckon . . .'

'Finally,' Grant Phillips announced, 'I order that the mother receive $2.9 million dollars, to be transferred into a bank account as nominated by her within twenty-eight days, to be characterised as damages for the psychological and physical abuse and their ongoing impacts, which I find on the balance of probabilities were more likely than not committed by the husband.'

This time the astonishment in the room was not discreet.

'Told you,' the barrister said to his friend.

'Damages! She actually did it!'

'Grant looks physically repulsed by the idea,' whispered someone else, and Jillian thought he indeed appeared to have just eaten something sour. He leaned down and whispered something to Christianne, who glanced at the detectives and nodded.

'I publish my reasons. My associate will hand copies to each of you shortly. We'll adjourn, thanks Christianne,' Grant Phillips announced loudly. The associate directed the attendees to stand and the judge briefly bowed and left the courtroom.

When everyone else had left, Christianne approached the detectives. 'His Honour says he'll come right back in as soon as I lock up. I assumed you wanted to speak to him?'

'Thank you,' Jillian said. 'We do. But could you just give us one minute first?'

The associate obediently disappeared behind the bench and they heard the door close.

Jillian pulled out her phone and called Mossman. 'Was I right?' she asked.

'You were.'

'About everything?'

'About everything,' Mossman confirmed.

'Great. Could you get her to talk to the law firm straightaway, and give them my email.'

'Yup, already done.'

Jillian looked at McClintock. 'We're good to go,' she said. 'They've got Harriet.'

CHAPTER 35

Grant Phillips burst back in as Jillian was explaining to McClintock the exact circumstances in which Harriet had been found. Christianne followed close behind him.

'Is it Harriet? Is that why you're here – you've found her?' the judge asked. He walked through the gate protecting his bench from the public gallery and met the detectives at the bar table.

'We have,' Jillian said, watching his face. A strange look flashed across it to be replaced instantly by nervous excitement.

'And is she alright?'

'She is.'

He sat down heavily. 'Thank the gods,' he said. 'I was so sure he'd have killed her. When can I see her? Where is she?'

'Our colleagues are taking her down to the station right now. We can take you to her.'

'Of course, wonderful. I don't have anything else listed. Can we just nick up to chambers? I'll get my jacket and phone.'

The judge shot the detectives a dozen rushed questions as they escorted him upstairs. 'Where did you find her? And how? When? Who was she with? I mean, who was responsible...' As they passed

Angela Hui's office, the registry manager caught sight of them and gestured for them to come in.

'I'll go,' McClintock said, 'I'll catch you up in a sec.'

As he walked into the room, Jillian heard Angela say, 'You were right. They are missing.'

In his chambers, Grant Phillips removed his judicial robe and retrieved his mobile. He put it in his jacket pocket, felt the left-hand side for his car keys and looked expectantly towards Jillian. McClintock reappeared at her side carrying a large box marked 'Shanahan exhibits'.

The judge's eyes twitched slightly and he reached up and rubbed at them.

He's nervous but playing it as cool as he can.

'How is she mentally?' he asked the detectives as they waited for the lift. 'Was she, you know, with it? Was she making sense? Has she seen a doctor?'

'Our colleagues have confirmed she's very delicate – no physical injuries, though, and we'll have her seen by a doctor as soon as we can. It sounds like she's been through a lot.'

'Oh Jesus,' the judge replied. 'Oh god. My poor girl.'

At level two the lift opened. 'Shall we keep going to the carpark?' he said. 'I can take my own car, that way I can take Hari –'

Jillian shook her head. 'We're going to drive,' she told him. 'Because we're arresting you for the murder of Kaye Bailey.'

Grant Phillips had a way of sitting that conveyed relaxed charm, even within the confines of a police interview room. His long legs were stretched out to the side of his chair, crossed at the ankle, and he sat back, one arm on the table. It was the way he had sat that first day at the court, when Jillian had watched the judges wait for Saul Meyers to deliver that terrible news. It was also an act, she now realised, an assumed informality designed to win others over. The anxious excitement he had initially played at was gone. However he might appear, he was now on the defensive, and, she was sure, making mental calculations about what exactly they knew and what Harriet might have told them.

How did I not see it before?

'Look,' the judge said as soon as they walked into the interview room, 'I don't know what Harriet's told you but I can assure you that I did not murder Kaye. Harriet will just be in the midst of an episode. Has she been given medical attention, has anyone spoken to her psychiatrist?' He said this lightly, as though it were obvious, as though this were something that could be quickly sorted out between friends.

'Well,' said Jillian, sitting down, 'interestingly, we've been trying to get in touch with her health services for the last few hours – with her permission, of course. And the curious thing is, aside from the family doctor, who says you always attend her appointments with her, no one else has really had much involvement with her. The Melbourne Clinic denied any knowledge of her, as did every psychiatrist we spoke to. There was really only the ED doctor you took her to a few months ago, about a very nasty burn on her left hand. He remembers you making a point of saying it was self-inflicted, another of your wife's self-harm incidents, but actually, he reckons you did it to her.'

Grant Phillips' pupils contracted fleetingly, but he recovered quickly. 'Look, she's said this kind of thing before, very convincingly too, but it's part of her illness.'

'Judge Phillips, we'd like to put some things to you now, information that we've put together over the course of our investigation. Did you want a lawyer?'

For the first time, Jillian witnessed undisguised anger on his face, the anger that Harriet Phillips had lived with for most of her adult life. 'No, I don't need a lawyer,' he said sarcastically. 'I seem to remember being one.' It was jarring, seeing this side of him, when he could be so skilfully amicable.

'Well then, let's proceed. We've finally obtained information from the law firm that Kaye engaged. For a long time we just couldn't figure out why they were being so obtuse, but we now know that it was because the funds Kaye transferred into their account weren't for her, they were for Harriet. For the application she's making for a property settlement against you, which we understand is going to be filed shortly. Harriet gave permission for the law firm to speak to us when we located her this morning. I expect you'll get served quite soon.'

The judge did not say a word, but his feet began to tap the ground with rhythmic urgency.

'They couldn't tell us earlier, of course, because they were obligated to protect Harriet's privacy. And, I imagine, they were probably concerned for her safety.' Jillian produced the photo from Kaye's phone of the bruised torso. 'That's Harriet,' she said. 'Taken the night of a gala function you attended on 16 December 2017 and saved on Kaye Bailey's mobile. That was the night your wife told Kaye what had really been going on. It was also the night Kaye began to help her plan her escape. We think you were probably a bit distracted that night, which meant Harriet was able to extricate herself briefly. We're told you were busy feeling up Helen McPherson in a stairwell.'

Still the judge did not respond, but his expression was icy.

'My best guess,' Jillian went on, 'is that Harriet was planning to make a run for it on the night of the retirement party. It was probably her first opportunity in ages. She couldn't leave from home; you had the house covered in cameras, alarms and locks that you could monitor remotely. She couldn't leave on the trip into court, either. She didn't have any money and I'm guessing she thought your driver would call you immediately if she tried to bolt. We think Kaye organised it so that there was a taxi waiting downstairs for her. We also think that was why Kaye slipped her the hundred bucks, to get her into a taxi and to the women's refuge in Preston that was expecting her. But she dropped the money and was worried you were suspicious, and that you wouldn't let her out of your sight. So she waited for the next possible time, which was the wake.

'The wake and the funeral were interesting for a few reasons, actually,' Jillian said. 'One thing that kept being mentioned was Kaye's persistence, how doing an alright job wasn't enough for her. It wasn't enough just to help Harriet escape from you, she wanted to ensure that you'd get as little as possible from the property settlement. I watched your face as you read out the award for damages in the Sharma judgement. You knew what those orders would mean for you if Harriet ever took you to court. You must have been so nervous after she disappeared, wondering whether she had actually attempted suicide or just done a runner and might turn up again in the future. You just had to hold out hope that you'd convinced enough people she was crazy.'

Phillips maintained his silence and his icy stare.

'Do you know what this is?' Jillian produced an unsigned affidavit for one Kim Surle of 42 Lane Street, South Geelong, retail employee.

Phillips leaned forward slightly to look at the document. 'Never seen it before in my life.'

'Kim Surle was an old client of yours from years back – I asked you about her, remember? You told Kaye at the end of the day in court that you'd be willing to forgo your fee, then you phoned Kim and told her in no uncertain terms how she was to repay you. It seems as though Kaye ran into her completely by chance. Kim refused to sign the affidavit, she told Kaye she'd put all that behind her, she didn't want to get involved. But there are seven others, all on affidavits that Kaye prepared herself. They all tell pretty much the same story from what we can see. That is, Kaye briefs you to act for a vulnerable woman – either the victim of abuse or just poor, and you agree, put on the charm offensive, and afterwards call in the favour. Pro bono for sex.

'Kaye sent all the affidavits to that law firm, ostensibly for Harriet's case, but part of me thinks she might have been a little worried something might happen to her. The thing I find particularly interesting about the affidavits is that the first one was prepared before Kaye knew anything about your abuse of Harriet. She'd been onto you for a long time. That's why she was so keen to have that meeting with Saul – not just about Virginia Maiden and her conflict of interest, or Kaye's fears for her own safety, but also because of you. Your old boss confirmed that she alerted him to your behaviour in early October last year. We think that was when one of her old clients called her out of the blue to tell her what had happened. She acted quickly. Saul wasn't keen to pursue it, obviously, and in normal circumstances Kaye would just have kept pushing – we think at one stage she might even have been planning to resign just to try and force his hand. But then once she realised what was happening with Harriet, she needed to balance Harriet's safety with her desire to show everyone who you were.

'Which brings us to the point of speculation and motive. This is what I think happened the night you murdered Kaye. Feel free to interrupt if I've got something wrong. I think Saul Meyers, who was very drunk and had no love for Kaye, tipped you off that she'd been trying to complain about you. He was angry with her for embarrassing him at this party and doubtless didn't realise just what you were capable of, so he spilled.

'You were absolutely livid. You probably wanted to kill her then and there, but couldn't go straight in and confront her, because there were people everywhere. You drove home, got Harriet safely contained, left your mobile behind and returned to the city on the fabulous Pinarello bicycle we saw hanging in your garage and which I'm guessing you still ride from time to time. You left the bike some distance from the courts. You knew there was no security that night – did that feel like the gods giving you permission? Whatever, by this stage, Saul and Virginia and the judgement were long gone.'

Jillian looked hard at him for a few moments, waiting for some acknowledgement of subsequent events to show on his face. 'So you showed yourself into her chambers, confronted her and killed her.'

When he remained close-lipped, she sighed. 'You know how to clean up a crime scene, of course, after all those years doing criminal law. You were meticulous. Then afterwards, in the early days of the investigation, you kept your ears open, waiting to hear what we were thinking, who we were suspicious of. My guess is initially you thought to frame Michael O'Neil – you didn't know he had a watertight alibi early on. Then you saw an opportunity in Brian Shanahan. You knew about the security breach last year, which was perfect.

'And then Harriet made a run for it. She was fearful of us discovering – you discovering – what the money paid to the law firm was for. But ironically her disappearance helped you, in one way; it created an opportunity for you to point us back to Shanahan. We've confirmed with Angela that the eyelash was part of one of his court files, it was an exhibit. An exhibit that weirdly went missing just recently. He did love sending strange things to his exes, one of whom got a whole collection of eyelashes, plus fingernails and two used condoms. The note was from his court file too. A little letter he'd sent to an ex that was conveniently vague but threatening.'

Still Phillips did not talk.

'I imagine that Harriet doing a runner scared you quite a bit, though. You didn't know what had happened, whether or not she had actually gone to kill herself. But you were confident that you'd undermined her sufficiently to anyone who mattered that no one would believe any stories about family violence. And that anything else she said would be dismissed as the delusion of a crazy person.'

She stopped. Waited. And finally Grant Phillips spoke.

'Look,' he said, as though trying to reason with an obstinate toddler, 'I can see you've worked very hard on this but the conclusions you've drawn are insulting and frankly ridiculous.' He spoke in the same pleasant tone he always used, except it was no longer smooth and comforting, now it was chilling. 'I'd like to talk to someone higher up.' He went to stand.

'Sit down,' Jillian directed. 'We haven't finished yet.'

He did not move.

'She told you to sit down,' McClintock growled, and Phillips reluctantly returned to his seat.

Of course – he needs a man to tell him.

While Grant Phillips remained in the interview room for the bureaucratic process that followed significant charges, Jillian and

McClintock met with Harriet Phillips, who had been brought into the station some hours earlier. Without the fear for her physical safety, she was ever so slightly more relaxed. She was rereading the draft statement Mossman had already prepared with her, in anticipation of signing before the day was through.

Taking a seat opposite her, Jillian felt ashamed of her earlier blindness to Harriet's suffering.

'I'm so very sorry,' she said, 'that I didn't realise what was happening sooner.'

Harriet mustered a half-smile and took Jillian and McClintock through a little of her history with the charming Grant Phillips. She told them how they had met when she was nineteen and he was twenty-four. How she had married him a year later and thereafter become his prisoner. She told them how she was expected to cater to his every whim in private and treated as some precious, delicate princess in public. When she displeased him she was made to sleep on the floor, and to eat dog food. She was trapped within the appearance of upper-middle-class respectability and trotted out on a thousand different occasions where she would be referred to as crazy and treated with contempt. Her self-esteem, already delicate, disappeared. The easiest way to exist was to capitulate. Phillips told her that if she left he would make sure she never saw their son again, and she believed him because he knew the law and she didn't. As soon as Damien was old enough she told him he needed to leave, and he did. Then Phillips told her that if she left, he would kill her. 'Every morning, I thought, "Today he'll kill me",' Harriet said. 'And until Kaye came along I completely believed that.'

She confirmed that on the night of the party, Kaye had arranged for a taxi to wait outside and had slipped her a hundred dollars. 'But then I dropped it, stupid clumsy Harriet, and after that he was really suspicious. It was as though he knew something was up and I was so spooked I didn't want to try and leave. That night, on the car ride home he said to me, "You know if you try and make a run for it I'll kill Brasher?" I decided that was it. I wouldn't try again, but then when I found out what had happened to Kaye, I figured it was probably him, and then, well, he killed Brasher anyway. It was punishment for burning his toast that morning. The funny thing was, after that I knew I had to go and I knew the funeral might be my only opportunity. And staying would have been so insulting to Kaye's memory.'

Her plan had been to remain at the refuge until she felt it was safe, then travel to Sydney to sign the court documents and begin the litigation process. 'Kaye had thought of everything,' she said sadly. 'She assumed I'd be able to get out the night of the party, and that she'd be able to help, but there was also a whole network of people she'd set up for me, all ready and waiting.' She began to sob. 'I will feel responsible for her death for the rest of my life.'

'You have nothing to feel responsible for,' McClintock said. 'Just feel grateful that you had the opportunity to cross paths with two such brave, clever women.'

'Two?' Jillian said, and McClintock smiled.

He's talking about me.

'And an excellent man too.'

EPILOGUE

A feeble sunlight pawed at the brown water of the Yarra River as Jillian waited for McClintock and Des. They did not typically do breakfast meetings, Des not being a morning person, but the events of the past weeks had unfolded with such cascading urgency that there'd been no time to debrief, to touch on the things that had particularly surprised or outraged them, to try to find some black humour in the misery.

It was just after eight and Jillian had been awake since five, when Ollie had emitted his first shriek of the day. She had taken him into the lounge room for breakfast, and they sat with the low murmur of the television news. She was creating an intimacy with her son, though it did not come naturally to her – the soothing, the petting, the purposeful affection. She was not a physically expressive person. Her new psychologist had insisted, however, that every interaction made a difference, brought her a fraction closer to Ollie, and that one day it would be incomprehensible to her that they had not always been bonded.

Things will get better. You just need to do the work and have a little faith in yourself.

Jillian had taken additional time off in the aftermath of Grant Phillips' arrest. It had been difficult, for a woman who so loved

319

being in control, to allow her colleagues to begin the next stage of proceedings without her, but there were more important things that required her attention.

She had obtained the referral for intensive treatment of the anxiety that she now acknowledged had continued to plague her. Three times a week she attended individual and group therapy. Three times a week Aaron came with her and held her hand as she recounted in detail the strain that becoming a mother had placed on her and her understanding of herself, how it had undermined her self-confidence in her capacity as an adult and her ability to love. Things were slowly getting better. There were times now, small and fleeting, when she would experience a pang of love for her child so strong that it hurt her chest. It was terrifying. It was invigorating.

She yawned as she swiped through the photos she'd taken of her son, her fingernails still the lightest brown from the hair dye she'd used the week before – a necessary step towards returning to her old self.

She looked around for her colleagues as she reached for her coffee. The first signs of spring were beginning to show themselves, in the tentative blossom buds, the nesting birds, the sweetness in the air. Commuters were belching out of Flinders Street Station subway at regular intervals. In another month or so these people wearing heavy coats and puffing condensation through lips dry with cold would be in short sleeves and sunglasses.

'You good?' McClintock asked, approaching from behind in his full riding kit. She had barely spoken to him in the days since Grant Phillips' arrest; he had been consumed with the process of moving things from the investigation to the prosecution stage and she with family.

'I'm okay, you?'

'I was up until three writing my law school application letter.' He yawned dramatically.

'Oh god, you should have cancelled.'

'Nothing a coffee won't fix.' He ordered with a beatific smile to the waitress and Jillian laughed.

He honestly can't help himself.

'There's the boss man,' McClintock said on seeing Des loping along the path. It was strange to see Des outside the comfort of his office at any time of day, but it was particularly odd at such an early hour.

'Morning,' McClintock said brightly.

Des grunted. 'What bloody time do we call this anyway?'

'He needs a coffee to warm up,' Jillian said.

When he was sufficiently caffeinated and meals had been ordered, Des was able to speak. 'You chat to the prosecutor?' he asked McClintock.

'Yup, she was happy. Obviously still wants a few more things from us, but she seemed optimistic. She said it was inevitable that he'd get home detention rather than being sent off to the Remand Centre.'

'That seems a bit unfair when Brian Shanahan is on remand – he didn't actually kill anyone.' The different holding patterns for the two arrests ate at Jillian. Grant Phillips, with his long history of domestic violence and harassment of women, and facing a murder charge, would be confined to his stately home where to some extent his life could carry on as usual. Meanwhile a man who had not killed anyone, however disgusting his other activities were, was now being held in a concrete box not much larger than he was.

Justice isn't perfect. Justice isn't even just.

'You'd prefer Shanahan back in his caravan plotting how to make his new wife miserable?' McClintock asked.

'Not at all, I'm just saying there's a disparity there.'

'At least,' McClintock said, 'Phillips' reputation is well and truly muddied now; even if he gets off on the murder charge, he'll still be a pariah. And Angela Hui told me the allegations against him have been referred to parliament. The allegations against Maiden too.'

'Saul Meyers ran a loose ship,' Jillian said. 'If Kaye Bailey had lived to take over that place...'

Their meals arrived – eggs benedict for Des, a protein bowl for McClintock, French toast for Jillian. The man at the next table began watching a YouTube report on the imminent cricket tour in South Africa.

'Smith'll get us over the line,' McClintock said confidently.

'He's a bloody idiot,' Des said. 'The whole lot of them are hopeless and he's the worst.'

McClintock signalled the waitress for another coffee then said to Jillian, 'Did you eat all my cashews? The ones in the green tub on my desk?'

'I did. But I bought you a new packet. They're in my bag.'

'I didn't mind, just wondering,' he said with a smile. 'Feeling pretty comfortable, are we?'

'I get very comfortable when there are snacks around.'

'You've opened a can of worms there, mate,' Des told McClintock. 'I once made the mistake of telling her where I kept my Tim Tam stash. She ate me out of them in a day.'

'Alright, alright!' Jillian said in mock annoyance. 'That's enough. I have more news – Harriet Phillips called me late last night. Poor thing, I don't think she really has anyone much to talk to yet, he basically controlled her every interaction for their entire marriage.'

'How's she going?' McClintock asked.

'She's okay. She's in Sydney. Her first hearing is next week. She said she's got a psychologist lined up, and that everyone believes her, which she sounded genuinely surprised about. I hope she finds her feet and he doesn't drag it all out unnecessarily.'

"Course he will, it's the last way he has of exercising control over her,' said McClintock. 'By the way, I still don't totally understand how she got out, of the wake, I mean, and over to the refuge.'

'Do you remember that woman at the funeral on crutches? Sigourney. Kaye had worded her up that Harriet might need to get to the refuge at short notice and told Harriet about her too. Somehow, Sigourney managed to have a quiet word to Harriet at the wake. Sigourney said she could have a car outside in ten minutes. It was a pretty risky operation, really. I suspect Harriet wouldn't have had the strength to go through with it if Grant had intercepted her.'

'When did you realise it was him?' McClintock asked. 'I still can't for the life of me figure out how you got to it after the interview with Shanahan, and his DNA match. He was too perfect for it.'

'A few things clicked the night we were at the pub,' Jillian said. 'The taxi driver who told me he was waiting for someone reminded me of the taxi outside the court the night of the murder. And then you'd been talking about your dad, Michael had talked about how people groom each other, there was the photo on Kaye's phone, and then I thought of Harriet dropping that money. Why would she react as she did? I realised I had accepted Phillips at face value, and I shouldn't have. He'd worked me, he really had. I began to suspect it was him but I didn't understand why he would murder Kaye. But slowly it all just fell into place. Then once he read out the judgement, I was one hundred per cent sure. Kaye had pinned him twice. She was going to ruin his reputation and, assuming her judgement was held up, ensure that Harriet would get almost everything they owned.'

McClintock whistled.

'How'd he get the earrings?' Des asked.

'Oh, she hadn't worn them to the funeral, they were another pair. He just needed something with her DNA on it, and of course he already had access to Shanahan's DNA and a bunch of his abusive letters, they were from the court file too.'

'He wasn't worried about the letters getting forensically dated? Or Shanahan having some incredible alibi?'

'I think he took a gamble that it would be too hard to date the letters. They were relatively recent – less than a year old – so it would've been hard to narrow them down. Bit different from something that was four hundred years old. And I think he probably took another gamble that we, and everyone else, would take his word over Brian Shanahan's, if it ever came down to it.'

'He's a sneaky bastard.' Des shook his head.

'Well, he spent years doing criminal law. He knew what to do. I have another update, too. An email came through late last night from Angela Hui regarding those colourful photographs Kaye had been receiving.'

'Oh yeah?' McClintock was interested. 'Who was it?'

'Tomir!' Jillian said. 'The security manager. Can you believe it? After Bailey died he started sending them to Angela, and one of the other blokes in the security team happened to see his phone, dobbed him in.'

'I never want to set foot in that place again,' McClintock said. 'It just changes so much of the way you see ordinary people.'

'I agree,' said Jillian. 'Rahul Sharma's so nice on TV and the wife presents as such a lunatic, and yet she's the better person of the two. She's a drunk but he's a violent narcissist – I have no doubt about that. Andrew Maiden was definitely reported to AHPRA, by the way.'

'Mummy will get him out of that one,' Des said. He looked at Jillian, eyes narrowed. 'Are you going to be like that with your boy? Always fixing his mistakes, babying him?'

The man at the next table got to his feet. Seagulls were already waiting to pick at his leftovers. 'I hope so,' Jillian said as one neatly collected a finger of toast and flew under the table to enjoy it privately.

I do. I really do.

ACKNOWLEDGEMENTS

With many thanks to the following people: my darling Benny and beautiful Mum for the most precious of gifts – time to write, patience through my bad tempers, and thoughtful feedback; Martin Shaw for taking a chance on a newbie who takes weeks to respond to emails; Cate Paterson for making the offer; Cate B, Bri and the lovely team at Pan Mac for gentle guidance and again, taking a chance; my boys for keeping me sufficiently humble by being utterly underwhelmed that their mother birthed a book and a baby sister concurrently; my family for their enthusiastic support. I was in the fortunate position of being able to donate a portion of my advance to two of the organisations that deal with some of the themes in this book – specifically, Our Watch and PANDA. Both do extremely important and under-recognised work and can be located online for those interested in some further reading.